DELTA

HUNT BROTHERS SEARCH & RESCUE
BOOK 5

JESSICA ASHLEY

HUNT BROTHERS CHRONOLOGICAL READING ORDER

While the Hunt Brothers are written in a way that you *can* read in any order, I do recommend you read in this order to avoid any possible spoilers.

Happy reading!

1. Bravo
2. Echo
3. Romeo
4. Tango
5. Delta
6. Lima
7. A Hunt Brother Valentine's Day *(Website exclusive available in 2026)*
8. A Hunt Brother St. Patrick's Day *(Website exclusive available in 2026)*

DELTA

By Jessica Ashley
Copyright © 2025. All rights reserved.

This book is a work of fiction. Names, characters, places, businesses, and incidents are products of the author's imagination or used fictitiously. Any resemblance to actual persons, living or dead, places, or actual events is entirely coincidental.

No part of this book may be reproduced or transmitted in any form by any means, electronic or mechanical, including photocopying, recording, or by any information storage and retrieval system without written permission of the author, except for the use of brief quotations in a book review.

This book was not created with the use of AI and is not to be used to train any kind of AI technology.

Scripture used in this novel comes from HOLY BIBLE, New Living Translation®, NLT®. Hymn from CHRIST BE OUR SURE FOUNDATION (public domain).

Used by permission. All rights reserved worldwide.

Developmentally Edited by The Editing Soprano
Edited by HEA Author Services
Proofread by Love Kissed Books, LLC
Proofread by Dawn Y.

Cover Design by Covers by Christian
Photographer: Wander
Model: Landon C.

BLURB

A second chance at love sparks a fight for redemption.

Dylan "Delta" Hunt thought he left his past behind when he returned from war. Haunted by all he's seen, he's built walls around his heart, convinced that peace and love are beyond his reach.

Emma has never stopped loving Dylan, even after the man she knew came back a broken stranger. She's spent years trying to reach him but has failed every time. Now, an unexpected revelation about her estranged family pulls her into a dangerous mystery, and Dylan might be the only one who can help.

When Emma vanishes without a trace, Dylan is forced to confront the feelings he buried long ago. But the real question is: Does he have enough light inside to bring them both home? Or will rescuing her cost him what little peace he clings to?

NOTE FROM THE AUTHOR

"But even if you soar as high as eagles and build your nest among the stars, I will bring you crashing down," says the Lord. (Obadiah 1:4).

There are moments in all of our lives when it feels as though we are up against an immovable mountain. When the enemy has convinced us that there is no way out. Where the flaming arrows just keep getting hotter as they hit closer and closer.

Whether it's an addiction wreaking havoc in our lives.

Chronic illness.

Pain that just won't ease.

Grief that feels never-ending.

Or maybe you're facing down someone who seems determined to see you fail.

In moments like that, when you feel overwhelmed and

outgunned, you need to remember that there is *nothing* our God can't do.

David didn't face Goliath alone. See, everyone else saw a giant, but David saw someone who was betraying God. He *knew* that God would fight with him and that he would not be facing Goliath alone.

There will always be mountains in our lives.

Moments where we feel like we're facing insurmountable odds.

But nothing we face is impossible with God.

He is always there. Even in the dark moments when we feel all alone, when we're crying in a closet, our car, the kitchen, long after everyone else has gone to sleep…we are seen.

Loved.

Cherished.

We are children of The KING.

His love for us as His children is never-ending. It's unceasing. And even in the darkness, His light is there.

I know that the world feels dark these days. That the trouble in the news feels unceasing, but just know that there is light, too. That, even amidst the tragedies, there is hope because, one day soon, Jesus will return.

He will wipe all the tears from our eyes, and there will be no more pain.

No more suffering.

Because God never gives up on His children.

He loves us.

And that mountain you're facing? That immovable wall? It's NOTHING compared to Him.

Our God can do anything.

So, give your worries to Him, and watch as He works in your life.

-Jessica

To those who smile in the face of the storm.
Because we know, God's got this.
Mark 4:39-41

CHAPTER 1

DYLAN

TEN YEARS AGO

The steady *drip, drip, drip* is slowly driving me mad.

Or maybe it's the fact that I haven't eaten in —I don't know how long.

Or the dehydration.

Or the putrid stench of the dead bodies decomposing on the floor of my prison. Even now, it sears my throat and lungs, burning me up from the inside. At least, I can't see them or stare into their dead eyes. This pitch-black hole we were thrown into ensures that.

No, I can't see them.

But I can *feel* them.

Death surrounds me.

They used to moan in agony. Used to plead with God for mercy.

Until, one by one, they fell silent. Leaving only the *drip, drip, drip.*

How long until I join them too? Why haven't I already?

I've begged for my life to be taken. Pleaded.

Yet, here I remain. Wrists chained in front of me, trapped in a cell of death, ready for whatever nightmare they have planned for me next. The upside to all the pain? Anything new they do is just background noise.

As they torment me, I let my mind drift back to home.

Back to her.

Blonde hair. Sun-kissed, freckled face. Eyes so blue that they make me want to swim in them forever.

My love.

My Emma.

Would she even recognize me if she saw me now? Would she see past the animal I've become to the man I used to be?

I've been bound so long that I don't even know what it feels like to be unchained. I'm a creature in a cage. A shackled monster. That's what they've made me.

Light assaults me when the lid covering my prison is opened. It burns my eyes, so I have to close them tightly, listening only to the yelling above in a language I can't understand.

Slowly, I try to open my eyes, but the moment I do, tears fill them. The light is so beautiful. Is this it? Am I dead?

Even before those thoughts can fully form in my mind, the light is momentarily blocked by two bodies rushing down the stairs toward me.

I grip the hilt of the blade I found when I was feeling around the cell for something to fight with. I'd pulled it off of one of the dead—then promised to use it to get justice for us all.

Even if it's the last thing I do.

"Get up," a man orders in a thick accent. I don't know his name, but I know he loves to play with fire. I have the burns to prove it.

I don't listen. *Get closer.*

"I said get up!" He raises a rifle at me. Does he not know that I don't fear death? It would be sweet relief for me to leave this world. Doesn't he realize just how dangerous that makes me? After all, a man with nothing to lose is hardly a man at all.

The buttstock of his rifle slams into my cheek. I barely feel the pain—though I taste the blood. Instead of letting him intimidate me, I tilt my face up.

And smile.

His dark eyes narrow on me. "You do not hold the power here, American," he growls. "Or have you forgotten?"

"We don't have time for this." The second man—one I don't recognize—rushes over and grips my arm to rip me up to my feet. With all the weight I've lost, it's not a struggle for him to do.

Together, they drag me out of the hole, my legs slamming into creaky wooden stairs as I go completely limp.

Once we reach the top, they throw me to the ground.

All around, chaos reigns. Alarms are screeching, and armed men are running around, shouting orders.

Drip. Drip. Drip.

I can still hear it.

Why can I still hear it?

"Let's go," the second man orders as he tugs me the rest of the way out of the hole.

"No!" With a feral roar, I slice out with the blade.

The man yells when it catches his arm.

"Idiot!" The butt of a rifle is slammed into my gut, and I fall forward, gasping for breath, but I don't remain down long.

Someone yells, but my gaze is focused only on killing the man in front of me.

On killing him, just as he killed my friends.

On killing *them all.*

The man raises his rifle and fires.

Two bullets.

One.

Two.

They tear through me, and I fall backward—down,

down, down—into the hole. The knife stabs into my side, but as soon as I catch my breath, I roll to the side and tug it free, the pain nothing more than a pinch compared to everything else my body has been through.

I can't feel much of anything anymore…except this thirst for vengeance. This desire to watch my enemies *burn.* Not even bullets can stop me now. Not after what they've done to me.

Two men descend into the hole again, shadows that momentarily block out the sunlight once more.

I can't see their faces, but it doesn't matter because they're *all* the same. Monsters masquerading as men. Threats that need to be eliminated. The world will be safer without them here. Isn't that why I went through all of this? Why my men were cut down? Because we were sent here to stop these monsters from committing genocide.

I remain still, waiting for my chance as one moves to my cuffs. *Bad move, enemy.* They think I'm dead. They probably want the cuffs for another member of the living. But they won't get that chance. I won't let them do to someone else what they did to me.

The cuffs fall off my wrists, clattering to the ground. Summoning what little strength I have left, I lunge to my feet and slash out with the rusted blade.

"Dylan!" someone yells, but I don't recognize the voice. "Stop!"

I can't stop. Don't they see that? They've turned me into exactly what I was always afraid of becoming—a killer. I slash out again, and large hands grip my arms. I'm slammed to the ground, face-first, a knee between my shoulder blades.

"Let me go!" I spit. "I'm going to kill all of you!" I thrash beneath them, but within seconds, all the energy leaves my body, and I fall still. Breathing is a struggle; it has been since well before this moment.

Honestly, I've been struggling to draw breath since I left home.

Since I left *her*.

"We need to get him out of here," a man says.

"I'll cover you," another replies.

Their tones are strained, tense. But they don't have the accents my abductors have. Does that make them different? Or are they merely here to take away what's left of me?

I'm flipped onto my back, then lifted and draped over a shoulder. The man carries me toward the steps, and I don't fight it. Instead, I close my eyes and let my thoughts drift back to the small shred of humanity left in me.

Golden hair.

Soft brown eyes.

Freckle-dusted skin.

Maybe this will finally be the end for me. Maybe I'll finally find peace—if that even exists. I'm beginning to believe it was all a lie. But as I drift away, letting myself come to terms with what will likely be my last moments, I picture her face.

And in my imagination, I get the chance to say goodbye.

CHAPTER 2
EMMA

PRESENT DAY

The fall sun kisses my face as I make my way down Main Street. A light breeze toys with the strands of hair that escaped from the braid I put it in this morning, and overhead, birds soar through the cloudless sky.

Man, it's so beautiful outside today. Such an absolutely lovely day to be alive. Reaching up, I gently touch the cross around my neck. *Thank You, Lord, for this day.* It truly is a gift.

Smiling, I let my hand drop as I head up the walk toward the diner. Lunch is *calling* me. Has been for hours —since I skipped breakfast. But I had a goal—and now that goal is met. My reward? Food.

Delicious food.

The door is propped open, and I can smell fresh apple pie before I've even fully entered. I don't know that I've ever been more grateful that I already got my run in this morning. Because that means *two* slices of Talia's delicious pie for me today. One for after lunch, the other for dinner.

"Good morning, Emma," Talia greets as I step inside. Her slightly graying hair is pulled back in a high ponytail, just as it always is whenever she's working. "I'll be right with you."

"No rush at all." I beam at her, then take a seat on one of the orange barstools at the counter before pulling out my list and marking off the last errand I finished. *Check on bounce houses. Check!* It's only just now lunchtime, and I've already made an impressive dent in today's to-do list.

It's been a great day.

"What can I get for you today, lovely?" Talia asks as she sets some wrapped silverware in front of me.

"Chai tea and a grilled chicken salad, please, ma'am. And two slices of apple pie to-go."

"You got it. We still on for your thirty-sixth birthday dinner tomorrow night?"

I wince. "You just had to remind me."

She laughs. "Thirty-six is the new twenty."

I laugh, though inside, my heart aches. I wanted to be married with kids by the time I was thirty. And now—who knows if that will ever happen. "I'll be there," I reply, forcing a smile. "My mouth is already watering."

"Good." With a smile, Talia heads into the kitchen, leaving me to glance around the diner to see who else is currently grabbing lunch. Sheriff Gibson is in a booth with his mother, both of them laughing happily as they enjoy their lunch. I offer him a wave when he glances in my direction.

Then there's Kennedy Hunt's parents, who both offer me kind smiles as they make their way up to the counter to pay their tab, alongside Alice Hunt's parents. They're relatively new to town, their daughters having married two of the five Hunt brothers. According to Lani, they bonded shortly after Alice's parents relocated here last year.

I've lived in Pine Creek my entire life—well, almost my entire life. I was born in Massachusetts but was placed up for adoption when I was only a baby, and the couple who adopted me moved back here, where they both grew up.

I was nine months old when we came to Pine Creek. For all intents and purposes, this place has been my home my entire life. I know everyone, and they know me. We all support each other, which I was certainly grateful for after my parents' accident thirteen years ago. I was barely eighteen when I lost them. But I had a town to rally around me. An entire family of people who made sure I didn't lose myself too.

That familiar knot of grief wells up inside of me, and I have to actively fight it back down. It was a season of grief and pain. One thing after another for three years after I lost them. God is the only reason I survived, and I believe wholeheartedly He guided the town to close in around me so I didn't feel so alone.

"Here you go, honey." Talia sets a mug down in front of me, the hot water already turning a pale brown, thanks to the bag of fresh spices steeping inside. "Food will be up in a moment."

"Great. Thanks." As she steps away, I slide my list back into my purse, then withdraw my latest read—a swoony romance about two people who survive a plane crash and end up marooned on an island. Rivals to romance—my favorite.

There's just something about that moment when they finally realize that *everything* they've been fighting against is everything they need.

If only things worked like that in real life. An all-too-familiar face swims into the front of my memory, but I bat it back down.

No. There's no time for shattered dreams and broken hearts right now.

This has been a good day, and it will continue to be a good day.

As I focus on the words printed across the pages, I completely tune out the world around me, letting myself be fully engulfed in the story, the characters, the everything. Here, I can block out all of my own problems and watch as the characters solve theirs. Here, things are easy. A safe formula I can count on.

Girl meets boy.

Chaos ensues.

Boy chooses girl over everything.

There is no life after the happily-ever-after, where things can still fall apart.

No broken promises.

"Hey there, bookworm."

I jolt a bit, then turn and smile at Riley Hunt as he slides onto the stool beside me. The third oldest, Riley has always been a bit more laid-back than the rest of his brothers. Not that they're overly serious…well, Tucker's not.

His dark hair is a mess as though he's been running his hands through it all day, and he's wearing his ranch clothes, which means he's been out working rather than running errands. Not surprising—the Hunts are hard workers and the first to lend a hand if things go sideways.

"Hey yourself, Mr. Hunt. No Romeo?" I ask, noting that his service dog, an adorable German shepherd named Romeo, is nowhere to be seen.

"Nah, he's with Jules today. She's meeting with one of her charges, and the girl loves dogs. She's hoping he'll help her open up a bit, and I know he'll keep my wife safe. Win-win all the way around."

After suffering trauma no one should have to go through, Jules turned her pain into strength and now spends quite a bit of time in Dallas at the center for Find Me, a company that rescues trafficking victims from all over the world.

Frank Loyotta, who runs Find Me, occasionally calls in outside help for particularly hard cases. All five of the Hunt brothers have been called in on more than one occasion to aid in rescue missions since they run their own search and rescue company. And now, Jules is the one who helps these victims transition back into whatever normalcy they can find. Because she's been through it too.

"It's so great that she's doing that."

"She loves it." His pride shines all over his face.

"I'm glad." I beam at him, then look at the book he set on the counter in front of him. "What did you bring today?"

"A thriller. You?"

"Romance." I hold mine up. "You know me."

He laughs. "That, I do."

I practically grew up alongside the Hunt family. First, it started out with me being friends with the youngest of the Hunts—Lani. We bonded over both being adopted and became friends despite the one-year age gap between us.

Then I met Dylan. And my entire world shifted. *If only it would shift back.*

"Riley. What can I get for you?" Talia asks, her friendly smile always warm and inviting.

"A burger and fries for me, a club sandwich with extra crispy bacon and a bag of potato chips for my dad, and another burger with no mayo and a side of onion rings, to-go, please." He doesn't add in who the last burger is for, and he doesn't have to. I know that Dylan prefers onion rings to fries, and he hates mayonnaise. The Independence Day parade picnic cemented that when the potato salad got left out too long and he got sick to his stomach.

"You got it." After making a note on her pad, she heads back into the kitchen.

"How are things going out at the ranch?" I ask, hoping he doesn't know what I'm *really* asking. *How's Dylan? Has he decided he misses me as much as I miss him yet?*

"Not too bad. Dad's truck is on the fritz, and since Elliot is out of town for a mission, I'm on mechanic duty until he gets back."

"I'm assuming Dylan is helping?" When he doesn't answer right away, I dramatically roll my eyes. "His name isn't a bad word, Riley. Since I happen to know he's the only one of you who can't stomach mayonnaise, I know he's helping you."

Riley shrugs. "Sorry, not sure where you stand."

"Nowhere," I reply. "We don't stand anywhere, and that's just fine by me."

He gives me a side-eye, not sure he believes my words. "Yeah, he's helping. If by helping, you mean humming every time he thinks I'm doing something wrong."

Humming. Dylan has an excellent voice. One of the best out of all the brothers. There was a time when we thought he was going to go into music. Then he'd chosen the military, and everything went sideways.

"Well, he does like to make you crazy."

"Yeah. We get blips where he's himself, and even as annoyed as I used to get, I'm just glad to see a bit of his old self shine through."

My heart aches. What I'd give to see that side of him again too. "Good. I'm glad to hear it."

Because I genuinely can't discuss Dylan anymore without completely losing it, I go back to reading, or at least pretending to read, and a few seconds later, Riley opens his book too.

Even as Lani and I have been friends for forever, and books are something Riley and I bonded over a long time ago, my real connection to the family lies with Dylan—the youngest of the brothers.

A man I've loved for as long as I can remember.

Pain blossoms in my heart, grief that just won't go away, no matter how many years pass. No matter how many times he treats me like I mean nothing, I can't let go of what we *were*.

I suppose that's my burden to carry.

I pray constantly for God to take it away…to remove my feelings for Dylan, but so far, that particular prayer has not been answered. Someday, maybe, but not today.

"Here you go." Talia slides the chicken salad in front of me, so I close my book and set it aside.

"Thank you."

"You're welcome. Shout if you need anything else."

"Will do." I bow my head. "Lord, I ask that you bless this food. Let it nourish my body. Thank You for the wondrous blessings you bestow upon me. I pray this in Jesus' name. Amen."

"Amen," Riley says beside me.

I pour the dressing over the top of my salad and mix it in, then take my first bite. It's the first time I've eaten today since my breakfast consisted of a protein shake after my run, then a mad dash out the front door so I wouldn't be late to the Saturday staff meeting at the school where I teach kindergarten.

"Any big plans today?" Riley asks.

I finish chewing and swallowing my current bite. "Just preparations for the school's fall festival. Then I'm headed over to Charlene's place for a bit."

"How is she doing?"

"Not great," I reply sadly. Charlene Thomas lost her husband of nearly sixty years last month. She's been struggling with depression, on top of the Alzheimer's that's been slowly pulling her further and further away from us. Most of the time, she forgets to do basic tasks, so even though she has a full-time nurse, I still head over at least once a day to sit with her and help wherever I can.

"I'm so sorry to hear that. Is there anything I can do?"

"Actually, if you have time, her back porch has a couple

of loose railings. She likes to take tea out there every afternoon, and I'm honestly worried that she's going to fall through one of these days."

"Consider it done." He smiles.

"Thanks so much." I open my notepad and check off the line that says *'Get Charlene's Porch Fixed.'* Because if one of the Hunts says they'll do something, it's as good as done.

"You had that on your to-do list?" he asks, amused.

"I did. It's been on there for the last couple of days. I've fallen a bit behind. It's actually happenstance I ran into you because I was going to call Bradyn this afternoon."

"You and those lists," he says with a laugh.

"Don't mock. They keep me organized."

"I bet you still add 'make a list' to your lists."

I glare at him, though a smile turns up the corners of my lips. "That happened *one* time. Dylan never let me live it down." His name used to roll so easily off my lips. Now, it's like a boulder falling on my toe. My happiness dies just a bit, so I turn my attention back to my salad.

"You okay?" Riley questions.

"Fine." I say it a bit sharper than I mean to, so I offer him a smile. "I'm completely okay," I add.

"Alright. Well, you know that I'm here if you need me. We all are."

"Thanks, Riley." Even though Dylan is their brother,

they all supported me during the months when Dylan was in rehab. During that whole year, after the initial hospital visit ended horribly, I'd waited for the day Dylan would call and want to see me again, but it's a call that never came.

"No problem." He offers me a smile, then returns to his book, so I finish eating in silence, all while my mind constantly replays the moments I had with Dylan before everything fell apart.

"WELL, well, Ma, what are you working on?" I playfully hold up a small pair of crocheted socks.

"I don't want to forget," Charlene replies, a sheepish smile on her aging face. The floral couch she's sitting on is one I've spent more than a few nights on since her husband's passing. It also happens to be nearly the same pale pink as the dress she's currently wearing.

"Forget what? How to crochet?"

"No, about the baby."

"What baby?"

Charlene's expression turns frustrated. Which means that she's grasping at something I'm not comprehending and doesn't understand why I don't understand.

"Hey, it's okay," I say quickly. "Sorry, the baby, of course. Tell me about the baby."

She laughs and rolls her eyes. "You know all about the baby, Emmaline. It is yours, after all."

Mine. "Oh?" I glance back at Ursula, her nurse, who simply smiles sadly.

"Yes. Yours and that Hunt boy—Dylan. How could I forget his name?" She snaps her fingers. "That kid was running around after you from the time he could walk."

My chest tightens. How many times did I dream about being married to Dylan? About carrying his child and being the one he turned to when things got hard? Instead, during his darkest moments, he pushed me away.

"Ma, Dylan and Emma aren't together anymore," her nurse says carefully. "Remember?"

Charlene looks at me, confusion in her blue gaze. "Not together anymore. Since when?"

"Quite a few years, Ma," Ursula says, once again using Charlene's pet name. She was an elementary school teacher up until she retired, and everyone has always called her Ma. Even the students called her Ma Thomas instead of Mrs. Thomas. "They haven't been together in a long time."

"But that doesn't make any sense. You were going to be married, remember? Baby's breath and lilacs."

It's a good thing I'm sitting down, because if I'd been standing, I imagine I would have fallen over, thanks to the weakness in my legs. Embarrassment, sadness, it all hits me as I look at her broken expression.

"Those were just plans," I tell her, trying to keep a

friendly smile on my face even as my bottom lip quivers just slightly. Walking her through this is like reliving it all over again. And the pain is just as fresh today as it was then. "Sometimes, plans don't work out."

"No. You two were more than plans. You were fated. Just like me and my love. I saw it. I saw it." She shakes her head, then lifts her crochet project again. As she begins working the hook through the yarn, she smiles and mutters happily to herself, lost in whatever daydream she's currently walking in. Maybe in her version of reality, Dylan and I are still together. Maybe we're having a child.

Would the young one have his hazel eyes? Crooked smile?

Because just thinking about it has me in desperate need of air, I push up from the chair and head into the kitchen to place my glass of tea in the sink. Outside, I can hear Riley working on the porch. The occasional nail being shot into place has taken up a good portion of the time I've been here. I keep meaning to pop out and thank him for being so quick to get over here, but I haven't had the chance yet.

"You okay, honey?" Ursula questions. She was close friends with my mom, having also grown up here in Pine Creek.

"Yeah. I'm okay."

"She's only thinking about Dylan since she saw him earlier."

"When did she see him?" Since Charlene doesn't tend

to get out, it would be unusual for her to see Dylan, who rarely leaves the ranch, aside from Sunday mornings or missions for Hunt Brothers Search and Rescue.

Ursula looks at me, confused. "He's outside." She points to the porch. "I thought you knew."

"I—" And then it hits me—*Riley. Mischievous trouble-maker. Ugh.* Despite not wanting to speak his brother's name around me, he's always trying to put Dylan in my path. Likely because he hopes that, one day, what's broken will be repaired. What he doesn't realize, though, is that, even if Dylan offered to give me the time of day, I don't know that I would be interested.

He broke too much of me to put back together.

She arches a brow. "Didn't you ask him to fix the porch?"

"I asked Riley. I'll be right back." Forcing a smile onto my face, I open the back door and step out onto the porch.

As I do, my mouth dries.

Dylan's back is to me, his white tank top drenched with sweat. Scars snake out of the edges of the shirt, climbing onto his shoulder blades. It's the first I've seen of the physical damage done to him all those years ago.

And my eyes fill at the sight of it.

The muscles of his back contract as he works with a piece of lumber that's straddling two sawhorses. He slips a pencil behind his ear, then turns to face me, stopping abruptly when he sees me standing there.

Hazel eyes so piercing they steal the very air around me level on mine.

He's always had this power over me. The ability to make everything and everyone else around me disappear— similar to how I feel when I read a book. Maybe that's why I loved him so much. His ability to block out the noise and ground me in the present.

"I asked Riley to fix this," I blurt.

"Riley's busy." He lifts the piece of lumber and carries it up to the porch, then lays it in place and uses a nail gun to fix it in place.

"I didn't mean for you to do it."

Dylan doesn't verbally respond, just nods.

"You don't have to do it."

"I don't mind."

It's hard to believe we used to talk for hours when he can barely utter three words to me in a single sentence these days.

"Fine." Hating myself for letting it get under my skin even after all this time, I turn on my heel and head back into the house. Ursula is getting Charlene to her feet.

"Emmaline! Dearest girl, when did you get here?"

Tears filling my eyes and emotions searing my throat, I force a smile. "Not too long ago, Ma. Are you off to take your afternoon nap?"

Her expression turns regretful. "I was, but you just got here. Why don't we have some tea?"

"You know? I actually just got a call and need to head out. Can I take a rain check?"

"Of course, honey. You go do what needs to be done. You're such a good girl. Give your parents my love, okay?"

"Okay," I choke out, still doing everything I can to keep the smile on my face and tears out of my eyes while Ursula guides her down the hallway and to her bedroom.

I grab my purse and head out front, walking right past the Hunt Family Ranch truck parked in front of my car. As I climb inside, I close my eyes and bow my head. "Lord, please grant me the strength. Please take this pain. I don't know how I can keep carrying it. I feel crazy. Please, God. In Jesus' name I pray. Amen."

After wiping the tears that I couldn't quite blink away, I pull away from the curb in front of Charlene's house and head back toward mine. Back to my carefully crafted world where everything makes sense and I've hidden away all traces of Dylan Hunt.

CHAPTER 3
DYLAN

The heavy bag swings, the chain creaking as I drive my fist into the side of it.

Again.

Again.

Every muscle in my body is warmed up, my skin slick with sweat, but I'm nowhere near tired, despite being out here for nearly four hours. It's not unusual though. Sleep eludes me more often than not.

I step back, then spin and kick, slamming my foot into the bag and sending it swinging wildly. The ache in my chest isn't unfamiliar either. Honestly, I'd be worried if I woke up one day and it was gone, but that doesn't mean it's easy to deal with. And ever since I saw Emma standing in the sunlight on Charlene's porch, her pretty dress flowing softly in the early fall breeze, it's felt like there's an anvil on my chest.

If only it would crush me already and get it over with. This slow, torturous pain is killing me anyway.

"I thought I saw a light on." Tucker, my twin brother, steps through the open door of the gym. His dog, Tango, rushes to greet my dog, Delta, and the two of them almost immediately start wrestling.

"Wanted a quick workout in before bed."

"Didn't you work out earlier today too?" Tucker questions, leaning back against the refrigerator holding all of our cold pre- and post-workout drinks.

"Yeah. So?"

"So, is everything okay?"

"It's fine." I slam my fist into the bag, wishing this conversation was already over. But Tucker being Tucker, he only pries more.

"You haven't been coming around as often, so I want to make sure you're good."

"You just got married a few months ago," I remind him. "So no, I haven't been around a whole lot. Seems to me you'd want some time to be alone with your wife." I undo the cap of my water, not bothering to remove the wraps from my hands because I'm nowhere near numb enough for sleep yet.

"Fair enough, but you know we like having you around." He crosses his arms.

I hate that he still feels like he has to take care of me.

And I hate it even more that I really do miss my brothers. All of them. Even if I am happy for all of them and the families they're starting, love just isn't in the cards for me. Not now. Not ever again. Which means this is the new normal, and I'd better start getting used to it.

They'll be starting families and living their happily ever afters while I grow old alone, waiting for the day I no longer have to live with the cement of my past caked around my ankles.

I set my water down and turn toward him. "Look, I did some work over at Ma Thomas' place earlier, and now I'm trying to get one final workout in today since I have to be up early to stain her new porch railing and likely won't get one in tomorrow morning, okay?"

Tucker doesn't look at all like he believes me. "You saw Emma over there, didn't you?"

I drop my head into my hands and let out a frustrated breath. "She's an off-limits topic, and you know that."

"Do I?" Tucker crosses his arms. "Did she say something that upset you?"

"Emma?" I ask. "Of course not. She never says anything mean to anyone ever." She's pure light. Always has been. Which is why I can't be anywhere close to her. The darkness in me will devour her light.

And this world *needs* her light.

It already has enough darkness.

"Tomorrow's her birthday."

"I'm aware," I growl.

"Just making sure." Tucker uncrosses his arms and pushes off the refrigerator. "Want me to hold the bag? Might be easier to beat it up if it's not going anywhere."

"No thanks." I unwrap my hands. "It's late, I'll probably just call it a night now."

"You sure?"

"Yeah." I hang my wraps up, then grab my bottle of water on my way out the door. "*Hier,* Delta," I call my dog, using the German commands they were all trained with as puppies. Easier to control your dog when few others can interfere.

He hops up from where he was lying and trots over toward me, ears perked, tail wagging.

Tucker whistles for Tango, who also joins us as we step out into the evening air. It's nearly eleven at night, and the moon is high overhead, casting a silver glow over the ranch that's been my home for my entire life.

If only it still felt that way.

Truth is…I haven't felt at home anywhere in a long, long time.

I doubt I ever will again.

"You sure your good? I can come hang for a bit. Alice is wrapping up some work stuff."

"Nah, I'm good. Thanks though."

Tucker offers me a nod before he turns away.

"Hey, Tuck?"

He turns back toward me. "Yeah?"

"I'm really happy for you and Alice, I hope you know that."

Tucker smiles. "I know, bro. Love you."

"You too."

Delta and I climb into the utility vehicle I drove over here earlier, then wait until Tucker has pulled his truck out of the way so we can head home. As soon as he's out of the way, I make the five-minute drive over toward the acre of land my parents gave me to build my house on.

We each have an acre—including our youngest sister, Lani, though she's still living in an apartment in town and hasn't started building anything on her land just yet. Personally, I think she's waiting until she finds her happily ever after, though she will never admit as much. Because that would mean having to admit to the torch she carries for our town's sheriff, Gibson Lawson.

My home comes into view, a quaint single-story three-bedroom cabin that's been my home since I built it a couple of years after returning to Pine Creek from my last deployment. It's a good house. Sturdy. But that's all it is to me—a structure built to protect me from the elements.

I thought time would make it feel more like home, but the truth is, no matter how many days pass—it's still just a house. And I'm still a man—barely alive.

Used to the routine, I don't have to call Delta as I climb

out. He simply falls into a walk beside me while we climb the porch steps. I unlock the door, and he trots inside, so I follow, hanging the UTV keys up near the door and retrieving my truck keys and wallet from the counter.

With them in hand, I grab the glass vase I'd picked up earlier, add some water, then head out and lock up behind me. The wildflowers I planted in front of my house are the only part of this place that brings me any spark of joy.

Because they remind me of *her*.

Colorful, chaotic yet organized, beautiful—they're Emma.

It's a sweet kind of torture to look at them and see her, but it's the closest I can get without dimming the light burning bright within her soul. So I take what I can, though it's never enough to satisfy the starvation I've suffered since losing her.

Tucker knocks on the doorjamb but doesn't pause before coming into the hospital room. I can't bring myself to look at him. Even though we're not identical, my twin is a painful reminder of who I was before hell descended upon me.

"Hey, brother. Look who's here."

I don't even have to look to know it's her. I can sense her like an animal can sense a storm headed their way.

That's what she is to me—a storm sent to sweep me away and carry me into a past that no longer exists and a future that will never come to pass.

"Hey, Dylan." Emma's gorgeous face comes into view as she steps in front of me. Her golden hair is swept out of her face and braided down over her shoulder. The light dusting of freckles on her cheeks is apparent even in the dim hospital light.

I don't respond. What can I say? I'm not who she's looking for. Not anymore. He died a horrible death in that cave when he was ripped out of me, leaving only a shadow.

She steps up beside the bed and reaches down to touch my hand. The moment her skin touches mine, I jolt away. My breathing turns ragged, and I clench both hands into fists as I close my eyes tightly.

I'm not in danger.

I'm not in danger.

But no matter how many times I repeat the mantra, over and over again, I'm still unable to put a leash around the panic clawing through me.

Fight. I need to fight. They'll kill me if I don't.

I'm not in danger.

They're going to take what little is left of me.

I'm not in danger.

"Brother, breathe."

"Get away from me!" I roar, shooting up off the bed.

Everything around me is gone, and all I see is red. My hand closes around skin, and I hold on.

A woman screams.

Hands grip my shoulders and shove me back down. But I will not be kept down. Not again. Never again.

"Stay down!" a man yells.

He'd like that. They all would. But I won't give up without a fight.

"Dylan, it's me!" That woman screams again. Her voice is familiar, but they'd want it to be, right? A trick to keep me from fighting.

"You're hurting her, Dylan!"

"Dylan, you're safe." That woman whispers to me.

The red begins to dissipate, and my surroundings return. I'm not in the pit—I'm in a hospital room.

I'm not alone…I'm with— Oh, no. I release the hold I have on Emma's arm, giving Riley the ability to rip her away from me. Tucker releases me, and he steps back too.

They're all staring at me like the monster that I am.

"Get her out of here!" I yell. "Now!"

"Dylan, it's—" Emma starts.

Hot tears sting my eyes. "Get out! I don't want to see you!"

Breathing is nearly impossible with the vise around my lungs, but I do what I can to draw in ragged breath after ragged breath while Riley ushers Emma out. Tucker remains where he is, but I barely see him as I curl onto my side, one hand gripping the hospital railing with such force my knuckles turn white.

I could have killed her.

I could have killed her.

I would have killed her.

Why couldn't they have killed me first?

CHAPTER 4
EMMA

"Happy birthday to you, our dearest Emmaline!" Mom leans into the camera lens and smiles. Her green eyes are so full of life, so bright and happy. Who would have known that, less than two months later, they would be forever closed?

"We love you so much, baby!" Dad calls out from behind the camera. He turns it on himself and waves; then the video ends. I've seen it so much that I know it's coming, yet when the camera cuts out, the loss hits me just as hard as it did that first year.

"Love you guys, thank you." Tears stream down my cheeks, but I let them fall, soaking up the grief from losing them as well as the happiness they gave me for the first eighteen years of my life.

Every year on my birthday, I watch that video right after waking. That way, I can spend my morning with them and get all my crying done before I head out into the world. Since church is this morning too, I imagine I'll get a whole mountain full of happy birthdays, and I want to embrace them with a smile rather than with the gnawing grief that sinks in when I remember that I won't get to eat my mom's chocolate cake with peanut butter frosting or enjoy the steak dinner Dad always made every year.

I stand and unplug the USB connecting the camcorder to my television, then place it gently in the cabinet where it will wait until next year to be used again. Then, I head into the kitchen for the tea I left steeping.

As I make my way toward the counter, my gray tabby, Ash, comes trotting out of my bedroom, his fluffy, squirrel-like tail swishing behind him. "Oh, hey there, bud. Finally decide it was time to wake up?" I ask as I squat down to run my hand over his back. He arches beneath me, already purring. "I know what you want. Breakfast, right?"

At the mention of food, he shifts his bright blue gaze up to me for a moment, then heads for the laundry room where I keep his food.

Chuckling, I top his bowl off, then return to my tea while he eats.

After adding some honey and a splash of milk, I carry my mug out onto the back porch to officially greet the day. The sun is just beginning to climb over the horizon, sending rays of gold, purple, and orange out over the world.

My backyard is a beautiful array of colors, thanks to the

Knock Out Roses I planted at the beginning of the season. With a smile on my face and my feet bare, I step out onto the soft grass. The breeze toys with my hair, and I close my eyes, taking a deep breath.

"Thank You, oh Lord, for this day," I say aloud. "Thank You."

I remain where I am for a few moments, letting serenity surround me. "It's going to be another great day," I whisper, then turn to head back in so I can get dressed for church. As I do, a vase overflowing with colorful wildflowers catches my eye.

It's sitting on the railing of my porch, closest to the gate that leads out to the front. Sunlight makes sparkles in the glass glitter wildly, but they turn into one massive blur as tears fill my eyes.

Every year.

He does this *every* year.

Yet he can't say more than three words to me.

Anger hits me out of nowhere. Whether it's due to the lack of sleep I got last night or Charlene's confusion yesterday, I'm not sure. But I know that I need to let him go. That I need to stop waiting for some miracle to happen and just move on with my life.

Because, even if I want to believe I wouldn't accept him if he told me he still loves me, I know—without a doubt—I would go running right back into the arms that broke my heart.

So I stomp over to the gorgeous flowers and carry them inside. Unlike years before, though, I don't display them on my kitchen island. Instead, I shove them into the same brown box I'd used to carry in the crockpot I just recently ordered online, then get beneath the counter and grab the other vases left for me over the years.

Ten of them.

One for every birthday he's been back.

By the time church is over at noon, my anger has dissipated, and the box full of vases in my car makes me feel a bit ridiculous.

I'd had every intention of driving to the Hunt Family Ranch this morning but changed my mind the second I got behind the wheel. Why should I give him the satisfaction of knowing just how deeply he cuts me?

What's worse is I know that's not what he means to do.

The vases are Dylan's way of showing me that he still cares. Even if it can't be what I want, he's trying to be kind.

But I'm so far past his gestures of kindness. I want him to just leave me be.

Desperately.

Or so I tell myself.

Because, maybe then, I can find some peace. Maybe

then, I can find a man who will love me in the way I wish Dylan would.

"Happy birthday, honey!" Talia greets me as she wraps her arms around me in the aisle between pews.

"Thank you."

"Dinner tonight, right?" she confirms once again.

"Have I missed a year?" I ask. "Besides, you asked me yesterday."

She laughs. "I just want to make sure." She and my mother ran in the same circle growing up, so after my parents died, Talia and her husband kind of took me under their wings. Since they couldn't have children of their own, and I was a bit of an orphan, it worked out.

We spend holidays together—and birthdays—whenever the mood strikes.

She looks past me and waves. "Oh, I'll see you tonight, okay? I need to catch Ursula before she leaves and I head into the diner."

"Sounds good. See you tonight."

I retrieve my purse from the pew, then start to leave right as Kennedy Hunt—Bradyn Hunt's wife—steps into my path and wraps her arms around me.

"Happy birthday, Emma!"

"Thanks," I reply with a smile as she releases me.

"Happy birthday, Ems," Bradyn says warmly. The eldest of the Hunts, he was always a surrogate big brother to me. Truthfully, they all were.

Everyone but Dylan. I never saw him as a brother. He was always—

That thought cuts off when he moves into my eyeline. It's distant, as he's standing beside his parents while they talk to Pastor Ford, but he's there. The proverbial elephant in the room. And when he looks up at me, hazel gaze locking with mine, I momentarily forget that Kennedy's talking to me.

We've always been this way—drawn to each other. Or, at least, I've always been drawn to him.

"So, what do you think?"

"Huh? Sorry, I didn't sleep well last night."

Kennedy smiles knowingly. "I know you have plans with Talia and Connor tonight, but are you up for a girls' night tomorrow to celebrate? Nova is still out of town and won't be back until next month, but Jules, Alice, Lani, and I are ready and available. Sound good?"

"Yeah." I smile. "That actually sounds great."

"Perfect. Then it's a date." She hugs me again. "See you tomorrow!"

"See you."

Kennedy and Bradyn walk out hand in hand. I hate the jealousy that sneaks into my thoughts. Jealousy that I'm not wrapped around Dylan's arm right now. That he's only across the room but might as well be a million miles away.

I need to get out of here.

I'm headed to Charlene's next, so I wave to Ursula and

Talia as I step out onto the front steps of the church. Manners dictate I should go to Dylan and thank him for the flowers. However, the first couple of years I did that, he acted like he had no idea what I was talking about.

He'd completely brushed it off, despite me knowing without a doubt it's him leaving them. He's the *only* one who knows how much I love wildflowers. The only one who ever took the time to choose each bloom carefully.

So, ever since that third year, I've just pretended that I didn't find the most beautiful assortment of flowers on my porch.

I won't ever forget that first year though. How happy I was, thinking he was reaching out, only to find out that he had no intention of ever moving past the chasm of brokenness between us ever since he got home. It made me feel like a fool, and I'd gone home a mess of tears.

Never. Again.

I'm just reaching for the handle of my car when Ruth Hunt calls my name.

With a forced smile, I turn to face Dylan's mother. She's one of the sweetest humans I've ever met, and I absolutely adore her, but if she's there, then Dylan's not far. He always rides with his parents on Sunday mornings.

Ruth rushes forward and embraces me, her floral perfume familiar and welcoming as she wraps both arms around me. "Girl, you are aging backward."

I laugh, appreciating the compliment while also grateful

that Dylan seems to not have followed her out here. Maybe he's inside with his dad. "I appreciate that, Mrs. Hunt, but it is so not true."

"It is absolutely true." She smiles at me. Growing up, I spent so much time with the Hunts that Ruth practically became a second mom to me. Between hanging out with Lani and my relationship with Dylan, the Hunt Ranch was my home away from home.

Though, ever since Dylan came home, it might as well be a foreign country. I barely set foot on the property, except for the times I help Ruth with charity stuff for the church or the occasional girls' night hosted by one of the brothers' wives.

"Well, thank you."

"You're welcome. Any big plans?" she asks.

"Dinner with Talia and Connor."

"That's so wonderful." She smiles, then eyes the box of vases in the backseat of my car. *Oh no. Does she know?* "Those are lovely."

"Thanks. They were a gift."

"A well-deserved one," she replies. "I hope you have a great day, sweetheart. Please, don't be a stranger. I miss seeing you."

The emotional war in my chest is all-consuming, but I fight to keep it together. I *have* to keep it together. "You too."

A man clears his throat behind me. "Uh, Emmaline Franklin?"

I turn at the mention of my name, the voice unfamiliar, and see a handsome, dark-haired man lingering off to the right.

"I'll leave you to it, honey. Happy birthday." Ruth gives me one final hug, then heads back toward the church. But the smile on her face as she surveys the man, then me, doesn't quite reach her eyes.

"Yes. That's me. Sorry. Do I know you?"

He smiles, and a dimple appears near the right side of his mouth. "No, you don't know me. Not yet, anyway." He outwardly cringes. "That was—wow. Sorry, I just—I don't know how to do this."

"Do what?"

He laughs. "Can we go somewhere to talk?"

I open my mouth to tell him that I have somewhere else to be, but then I notice Dylan lingering near the porch steps, staring intently at me. Both hands are curled into fists at his sides, but he makes no move to close the distance between us.

Is that jealousy?

Good. Which, of course, I know isn't a kind way to think about it, but right now, I'm struggling with who I should strive to be and the pettiness of knowing he'll suffer, not knowing why I'm talking to this man wins.

"Sure. We can walk over to the diner, if that works? It's

right there." I point toward the diner, and he turns to follow my gesture.

"That works. Thanks." He waits for me to start walking before following along, and I'm so struck by Dylan's gaze fixed on us that I don't even realize I haven't asked this man his name until we're crossing the street together.

"I'm sorry, I didn't ask you your name."

"And I'm sorry that I completely forgot to tell you." He reaches for the door and pulls it open. I move inside, and he follows.

"Hey, honey," Talia greets.

"Hey, Talia. Did you find Ursula?"

"I did." Her gaze shifts curiously to the stranger. "Table for two?"

"Yes please. Thanks."

"Of course. Sit anywhere you like."

The man leads us toward a booth near the back, then slides into the side that places his back near a wall. It's a move I only recognize from the time I've been out with the Hunts. None of them wants his back to a door.

Prior military, perhaps?

I sit across from him. "Your name?" I press again.

"Mattheus Karver," he replies with a smile.

"Karver, I don't recognize that name. Are you from around here?"

He chuckles. "No. Regrettably, I grew up on the other side of the country."

"What can I get you two?" Talia asks as she sets two wrapped silverware sets in front of us.

"Uh, just chai tea for me, please," I ask.

"Sweet tea," Mattheus says. "Thanks so much."

"You got it." Talia leaves the table.

"So you know me but didn't grow up around here. I'm a bit confused."

He smiles and runs a hand through his dark hair. "It's actually a long story."

"I have time." *Not really, but I'm here.*

"Happy birthday, by the way. I was so shocked to see you standing there that I completely forgot to say it."

"Thanks. But you were shocked to see me standing in the place where you came to find me? Since I haven't ever seen you at church before, and you're not from here, I'm assuming you were there because of me." I realize after I say it just how presumptuous it sounds, and my cheeks heat.

"I was. Um— I did not think this through." He reaches into his pocket and withdraws a folded-up photograph, then slides it across the table at me.

Lifting it, I stare down at the old photo of a blonde woman wearing a hospital gown and cradling a baby in her arms. "Who is this?"

"Your mother," he replies. "Birth mother, that is."

The blood drains from my face, and my stomach turns into a pit. "Excuse me?"

"Here you go." Talia sets my mug of tea down, alongside his sweet tea. "Aww, who is that?" she asks as she looks at the photograph.

"My birth mother," I whisper.

"What?" Talia asks, surprised. "Seriously?"

Mattheus clears his throat. "Yes. Her name is—"

"Wait." I put my hand up. I made up my mind a long time ago that I didn't want to know the name of the woman who decided—before she ever really knew me—that she didn't want to keep me. As far as I'm concerned, Patricia and Emmit Franklin are my parents.

Mattheus reaches out and gently touches the hand that I have resting on the table. "I know you probably have a lot of questions, and I can answer all of them. Well, most of them." He smiles at me, then glances up at Talia, who rests a hand on my shoulder and squeezes lightly.

"You know where I am if you need me," she says.

"Thanks."

"Anytime, sweetie. You two holler if you'd like anything else." She hesitates a moment but then turns to leave.

As she walks away, I keep staring down at the photograph. The woman is looking down at the infant as though she's the single most important person in her life. So, if this really is my mother and me, then why didn't she keep me?

"You said you can answer my questions?"

He withdraws his hand. "Anything. And if I don't know, we can find out together."

Slowly, I set the photograph down and level my gaze on his. "Why didn't she keep me?"

"Oh, Emma," Mattheus says softly. "Your parents were told you died right after birth."

Horror mixes with my sadness, and I gape at him. "What?"

He nods, expression turning somber. "A nurse stole you from the hospital. We're not sure what happened after that, but at some point, you were placed up for adoption."

"Someone *stole* me?"

He nods. "Your adoptive parents wouldn't even have known. When police couldn't find your family, they placed you in a foster home. All the while, your parents had no idea you were still alive. There was a funeral and everything." He reaches into his pocket and withdraws a cell phone, then taps the screen a few times. "Here."

Mattheus offers me the phone, so I take it. A marble headstone gleams beneath bright sunlight.

GWENDOLYN VICTORIA KARVER

Born October 2nd, 1989. Died October 2nd 1989.

Gone but never forgotten.

"Karver." I look up at him. "That's your last name."

He smiles and nods. "I'm your older brother." His dark eyes glisten beneath the lights overhead.

"Brother?" I somehow manage the single word despite the lump in my throat. "I have a brother?"

"Yes. I've been trying to find you for the last six months, ever since we learned that you were alive."

"How did you find out?"

"We were contacted by a woman who knew the nurse who kidnapped you. She wouldn't give us a name but told us that you were alive and had been placed up for adoption shortly after you were kidnapped from the hospital. She said she couldn't live with herself anymore, then hung up without giving us anything else. Mom and Dad are— they're beside themselves."

"Mom and Dad. They're both alive?" Is it possible that I still have family out there? That what Mattheus is saying is true, and I'm not really all alone?

"Yes." His gaze softens. "I read about what happened to your adoptive parents. And I'm so sorry for your loss. Were they good people?"

"The best," I reply softly as I try to blink away tears.

"You had a good life, then?"

"So good." I smile, then pick the photograph up again after sliding his phone back over to him. "Why didn't they come?"

"They don't even know I'm here. Neither of them wanted to disturb your life. But I needed to meet you. I mean, a sister! I have a living sister. That was a cool revelation to have in my late thirties."

"Tell me about it." I look back down at the photograph. She has the same color hair as I do. Are her eyes the same too? Does she have freckles? "How long are you in town for?"

"Just until tomorrow night," he replies. "I need to get home, but I'm—" He trails off. "I'm hoping you'll come too. Even if it's just to meet them. They would love to know you."

"I don't know." The truth is that I would love to go and meet them. But I'm scared.

What if they don't like me?

What if they don't want a relationship with me?

We sit in silence for a few moments, and I'm unable to tear my gaze away from the photograph between us. Is that really her? The woman who brought me into this world?

"Just think about it, okay? Please?" He reaches into his pocket and puts some bills on the table.

I look up, startled to see him standing already. He just got here. Why is he leaving already? "You're leaving?"

"I want to give you some time. It's what I would want if I were on that side of the table. But don't worry, sis, I'll see you soon, okay?"

I smile up at him, appreciating him anticipating that I'd need time. "Okay." I offer him the picture back, but he shakes his head.

"Keep it." He sets a piece of paper with a phone number on the table between us. "This is my cell. Call me when you've made up your mind, okay? No pressure though. It was enough to just get to meet you." With one final smile, he turns and leaves.

The second the door closes and he's on the street, Talia slides into the booth. "Okay, girl, spill. Who was that?"

I stare down at the photo, then smile. "My brother. That's my older brother."

CHAPTER 5

DYLAN

Forty-five minutes.

That's how long I've stood in this church parking lot, waiting for Emma to leave the diner. Riley joked that it's because I'm jealous, but it's not. Not entirely, anyway. I'd noticed the man who approached her as he lingered in the back of the church during the service.

He wasn't there for the Gospel, but rather, the entire time, his gaze had been trained on Emma. At first, I brushed it off. She's gorgeous, so the fact that she captured his attention doesn't surprise me.

But when he'd beelined for her after service, something felt wrong.

Off.

So here I wait. Watching. Making sure she leaves safely.

The stranger left a few minutes ago, and I snapped a

couple of cell phone pictures for Tucker to run through facial ID. I know the man doesn't live here, which makes him a potential threat—at least in my opinion.

Unknowns are unpredictable.

I like my life to be predictable.

She steps out onto the street like a ray of sunshine in her yellow-and-white striped church dress. After waving goodbye to Talia inside, Emma makes her way across the street, a smile on her face. But as she gets closer, I note the red rimming her gorgeous eyes.

Eyes that are currently narrowed on me.

"What did he do to you?" I demand, already prepared to hunt him down and make him pay for causing her pain.

"Nothing." Emma crosses her arms. "What do you want, Dylan?"

What am I supposed to say? That I was worried and wanted to make sure she was safe? Or that the idea of her sharing a meal with someone else makes my skin crawl? "I didn't recognize him, and I wanted to make sure you were okay."

Emma's glare turns molten. It's something about her that's always fascinated me. Emma is the happiest person I've ever met, but her temper, while slow to come by, is a force to be reckoned with. "You don't care whether or not I'm okay, Dylan. So stop pretending otherwise." She tries to walk past me to her car, but I remain where I am.

"I do care."

"Why? Because you bring me anonymous flowers every year? You think that earns you the right to ask me about my life? To pry when it's none of your business?"

How do I explain to her that I'm doing everything I can? That those flowers are the only way I can safely show her how much she means to me?

"I can't keep doing this anymore, Dylan."

"Doing what?"

"This." She gestures between us. "Whatever this is, I'm done with it."

"Nothing." The moment the word leave my lips, I wish I could take it back. "We're just—"

"Just what?" she demands, tears filling her eyes. "Go ahead, I would *love* to hear what you have to say about it. What are we? What am I to you? Because, as far as I know, we never even officially broke up. You just told me to get out of that hospital room, then told your family not to let me see you."

I swallow hard. *You're the only piece of joy I have left in my life, and I'm so afraid to taint it that I can only watch from a distance.*

"Who is he?"

She gapes up at me, her broken heart right there for the world to see. *I* did that. I'm more of a risk to her than anyone else, so why did I do this? Why did I linger around when I bring her nothing but pain?

"He's none of your business."

"Emma."

"No." She glares up at me, standing closer than she's been since I got back ten years ago. So close that I can see each and every color variation in her gorgeous eyes. "You don't get to care anymore, Dylan. You threw that away when you decided I wasn't allowed to be a part of your new life." She shoves past me and unlocks her car, then tosses her purse inside before whirling on me again. "You are going to leave me alone. Do you hear me? No more sneaking flowers on my birthday, no more showing up when I'm working late. You don't want to be in my life? Then *don't* be in my life!" She's yelling now, so loud that people who are walking by the church pause to look.

The edges of my vision begin to cloud. "You're making a scene." I need her to stop yelling. I need to regain control of myself. Of my racing heart.

She seizes up, her already furious gaze darkening like the sky before a storm. "Oh, I'm making a scene? Fine." Emma rips the back door of her car open and pulls out a box containing what are now wilted flowers, along with all ten vases I've brought her over the years. "Here's your scene." She shoves them into my hands. "Take these back. And don't even think about pretending like they aren't yours." Angry tears stream down her cheeks. "How dare you ruin this for me, Dylan Hunt. How *dare* you act like you care when we both know I'm nothing but a guilt project for you."

I toss the box to the side, not caring when I hear glass shatter as my own temper flares. "A guilt project? What is that supposed to mean?"

"You know exactly what it means. Poor little Emma had her heart broken. Poor little Emma still needs big, strong Dylan Hunt to look out for her." She rams her finger into my chest, and my consciousness slips.

My breathing grows ragged, and tunnel vision takes over.

All while she's still yelling at me.

I can't breathe.

I can't see anything but anger.

Red.

Fury.

"Hey! What is going on here?" *Bradyn.* His voice grounds me, but it's not enough.

Emma is still yelling.

"I don't need or want you around me, Dylan. You got that? Keep your distance, and stay out of my life!" Her door slams.

"Dylan."

"I can't—I can't breathe." I try to suck in some air, but it's strained, as though I'm trying to breathe through the hollow part of a pen.

"Come on."

"Don't touch me. Please. I just need a minute." The voices are loud in my head—the yelling. The *anger.* Black spots have infiltrated my vision, making it nearly impossible to see anything but the darkness.

Faceless men reach for me.

I clench my hands into fists.

"I'm not going to touch you," Bradyn says, his voice an echo in my mind. "But we need to get you in my truck, okay?"

Drip, drip, drip.

"Dylan, come on. Let's get you off the street."

I take a deep breath. "Yeah."

Bradyn lifts the box, and I follow him over toward his truck. By the time he's set the box in the bed of his truck, my heart rate has slowed, and my breathing has regulated—something my older brother realizes as we both climb inside.

"What happened?" he asks.

"She poked me." I touch my chest where her finger hit. Even through my shirt, I can feel the puckered scar beneath. A scar that exists because I had a dagger driven into my chest so slowly I could feel it tear through each muscle fiber.

"What was the fight about?"

"Some guy was talking to her," I say, keeping my gaze trained down at my clasped hands in my lap. "I waited around to make sure she was okay. She's right though. I lost the right to care a long time ago."

"You didn't lose the right to care," Bradyn corrects.

"But you did lose your ability to be a part of her life when you closed the door on her."

None of my brothers pull punches. I don't either. It's just not how we were raised. But right now, I wish that Braydn would let me have this one. At least until my breathing regulates.

"What's with the box?"

"Gifts."

"From you?"

I nod. "I leave flowers on her porch every year for her birthday."

"Aww, so that *was* you. Riley owes me fifty bucks."

I glare at him as he puts his truck into drive. "You bet on me?"

"Yeah. Riley overheard her quite a few years ago, thanking you, and you denying. So we made a wager."

"On whether or not I was taking her flowers."

"Yeah. None of us could catch you in the act. Kudos there, brother."

As we hit Main Street, we fall into silence. All I can see is her furious expression. Pink cheeks, wide eyes—she was hurt. Was that really all because of me? Or did that stranger say something to her that upset her?

I can't keep living in this messed-up nightmare of what my life used to be. But I don't know how to make it stop.

How do I get off this twisted rollercoaster?

"Why were you back in town?"

"Mom said you asked to linger behind. I figured you'd need a ride home, so I came into town looking for you."

"Yeah, I guess that was good foresight."

"I thought so. Call it brotherly intuition."

"It's good you got there when you did. There's no telling—" I trail off, not even wanting to think about what could have happened had he not shown up when he did. Would I have completely lost myself to the past? Would I have fought back? Hurt her?

"You wouldn't have done anything to Emma, Dylan."

"In those moments, I'm not me anymore."

"You wouldn't have hurt her," he repeats. "When I got there, you were doing everything you could to put distance between the two of you. Which means you were rational enough—even in the panic—that you knew who she was."

"I was on the way out," I tell him.

He doesn't respond.

"I need to keep Delta with me. I got comfortable and left him at home." He can sense when I start to lose myself, and so far, he's one of the only things that grounds me in the present. Even my brothers struggle to bring me back from the brink.

More than once, I've attacked them in the middle of an episode.

Which is something Emma will never understand. It's not that I don't want to be a part of her life. Honestly, it's the exact opposite.

Emma is *everything* to me. Whatever tattered remnants of my heart remain will belong to her until they put me six feet under. Maybe even after that.

She's the air that I breathe.

The sun in my sky.

But that time in captivity changed me.

It made me a monster.

Someone unworthy of even existing in the same space she does.

No matter how badly it hurts, I know that she deserves a lot better than half a man.

CHAPTER 6

EMMA

"He's alive."

I remain rooted in place, the receiver pressed against my ear, because I'm sure that I heard Tucker wrong. Even as I'm sure I misheard him, hope burns a hole in my chest. Straight through my broken heart. "What?"

"Dylan's alive, Emma. We found him."

"You—" Tears fill my eyes, but I try to keep my voice level as I set the flowers I was arranging aside and grip the receiver with both trembling hands. "How is he? Is he hurt?"

Tucker hesitates. "It's not great."

"Oh no." I choke on a sob. "How bad?"

"I don't want to get into the specifics, Emma."

Which means it's horrific. "He's alive, though?"

"Yes. Lani thinks he'll pull through, even with the injuries."

"Injuries. Where did you find him?"

"He was being held in an underground prison."

"He was being held captive?" I choke on that last word. Are the injuries because of the escape? Or did they—

"Yes. Like I said, he's in bad shape, but we got him back, and that means there's hope."

"When will you be back? When can I see him?" Hope shoves aside the grief I've carried since we were told he was killed in action.

"We'll be back stateside in two days. But I think you should wait a bit before seeing him."

"Why?" When he doesn't answer me, I become more frantic. "Why, Tucker?"

"He doesn't remember who we are. Whatever they did to him was bad, Ems, and we need to stabilize him—both physically and mentally—before you see him."

"Are you saying that for my safety or his?"

"Both," he replies. "Look. If he were to accidentally hurt you, he'd never forgive himself. I want my brother back, and I know you do too, so we need to move slow, okay?"

Tears stream down my cheeks. The pain in my chest is nearly unbearable as I imagine all of the horrific things that may have happened to him while he was held in captivity.

My Dylan.

The man I love with everything I am.

How could this happen to him?

"Okay," I whisper.

"Thank you. I'll let you know when we get back, okay?"

I nod even though he can't see me. "Tucker?"

"Yeah?"

"If you can, will you tell him I love him, please? I need him to know."

Tucker pauses a moment. "I'll tell him."

THERE'S NOT a single part of me that doesn't ache as I refill my mug for the third time, then steep a fresh bag of herbs inside. Even the hot tea can't soothe the pain in my chest. I've never lost it like that.

Not once, in my entire life, have I been so angry. I screamed at him. Yelled until my throat burned, all while he stood there like stone.

A statue that cannot be bothered by anything anymore.

What's worse is that my pain isn't even entirely about me. It's about how far he's fallen. Dylan was the most sensitive person I'd ever met in my life. He was kind, loving—feeling. And now? He might as well be made of marble.

Cold. Immovable.

I glance at the shoebox I'd pulled out from beneath the bed in what used to be my bedroom but is now a guest room. The lid is firmly in place, the contents still hidden from view. Just like they've been every day for the last ten years.

Maybe it's time to face it though.

With a deep breath, I lean forward and lift the lid.

A withered corsage made of lilacs and baby's breath is the first thing I see. Since Dylan was homeschooled and I wasn't, he'd gone with me to my prom. It had been a perfect night.

I toss the corsage into the trash can beside me.

Next, I lift a photograph of the two of us. Taken by Tucker right after Dylan smeared some vanilla ice cream onto my nose.

Straight into the trash can.

With each discarded memory, I expect relief. Instead, I only feel more pain.

My phone rings, ripping me off of memory lane. I check the readout. When I see Kennedy's name on the screen, I take a deep breath. She's called nearly half a dozen times in the last hour. Same thing with Lani, Alice, Talia—they've all called nonstop. And I know that if I don't answer at least one of them, the calls won't let up. "Hello?"

"How are you?"

"Fine."

"Emma."

Embarrassment heats my cheeks. "I'm assuming Bradyn told you what happened?"

She lets out a sigh. "He did. And now I'm going to ask again, how are you?"

"Mad. Hurt. But it doesn't matter. None of it does, and I think I'm starting to realize that."

"What do you mean, it doesn't matter?"

"Dylan will never be the man he was again, and I am finally coming to terms with that. Maybe now he'll leave me alone so I can move on."

She pauses a moment. "Look, I know I wasn't around when everything between you two went sour, but I hope you know—he's hurting too."

"I really want to believe that, but I don't. I need to go, okay? I'll talk to you tomorrow. Thanks for calling."

"I'm here if you need me."

To defend Dylan. "I know. Thanks. Bye." Without waiting for her to say anything, I power down my cell phone and toss it onto the counter. After adding honey and milk to my tea, I take the mug into my living room and sit down on my couch, tucking both knees up to my chest and wrapping my arms around them.

I can't get the image of him out of my head.

Standing there, unmoving, completely unaffected by the pain he's caused over the years. Pain that I've buried because I know that, even with what I'm feeling, it's *nothing* compared to what he suffered over there. He could break my heart a thousand times over, and it still wouldn't match up.

But I'm so tired of pretending that I'm okay. Of not wanting to fully grieve because it means I have to really let him go. Maybe that's why God hasn't healed my heart yet. Because I wasn't truly ready to surrender my feelings for Dylan Hunt or the love that I still carry for him, despite everything.

Will I ever be able to move on?

My gaze lands on the photograph sitting on top of my coffee table. A woman and her baby. Me and my mother. Unfolding my legs, I reach forward and take it into my hands. The truth is that I have an entire family out there waiting to meet me.

People who won't remind me of everything that went so horribly wrong.

But am I really selfish enough to leave my friends behind in search of a past I never thought I wanted to know?

Someone knocks on the door. Even though company is the last thing I want, I get to my feet and pull it open, fully expecting it to be Pastor Ford coming to check in on me after the very public fight in the church parking lot.

What I'm not expecting is Mattheus on my porch, a

bouquet of bright white daisies in his hand. He smiles at me widely. "Hey, Emmaline."

Alarms screech somewhere in my mind. *How did he find me? Did he follow me?* "Hey. How did you know where I live?"

"Asked around. Small town." He offers me the flowers. "For you. I know I said I was going to give you time, but I realized that I never gave you anything for your birthday. Since it's the first one I've actually been able to somewhat celebrate with you, I didn't want to mess it up."

"Thanks." I take the flowers, feeling a bit of my pain ease away thanks to the distraction of having my brother here.

My brother.

It is a small town. And since Talia knew who he was, it wouldn't be unusual if she told him where to find me, right? Honestly, he could have asked the florist. Genny has known me since I used to work there.

I always wanted a sibling. And here one is, on my doorstep. "Won't you come in?"

"I would love to. Thanks." He closes the door behind him as I carry the flowers into the house. "They smelled amazing in the floral shop, so I hope you like them."

Leaning in, I sniff the flowers, drawing in the delicate scents. "They do smell amazing." Reaching under my sink, I pull out a vase I bought at the farmer's market last year and move to set it on the counter. But as I straighten, my vision swims, and the vase falls to the floor.

Glass shatters.

My stomach rolls as the ground sways beneath me.

"Oh no, I'm sorry." I try to lean down to grab it but lose my ability to stand. Mattheus is there though, wrapping an arm around my waist to steady me.

"You're okay," he says. "Just ease into it."

Ease into it. Fear ices through all other emotion, those alarms louder than they've ever been.

Because he's not surprised. Or worried. Which means — "Did you do this?" I ask, my voice wavering.

"You'll come to forgive me one day," he says. "Maybe." Reaching into his pocket, he withdraws his cell and taps the screen. "Yeah. It's me. We're going to be wheels up in twenty minutes. Got it? Great."

"W-w-what are y-y-you doing?" I stammer, slurring my words so badly they're barely audible.

"Putting my family back together."

He reaches into his other pocket and withdraws a syringe. "Sorry about this. You shouldn't feel it now, but it's going to leave you with one nasty headache when you finally wake up."

"Please don't."

"Too late." Cold surges through my veins, spreading from the side of my neck. And as it does, my vision goes completely dark, leaving me with only one final thought.

What will this do to Dylan?

CHAPTER 7
DYLAN

Throwing hay bales is a poor way to blow off steam when your mind is a firestorm.

Even though it's barely eight in the morning, sweat is already slicking my skin. I toss another bale onto the stack, then head back to the trailer to repeat the process. Hopefully enough times to wear myself out so much that I won't be able to think straight.

Maybe then I can get her out of my head so I can sleep longer than the thirty minutes I got last night. Never in my life have I wished meds worked for me like I do now. I've tried them all though.

Everything from prescriptions to herbal blends, and *nothing* has eased the monsters in my mind. The creatures that stand ready to devour me the second I let my guard down.

The scent of alfalfa surrounds me as I toss another bale

into place, rip the hay hooks free, and turn back toward the trailer once again. But as I do, I catch sight of Gibson Lawson in his sheriff's uniform, walking toward me with Bradyn and Tucker at his side.

All three men have strained expressions, their shoulders squared as though they're prepping for a fight. *Fantastic.* I toss the hay hooks as far from me as I can, not wanting them anywhere nearby because there are times I don't trust my own mind.

And it doesn't look like whatever news they have to deliver is going to be easy.

"What is it?" I demand as soon as they're close enough.

"Hey, Dylan," Gibson starts. "I need to ask you a few questions."

"What about?"

"Just answer them so we can move on," Tucker snaps.

Gibson tosses him an apologetic glance. We've known Gibson his entire life. He and Lani were best friends growing up, so he spent a lot of time here with us. Which only makes his tense expression even more worrisome.

"What's this about?" I demand.

"Where were you last night?" he asks.

"Home."

"Can anyone verify that?"

"This is ridiculous," Tucker snaps.

"I agree, but I have to ask. Their fight was public, Tucker. Dozens of people saw it."

His word choice sends me spiraling. My heart begins to race, and spots dance at the edges of my vision. *"Where were you last night?"* He would only be asking that if something happened, right? Determining whether or not I had an alibi. What if— I charge forward. "What happened? Where is Emma?"

Gibson glares at Tucker.

"We don't know," Bradyn answers.

"What do you mean you *don't know*?" I demand, hands clenching into fists.

"Breathe, Dylan."

"I'm breathing fine!" I yell at Tucker. "What I want to know is what happened to Emma?"

"Talia Matthews called me late last night. Emma never showed up for her birthday dinner at the diner, so she and Connor went to check on her. They found her door unlocked, a full mug of tea on her coffee table alongside a box of mementos surrounding your relationship, and broken glass in the kitchen, but she was gone."

"Gone." The air is sucked from my lungs.

"Yes. And because of your *very* public fight yesterday, I need to ask the right questions. I know you wouldn't hurt her, but—"

"It's your job," I reply, my tone going flat. *Keep your head. It's a mission like any other. Find her.*

I have to find her.

Find her. And make whoever took her pay.

"As I said, I was here. Had dinner with my parents, then went home."

"What time was that?"

"Ten," I reply.

"So you were with your parents until ten."

"Yes."

"Talia and Conner discovered she was missing about seven thirty." Gibson slips his notebook back into his pocket. "Which means you couldn't have done it."

"Of course he couldn't have done it," Bradyn growls. "We told you that."

"Yes, but now that I have confirmation, I can officially ask for your help in tracking her down. I don't have the manpower for an all-out search."

"Is it possible she left for a walk?"

"No," I tell Tucker. "Emma doesn't like to be out at night. She wouldn't have gone for a walk. Why did no one come here last night? Why wait until this morning? That's a massive head start you gave to whoever took her."

"We checked the woods behind her house, the library, everywhere she could have gone. I checked with neighbors, and we were searching her house until nearly two in the morning. Then, we spent the rest of the time scouring all security cameras in town to see if we could see anything."

I withdraw my cell and toss it to Tucker. "The last picture I took is of the man who wanted to talk to her in the diner. It's distant, but you should be able to run him."

"On it."

"Let me know when you have a name," Gibson says. "And send me that picture."

"Will do." Tucker jogs off in the direction of his house, which is less than a mile from mine.

"That man was in the diner with her. Did he give Talia a name?" I ask.

"She didn't get a name," Gibson says. "There's more to it too. Another reason why I don't think I can call her a true missing person yet." Gibson removes his hat and runs his hand through his hair.

"What is it?" I demand.

Gibson looks from Bradyn to me. "Talia said that she overheard some of their conversation. The mystery man told Emma that he knew her birth mother. Dylan, you know her better than anyone. Would she run off like that without telling someone?"

"No. And she would never stand Talia and Connor up like that."

"That's what I thought too." He shakes his head. "I need to get back to the station. Let me know when you have something."

I don't even wait for him to walk away before I'm turning, hands clenched into fists, making my way to my UTV. *I will tear him apart for hurting her.* Red floods my vision at the mere thought of what I'll do to him if even a single hair on Emma's gorgeous head is missing.

For the first time though, I don't fight the anger. I let it seep into my system, driving me toward the mission they'll have to kill me to keep me off of. I climb behind the wheel, and Delta hops in the back. Before I can take off, Bradyn jumps into the passenger seat and grips the stability handle.

Since he doesn't say a word, I don't hesitate before pulling away from the barn and heading toward my house. I'll gear up and head out, then let Tucker guide me if he finds anything else. But I know better than most that sometimes you have to start right back at the beginning. Which means I need to see her house.

In silence, I park in front of my house; then Bradyn and I head up the porch steps. He waits while I unlock the door and follows me inside.

"If you're going to try to talk me out of this, then you should know that there's not a force in this world that will keep me from finding her." I grab my tactical backpack, the one I keep stocked with emergency supplies, setting it on the counter to go through it and double-check that everything I need is here.

"I'm not going to talk you out of it." Bradyn crosses his arms. "But I need to know where your head is at. Yesterday, you lost it because she poked you in the chest. What if this is worse? I won't lose you again, Dylan."

After setting down a bottle of water I was preparing to shove into the bag, I turn toward my oldest brother. His expression is all concern, and I love him for it. "Do you remember when Elliot and Nova were getting married? In his vows, he told her that she was the only one who could calm the storm in him.”

“I remember.”

I take a step closer. “Emma *is* my storm, Bradyn. She is the wind that tears me apart, the rain that hammers against my skin, the lightning that shoots through my blood, making me feel completely alive and torn apart all at the same time. She is the *only* thing that had me clinging to life when I was in that pit. I can’t trust myself around her, Bradyn, but I know who I’ll be without her. She’s the only thing grounding me, and if anything happens to her—” I trail off. “You might as well put me down too.”

“Then we need to make sure nothing happens to her.” Bradyn clasps a hand on my shoulder. “I made a call, and Elliot and Nova will be back later tonight. I’ve already let Riley know we need to meet, so he’ll join us at the office. Don’t go after her without checking in with us first, okay? We need to treat this like any other mission. Even though it’s not.”

I nod. “I’ll check in with you all after I head to her house.”

“Sounds good.” Bradyn heads for the door. “We’ll find her, Dylan.”

“I know we will.”

He leaves the room, and, alone for the first time since hearing the news, I sink back onto the barstool and close my eyes. In the silence, I sit, letting my mind replay every moment while I waited for her to step out of the diner.

What would have happened if, instead of arguing with her, I'd told her how I felt?

What would have happened if we hadn't gotten into that fight?

Would she still be gone?

How soon after that moment did he take her?

The weight of knowing I may never see her again settles in, and for a brief moment, it's not me who suffered in that pit—it's Emma.

Her blonde hair streaked with blood and dirt.

Her face bruised.

It's her blood that falls to the ground.

Drip. Drip. Drip.

Delta rubs against my legs and whimpers, then paws at me. Without thinking, I sink out of the stool and onto the ground, then wrap my arms around Delta. He leans against me.

"I can't lose her," I whisper to my empty home. "I can't lose her." And even though I'm not entirely sure He listens to me, I add, "God, please don't let me lose her."

EMMA'S HOUSE looks nearly the same as it did when we were growing up. The same photos are on the wall, the same throw pillows on the couch. There are a few differences now—a new blanket on the back of the couch. New patterns on the dishes displayed behind glass in her mother's china cabinet.

But it's almost like stepping back in time. After slipping gloves onto my hands, I move farther into the house, looking for anything that might be out of place. It's been years since I was in here last, but I know Emma. She likes everything to be in its place. Always.

I start in the living room where a box is sitting open. Leaning to peer inside, I feel the dagger slicing through my chest all over again. Pictures of us when we were kids. Teens so in love they never thought it would end.

I lift the top image, staring at the man with my face. He looks just like me, his eyes the same color, but there's no darkness in his expression. No shadow overcasting his soul. Dropping the photo, I peer into the trash can. It's nearly empty, a photograph upside down on top. I reach in and withdraw the image of us from the summer before I left for the military.

I'd playfully bumped her ice cream cone and smeared vanilla all over her face, and Tucker had snapped the photo.

My stomach churns, and I set the image back into the box instead of throwing it away. She can do that later, but I can't.

Beneath it is the corsage I gifted her for her senior

prom. We'd gone together and spent the night laughing and dancing. I never wanted it to end.

I place it in the box, right on top of the picture.

Was she looking at this when he came for her? Was her broken heart the last thing she thought of?

Stay focused, Dylan.

Taking a deep breath, I leave the living room and move into the kitchen. Glass crunches beneath my boots as I walk around the island. Kneeling, I lift a piece of broken glass, along with a floral stem that fell from the bouquet of daisies on the counter.

Is this how he got her to open the door? He offered her flowers for her birthday?

My stomach twists, and bile rises in the back of my throat. Straightening, I set the bloom back on the countertop and survey the rest of the kitchen. Nothing else seems out of place. Aside from the broken glass and the flowers, I don't see any signs of a struggle.

My gaze lands on the hall leading to her bedroom.

Heart racing a million miles a minute, I start in that direction. Gibson didn't say anything about there being signs of a sexual assault, but he didn't say anything against it, either. And if she was taken prior to seven thirty, her bed should be made.

The door is partially closed, and I pause outside of her room for a moment. *Please let everything be in order.* Placing my hand gently on the door, I push it open and breathe a sigh of relief when I see her pristinely made bed.

It doesn't rule it out, but it's a bit of hope.

The delicate scent of her jasmine perfume fills my lungs as I step through the threshold of her room. She surrounds me, almost as though she could step out of the adjoining bathroom at any moment and demand to know why I'm standing in her bedroom.

I gently lift the book on her bedside table and run my fingers over the cover.

Will she ever get the chance to finish it?

Something brushes against my leg, so I take a step back and find myself staring down at a pair of wide blue eyes.

"Who are you?" I ask as though the cat could answer me himself.

It meows and rubs against my legs, so I kneel down and touch its head.

"Are you hungry? Did anyone feed you last night?" Gibson didn't mention a cat, did he? What if he didn't know he was here?

"Come on, let's go find you some food." Straightening, I take one last look around the bedroom before heading back out into the hall and making my way into the kitchen. Since I keep Delta's food in the pantry, it's the first place I look. I'm grateful when I see the cans of wet cat food lined up neatly on the shelf.

After retrieving the animal's bowl, I dump the food into

it, then toss the empty can into the trash bin, and place the bowl onto the floor. The cat eats happily, fluffy gray tail swishing as he does.

How did he get her out of here without a fight?

Emma's no soldier, but she's extremely competent with self-defense. She and Lani took classes together when they were juniors in high school. She excelled too. Even taught a few classes up until I left for the service.

Given there's no blood on the floor or any signs of a struggle anywhere but the kitchen—she must not have been able to fight. The lack of blood doesn't mean she left alive though. I know all too well that you can kill without spilling a single drop.

But the fact that he moved her is a sign that maybe he took her alive. Somehow.

My gaze lands on the flowers.

Those had to be his way in.

I lift another bloom, and a scent that doesn't belong teases my nose. Pushing it away, I study the tips of the flowers, running my gloved fingertips over them. When I look down at the blue, I notice it's dusted with white.

Drugs.

She was drugged.

Which means he took her alive.

Carefully setting the bloom aside, I reach into my pocket and withdraw my cell phone.

"Lawson," Gibson answers on the first ring.

"Did you bag one of the flowers?"

He's quiet a moment. "The flowers?"

"You said you had your crime scene tech here; did he take one of the flowers near the broken vase?"

"Let me check." I can hear papers ruffling in the background; then he mutters something under his breath. "They were noted in the description of the scene, but I don't see that any were bagged."

"You need better resources," I say, not caring at all whether he takes offense to it or not.

"You're telling me. My usual guy is out on vacation, and the county sent someone over who I'm fairly certain can't even tie his own shoes. What's with the flowers?"

"There's a powdery substance on the petals. Likely a drug that he used to subdue her without a fight. I want to know what it is."

"You and me both. I'll head down there myself and bag one."

"No need. I'll do it for you and drop it by."

"Great. Tucker get any leads on the image you took of our mystery man?"

"He's running him now. I'll check in on him once I leave here."

"Okay. Thanks. We're running prints from the house too."

"Let me know if you find anything." I end the call without saying goodbye, then search Emma's drawers until

I find a plastic Ziplock bag. After sliding the flower carefully inside, I set it on the counter.

The cat comes meandering in, and I reach down and scoop him up before he can step on the glass or the drugs. Without knowing what it is, I can't be sure Emma's cat would survive exposure. Which also means he can't stay here.

"Looks like you're coming home with me," I say to the animal. "I hope you like dogs."

CHAPTER 8
EMMA

In my nightmare, I fight for my life.

But when my eyes flutter open, there's no one around but me. Head throbbing, I sit up out of bed, ready for a mug of tea and a shower that will hopefully clear my brain fog. But the events of the last few hours slam into me one by one, and I realize that it's not my bed I'm in—and the panic kicks right back in.

Heart racing, I throw the covers aside and jump out of the plush four-poster bed, complete with what I used to call fairy-tale curtains surrounding it. The room I'm in is *huge*. As in presidential-suite-at-a luxury-hotel huge.

This is all wrong.

The carpet is red with golden flowers—a relatively obnoxious pattern that makes my already throbbing headache intensify. The walls are covered in cream-colored wallpaper with light golden swirls. There's a nightstand, a dresser, and a door that leads to an adjoining bathroom.

Where am I? Where did he take me?

I rush toward the door first, but when the handle won't turn, I head for the window and throw the curtains aside. An audible gasp leaves my lips when I find myself staring down at waves crashing into jagged rocks. I'm at least three floors up and on a coast somewhere. *But where?* I don't remember ever leaving Texas, and I certainly don't recall any part of the Lone Star State looking like this.

Then again, given that I can't swim, I tend to avoid water vacations.

Unsure what else to do, I rummage through the drawers and closet, searching the room for a weapon. Anything I can use to defend myself against the liar who brought me here. *Brother.* How could I have been so stupid? I let him into my house. I went against my better judgment and ignored the fact that it was creepy that he tracked down where I live.

But, hey, I just invited him right on in, didn't I? All because of the picture and a pretty story about how I had a family out there that wanted me.

That photograph could have been of anyone, and I fell right into his hands because I'm so desperate not to be alone.

So desperate, in fact, that I forgot that I'm *not* alone. I have people who love me. People who care about me. Tears fill my eyes, and my throat constricts. *Will I ever see them again?*

God, where am I?

Muffled voices sound outside the door, so I rush back toward the bed and lift the closest thing I can find—an ornate lamp that probably cost more than my entire collection of furniture. It's heavy, so at least I know it'll do some damage if he gets close to me.

Seconds later, a lock clicks, and the door is pushed open.

"You," I growl as Mattheus steps into the room. He smiles at me, seemingly unbothered by the fact that he kidnapped me.

"I am so sorry for what I had to do to get you here, dear sister. But time was of the essence, and I was worried you wouldn't come."

"Sister? I am not your sister. You lied to me. Who even are you?"

"I'm—" He glances away from me to someone standing just out of sight of the doorway. I can't quite see whoever he's looking at, but his expression turns serious as he nods and moves toward the side of the room. "I think our father can explain things better."

A second man walks into the room. He's tall and middle-aged—his hair already turning a salt-and-pepper gray at the temples. His eyes are soft blue, and when he smiles at me, he seems almost genuinely delighted. But there's something there—something about him that makes the hairs on the back of my neck stand on end.

Probably the fact that he had a hand in my kidnapping.

"My dearest Gwendolyn," he says softly. "It is you. You're the spitting image of your mother."

I stare at him, unsure how to respond. Mattheus showed me the gravestone with Gwendolyn written across the cool stone, so the name isn't a surprise. But am I really going to believe him?

Am I really going to believe that the guy who kidnapped me is my brother?

"I'm sorry." The man presses both hands to his heart. "You are Emmaline now. I'm just so thrilled to see you." Tears fill his eyes, and he takes a step closer. "Mattheus *is* your brother," he says. "And I'm Gio Karver. Your—" He trails off, as though he needs to catch his breath. "Your father."

"My father." I look from him to Mattheus, who is smiling proudly as he watches the entire exchange. "I don't believe you. What kind of brother kidnaps his sister?"

"It's the truth. I told you, time was of the essence." Mattheus reaches into his pocket and withdraws his cell phone. "And while you were sleeping, I took the liberty of swabbing your cheek for your DNA. Which I had run against mine. I have the proof here if you want to see it."

"While I was sleeping? You mean, while I was under the effects of whatever you used to drug me? Why would I want to see it?" I demand. "You kidnapped me! For all I know, it could be fake!" My hand tightens around the lamp, though I'm not entirely sure who I should throw it at first, given they're both blocking my only exit.

"You *drugged* her? Mattheus, you said she wanted to meet us," Gio snaps, turning toward Mattheus, who visibly pales. "That she was excited and came willingly."

"No. None of that is true," I snap. "Well, the meeting part might have been if I'd been given time to actually process the news that I had a family out there."

"She seemed excited to meet all of us. And after the fight she had with her boyfriend, I assumed she was going to delay things. With Momma in the state that she's in, I didn't want to wait too long. I truly am sorry, Emmaline. What I gave you was a natural sedative. Nothing too strong."

"Are you even *listening* to yourself?" I snap.

"Please, Emmaline, give us a chance to explain," Gio urges. "And please do *not* tell your mother how you were brought here. I fear she won't be able to handle it. We can absolutely do another DNA test if you'd like. This one while you're alert and consenting." His tone is so strained that I narrow my gaze on him, trying to read the situation as best I can.

How would one of the Hunts take this?

What would they do?

Truthfully, I have no idea. I'm a kindergarten teacher,

not a trained soldier. One thing is certain though. Right now, I am out of my element. I'm nowhere near my home, friends, or anyone who can help me. Which means pretending to play ball might just be my only chance at surviving this.

So I take a deep, steadying breath. *Lord, help me, please.*

"What do you mean 'in the state that she's in'?" I look to Mattheus. "That's what you said, right?"

Gio clears his throat. "Your mother, Felicity, has been inconsolable since we discovered you were alive. She blames herself for losing you."

"Mattheus said I was kidnapped by a nurse in the hospital."

"You were. While you were in the nursery. Your mother had a difficult pregnancy that left her unable to have any more children after you. While she was recovering, the nurse offered to take you to the nursery so she could sleep. She agreed, and that was the last we ever saw you alive."

"Alive. Meaning you saw a baby you thought was me."

"From a distance," he explains. "Neither of us could bring ourselves to get any closer. Something I blame myself for. If I had just been strong enough, then maybe I would have noticed something and realized that baby wasn't you. That you were still alive." He trails off. "But you're here now, my darling daughter. And look at you! Just as beautiful as your mother."

I want to believe him.

I want so badly to believe everything he's saying.

But the kidnapping is making it really, really hard.

"I want to see those results, and I want to go home."

"Of course, of course," Gio says. "Can I ask that you at least meet your mother first? She's waiting for us in the dining room for dinner but has no idea you're here. I would love for her to meet you. Then, if you still choose to go, I'll have our private plane deliver you home as soon as possible." When I hesitate, he adds, "Please. I apologize for how you were brought to us, but I'm so grateful you're here."

I consider what would happen if I pushed back. If I were to demand that he take me home right now. Would they want to see me again? Does it matter? Whether he approves of Mattheus's methods or not, I was kidnapped. Not only that, but I was drugged too. Drugged and abducted from my living room.

Meaning I definitely can't trust Mattheus.

Given that Gio raised him, can I trust him? Or the woman they claim is my mother?

Play ball, Emma. Get the lay of the land; then find a way to escape.

"I want to make a phone call." I continue to cling to the lamp. "If you allow me that, then I'll stay for dinner while you get your pilot ready to take me home."

"Of course. Mattheus, allow her to use your phone."

"Here you go." He unlocks it, then hands it to me, so I

remove one hand from the lamp to take the phone from him.

I stare down at the phone. *Who do I call?* It's not like I have anyone's number memorized. Everything's saved on my contact list. What a fun side-effect of not needing to type in a phone number. Aside from 9-1-1, I have nothing memorized.

There's an idea.

Except—what if they take that as a threat? What if they silence me before I can even utter a single word?

Think, Emma. And then it hits me. There is *one* number I do have memorized. Because, once upon a time, I was a love-stricken teenager calling to talk to her boyfriend every few minutes.

Please answer. I type in the numbers, then press the phone to my ear as it begins to ring. *Come on.*

"Hello?" Ruth's voice is like a beacon. A familiarity that brings tears to my eyes and releases some of my fear.

"It's Emma," I choke out, my words strained with emotion.

"Emma! Oh, thank God above. You're okay. Where are you? Call Dylan," she adds, likely to her husband, Tommy. Where she is, he's never far, and vice versa.

"I don't know where I am yet, but I'm okay." I look to Gio for confirmation on where we are, but he doesn't say a word. Just watches me, expression serious.

He's nervous. As he should be, I suppose. Given how I was brought here.

"The boys are trying to find you. Everyone is. The sheriff has combed through most of the county by now."

"I'm fairly certain I'm not in Texas anymore."

Gio shakes his head.

"And I'm with my birth family. Maybe. I need to see the DNA results first."

She pauses a moment. "Your birth family," she repeats slowly.

"Yes."

"Are you there willingly?"

"No. But they said I can come back tonight."

"Tonight. That's good. Why don't you tell us where you are, and we'll send the boys to get you. That pilot they use is already fueled up and on standby."

"He's coming," Tommy says urgently. "Put her on speaker."

The phone shifts, and there's some crackling before the tone changes.

"Are you hurt, sweetheart?" Tommy asks.

"Aside from a nasty headache, thanks to whatever I was drugged with, I'm okay. No one has hurt me."

"Drugged and kidnapped," Ruth snaps.

"Dylan told us what your house looked like. That man who abducted you, what's his name?"

"Mattheus Karver," I tell them. "He claims that he's my

brother." As I say it, I glare in his direction. He offers me an awkward smile and shoves both hands into his pockets.

They're both listening to everything I say, but since I'm too afraid to turn my back to either of them, I remain where I am.

Gio steps forward. "May I?" He holds out his hand.

But I don't relinquish the phone. Instead, I put it on speakerphone.

"This is Emmaline's birth father," he says. "I'm afraid my son got overzealous in his attempt to surprise my wife and me with meeting our daughter."

A door slams, and I know—without a doubt—Dylan is there.

I can sense him, just as I always can.

Even with however many miles are between us.

"Overzealous?" Dylan growls. "He drugged and abducted her."

"Who is this?" Gio asks.

"Her boyfriend," Mattheus chimes in. "I recognize the voice."

"Not her boyfriend," Dylan corrects quickly. It's a dagger to my heart, even though it's the truth. "But I am someone who will hunt down anyone who so much as lays a finger on her." The ferocity in his voice is not something I'm accustomed to. Even this new version of Dylan, the cold one, has never held such anger in his tone.

Gio glances back at Mattheus. "There's no need for

that. As I said, my son was merely excited to find his sister and didn't want to risk losing the chance to bring her home. My wife is not doing well since she discovered our daughter is alive. He was worried about his mother. I'm sure you can understand that."

"Pine Creek *is* her home."

Gio's smile fades. "We merely wanted to ensure that those who know her back in your small town are aware that she is fine and not being held against her will. Should she choose to return home, we will escort her safely."

Should she choose. My stomach churns.

Play it cool. I have to keep my composure. Trust in God. He'll get me through this.

"Emma." My name rolling off Dylan's lips has always held such power over me. It's the way he says it, as though it's his favorite word in the entire world. But now—after our fight and his very quick declaration that I am not romantically involved with him whatsoever—I shove that power away.

Because he's not mine. Just as I'm not his.

"I'm fine, Dylan. I apologize for calling, Mrs. Hunt. I didn't know anyone else's number by heart, and I wanted everyone to know that I'm okay."

"Honey, I'm so glad you called. Please know that we all love you, and we only want to know that you are safe."

"She is," Gio says. "I can assure you of that. No one will harm Emmaline while she is with us."

"Where are you?" Dylan demands.

"I'm not at liberty to share that with you," Gio says coolly. "Given that I don't know you and you've been nothing but aggressive on this call, I have no interest in telling you where you can find the most important people in the world to me. Your declaration to hunt someone down was a threat, and I don't take too kindly to those. However, as I said, Emmaline is safe, and she will contact you all when she chooses to return home." He takes a step back.

"Listen up—"

I take the phone off speaker and press it to my ear again. "Dylan, stop. I'm fine right now, okay? As soon as I can, I'll make sure you know where I am. Please make sure someone takes care of my cat for me."

"You're not safe. Anyone willing to go to those lengths to get to you is not trustworthy."

"I know." *Tone calm. Words chosen carefully.* "If I could swim, this place might feel like paradise," I add with a smile, hoping he'll read between the lines. *Ocean.* I am somewhere near the ocean.

Dylan is silent a moment. "I'm coming for you," he says. "I promise."

My hand tightens on the phone. "Talk soon." I end the call.

"That boy sounds dangerous," Gio comments as he turns to Mattheus, who nods and slips from the room.

"He's just temperamental. Always has been."

"And he is not your boyfriend?"

"Just a really good friend who cares about me. Can you blame him? It's not like Mattheus approached me and asked me to willingly go with him."

Gio runs a hand through his hair. "That is fair. I apologize."

I want to call Dylan back. Stay on the phone with him until someone comes to get me—but I get the sense that would just not be possible. I have to put my trust in him that he'll somehow find a way to locate me.

Until then, I have to play ball. And a deal is a deal.

"The results are on this phone?" I ask.

"Yes. In the text messages, there's a photograph sent from the lab. The certified results will be in tomorrow. The packet was sent overnight through the mail."

I open the messages and stare down at the image sent through the only message on the phone. It's a screenshot of a medical document, and I have to zoom in to read.

There are four columns with a bunch of things I don't understand, but multiple markers are circled in red. *47% out of 50% shared DNA. Sibling match.*

So it is true. Regardless of how I was brought here, according to this document, Mattheus is my brother.

"Can we go see your mother now?" Gio questions. "I fear, if I keep her waiting much longer, she's going to come looking for us and spoil the surprise. You can always call them back. Feel free to keep the phone if it will make you more comfortable."

"Okay. Thanks."

"Anything for you," he says with a kind smile, then takes my hand and loops it through his arm. It feels strange to be walking so close to a man I just met. But I imagine that had I not been kidnapped all those years ago, this would likely feel as familiar as breathing.

Kidnapped away from my family.

Kidnapped and brought back.

There's some irony in that.

We step into a brightly lit hallway with sconces placed every few feet along the walls. The wallpaper is a cream color with faint golden stripes. The flooring out here is a dark wood, which gleams beneath the light.

"This is beautiful."

"Thank you. It has been my home since I was a boy," he says. "I always wanted to raise my family among the history here." He leads me down the hallway toward a set of stairs. We descend slowly. "The family who raised you —were they kind?"

"Very. God blessed me by placing me with kind people. I know that a lot of kids who end up in the system don't get so lucky."

"Yes, well, I'm glad you didn't suffer as a child, though I wish we'd been able to raise you."

"I'm sorry, that's not what I meant." My cheeks heat.

Regardless of how I got here, I feel a little guilty. And how twisted is that? They kidnapped me, but *I* feel guilty because I loved my adoptive parents.

He pats my hand. "I know it's not." He pauses outside a set of double doors. "Are you ready?"

I take a deep breath. Why does this feel so intimidating? "Yes."

Gio reaches forward and pushes the door open. A long table gleams beneath a chandelier hanging above, flickering lights that mimic candlelight. Mattheus is already here and is sitting on the left side while a woman sits directly in front of me, her back to me.

"My dearest, I have someone to introduce you to."

"Who, my love?" the woman turns, her blonde curls swaying as she turns to face me.

The moment our eyes meet, my mouth falls slack. It's like looking into a mirror, and any doubts I still had vanish as I stand here, staring at my mother.

Her gaze darkens a moment. "Who is this?"

"Do you really need to ask?" Gio says. "This is our dearest Gwendolyn," he says softly. "Our darling daughter who was stolen from us. Mattheus found her and brought her home."

The woman—Felicity—stands slowly, then crosses over toward me on tall heels that click as she walks. The black dress she wears is so different from what I normally wear—its tight fabric hugs her curves, while I prefer to wear looser fabric.

But her eyes—they're the same shade as mine.

Her nose is dusted with the same freckles.

And for a moment, I forget all about the manner in which I was brought here and let myself sink into the knowledge that I have a living family. That they didn't toss me aside at birth. They wanted me.

Truly wanted me.

"Hi," I manage.

She comes to a stop before me, her eyes filling with tears as she reaches up and cups my cheek. "My darling daughter," she chokes out. "You *are* alive."

CHAPTER 9

DYLAN

"*If I could swim, this place might feel like paradise.*" It was a code. Emma's trying to tell me something about where she is. "She's near an ocean," I tell my mom as I set the phone onto the counter.

"An ocean. That could mean practically anywhere," my dad replies, frustrated. "How do we even begin to narrow it down?"

"Tucker's working on a trace," I tell them. "I called him right after you called me. He hacked into the call."

"Of course he did," Dad replies proudly. "Then he should have a lock on her, right?"

"Maybe."

"She's okay," my mother says. "That's what matters, right?"

"She's in an undisclosed location with a man who

kidnapped her. Blood relatives or not, that's a far cry from okay." After withdrawing my cell phone, I snap a picture of the caller ID readout, then set the phone back onto the receiver. "I need to get over to Tucker and see if he has a location yet. Call me if she calls again."

"We will," my dad assures me.

As I try to walk past my mom, she reaches out and touches my arm. The contact is sudden, as is the jolt of panic that shoots through me. If I know a hug is coming, I can be prepared for it, but the random touches always push me closer to the edge.

Still, she's my mom, so I try to take a deep breath and turn toward her, resisting the urge to pull away.

"Honey, she's okay."

Is she? "Yeah. Thanks for letting me know she called." I step away now and make my way toward the front door, Delta on my heels. The sun is already beginning its descent, though sundown is still hours away. Every minute that passes without me knowing her location is another minute that she could end up hurt.

Who is this guy who drugged her? Is he really her brother? Then why the drugs? I'm betting the phone call was a proof of life for us. That way, we'll think she's okay and stop looking for her.

It won't work.

The only way I'll stop looking for Emma is if I'm buried six feet deep in the cold, hard ground.

I hop into my UTV while Delta jumps into the back. As soon as he's lying down, I take off toward Tucker's house. His wife, Alice, is sitting on the porch, a book in her hand. When I pull up and shut off the engine, she glances up and smiles at me.

"Hey, Dylan. How are you?" Her smile fades just a bit when she sees my expression.

"Fine."

When I first met the woman who would marry my twin, I didn't trust her. She'd been accused of murder, and all the evidence pointed toward her. But once we'd proven her innocence, she became one of the few people I'm comfortable enough around to really let my guard down.

Most of the time.

"You're not, but we don't have to talk about it," Alice says. "Tucker is inside. In his office."

"Thanks."

"You're welcome." She smiles softly, then returns her attention to her book as I make my way inside. Delta runs off toward Tango, who jumps up when he sees his brother. As the two of them start wrestling, I withdraw my cell phone from my pocket and step into Tucker's office.

In true Tucker fashion, he doesn't even notice that I'm here—something that's not at all surprising. When Tucker is in front of a computer, the rest of the world doesn't exist. I tell him all the time that he might as well be part computer for how thoroughly he 'plugs in.'

"You got a location?"

He glances over at me. "Huh? Oh, no. Not yet."

"How is that possible? You couldn't trace it?"

"It wasn't made over a cellular network. Whoever let her make that call didn't want us to be able to find her."

I hand him my phone with the photo of the caller ID on the screen. "This is the number. Can you track it using this?"

"Already got it from the call," he says, tapping his computer. "So far, no luck. I'm sorry, Dylan, I'm trying."

"I know you are." But it's not enough. It won't be until she's safely back in Pine Creek.

"She sounded okay. Calm, considering."

"The man that came onto the call right as I was going into Mom's, did you hear what he said?"

Tucker shakes his head. "Not at first. I came on right as you were threatening him. Nice move, by the way."

I let the slight roll off my back. Should I have threatened him? Probably not. It's better to keep everyone involved in captive situations calm—that way, no one makes any rash moves. "He said he was her birth father."

"Whoa." Tucker shakes his head. "What is going on?"

"I don't know, but we need to find out."

"I texted Gibson and let him know you were talking to her and I was trying to get a trace. He's waiting to hear from us."

In my desperate need to get here and have Tucker trace the number, I hadn't even thought to call up the sheriff. So, I do that now.

"Tucker get a lock on her?" he asks after answering on the first ring. Likely because he was staring at his phone, waiting for a call. Emma is family to everyone here, and everyone wants her home.

"No. They're bouncing it all over the place via Wi-Fi. Or something like that. Tucker can give you the specifics. She did try to give me a hint, though. Said that if she could swim, the place she's being held would be paradise."

"Tropical locations, then?"

"That would be a good place to start. Have you looked into flight records?"

"Yes. One private plane left yesterday, but it was a fake flight log. I'm still trying to find out where it really went."

"Okay. She did say she's not in Texas. Or, at least, she didn't think she was."

He's quiet for a moment, and I imagine he's likely writing down what I'm telling him. "Anything else?"

"A man came on the phone as well, claiming to be her birth father. He said that his son got overzealous in his desire to have his sister home."

"The drugs."

"No normal person drugs someone—overzealous or not."

"I agree. I've been trying to get my hands on her adoption records, so I'll apply some more pressure now that we have confirmation she's with them."

"Thanks. Tucker is still trying to trace the number, but I'll text it to you too so you have it."

"Great, thanks."

"Yeah." After ending the call, I fire off a text to Gibson with the image I took of my mom's caller ID, then shove my phone back into my pocket.

Tucker's still heavily focused on the screen before him. Even though I have no idea what he's doing to track down the number, the furrowed line of his brow is enough evidence that he's not finding what he wants.

And then—"Okay, I've got it narrowed down to the Northwest Hemisphere."

"That's the closest you can get?"

"That's it. I'm sorry, brother. If we can get her on the phone again, then maybe I can narrow it down further."

I withdraw my phone and type in the number.

But it comes back disconnected.

"They shut it down."

"Of course they did." Tucker groans.

"There's nothing else you can do?"

"'Fraid not, brother. But I'll keep an eye on it."

"Gibson said he's trying to get his hands on Emma's adoption records."

"Adoption records!" Tucker snaps. "Why didn't I think about that before?"

"Think about what?" Alice asks as she breezes into the office and comes to stand behind Tucker. She rests both hands on his shoulders and leans in. "Adoption records?"

"Emma was adopted," I explain. "Gibson is having trouble getting through the red tape to get his hands on the information."

"Ah, hence the whole hacking into confidential servers. Got it." Alice kisses Tucker on top of his head, and he casts a quick grin over his shoulder. Right before his gaze drops to her stomach.

It's brief.

A tiny blip of a moment, but the small smile on his face screams the underlying secret.

"You're pregnant."

Alice pales. "What?"

"Dude," Tucker says, a wide grin spreading over his face.

"How did you know?" Alice demands, then smacks Tucker gently on the back of the shoulder. "You said we could tell him together!"

"He didn't tell me." Even with as thrilled as I am, a pain spreads through my chest. Pain that I won't ever get to experience that type of love. The excitement that surely comes when you bring another human being into the world. "I could tell."

"How?" Alice asks.

"You were drinking tea on the porch instead of coffee, and Tucker briefly glanced at your stomach just now."

Alice narrows her gaze and crosses her arms. "Okay, Sherlock. First of all, you didn't get close enough to my cup to see what was in it."

"There was no coffee scent in the air when I came in."

"Coffee scent?" Tucker laughs. "You need a hobby."

That proverbial knife that's been lodged in my chest for over a decade twists as I try to shove aside all of my feelings and focus only on the fact that I'm happy for my twin and his wife. "So when are you due?"

"The end of April," she replies. "We only just found out yesterday." Alice reaches into her back pocket and withdraws her cell, then shows it to me. On the screen is a black and white sonogram photograph. The baby is little more than a blurred shape, but it brings a wave of emotion over me regardless.

"A baby." I smile. "Tucker is barely responsible enough for himself."

Alice laughs. "That's why he has me."

"Who else knows?"

"Just you," Tucker replies. "We were planning on telling everyone together, but then—" His expression falters.

"Emma," I say, knowing that he wouldn't want to

deliver news like this amidst something as serious as a kidnapping.

"Emma," he repeats. "I'm sorry, brother."

"For what?" I hand Alice back her phone. "I'm happy for you both. Truly. I think a baby is great."

"Thank you." Alice smiles, then steps toward me but hesitates.

I know what she's looking for, and I wish I could give it to her, but even something as simple as a hug might just push me right over the edge of the cliff I'm currently standing on. So I remain where I am and do my best to ignore the slight disappointment on her face.

"Uh, will you let me know if you get anything? I need to go burn off some of this steam before I pop."

"Sure thing, brother. Go."

"Thanks. And congratulations, you guys."

"Thank you." Alice steps back toward Tucker, so after forcing another smile, I turn toward the door and head out of their house. Even though the air is fresher here than anywhere I've been, there might as well be no oxygen.

A baby.

I'd wanted to be a dad.

Emma and I talked about having kids after we got married.

And then— I leave my UTV where it is and just start running. Delta races beside me as we crest the hill and take off toward the nearest pasture. My boots hit the ground with a heavy thud, my jeans slick to my skin within minutes, thanks to the sweat forming along my skin.

But I keep pushing.

Change happens during moments of discomfort. So maybe, if I'm lucky, I can exhaust myself so much that I'll become the version of me I could have been if the world hadn't detonated around me.

CHAPTER 10
EMMA

After what I have to admit was probably the tastiest meal I've ever had, I finish my glass of water. Gio had it brought in for me from the kitchen by a woman in a black dress and white apron. Though she didn't say a single word to anyone, she anticipated their needs in a way that I always thought only happened in movies.

Apparently, you just need a seemingly endless amount of money.

"So you're a teacher then?" Felicity asks.

I nod. "Kindergarten."

"Do you enjoy it?"

"Very much so. I love my students as if they were my own children."

"But you have no children of your own?" Gio questions. "Never been married?"

"No. Just never met the right guy, I guess." I take another drink of water, the glass already freshened by one of the wait staff.

"So no husband, but what about the boyfriend?" Gio asks. "He seemed—angry."

"Dylan's not my boyfriend," I reply quickly. "We dated a bit in high school, but that was it."

"Yet it was him you called," Gio presses.

"I—"

"Darling, let the girl breathe. She hasn't been a part of our family for even a full day, and you're grilling her over boys as though she's in her teens instead of her mid-thirties," Felicity scolds with a smile and a click of her tongue.

Gio seems unfazed at first, but then he leans back and wipes his mouth with a cloth napkin. "Yes, well, I suppose I'm trying to make up for lost time."

The doors open, and a man wearing a black suit walks into the room. He has a tattoo that climbs up his neck, and his eyes are shielded behind dark glasses even though it's well past sundown outside.

My stomach twists as he leans in and whispers something to Gio.

"Aah, okay. Thank you." The man turns to leave, and even though I can't see his eyes, I get the faintest impression that he's sizing me up as he leaves the room. "Emmaline, I'm afraid that my pilot has grounded the plane for the evening due to storms."

"Storms?" I turn to look at the open balcony doors. There's a soft breeze coming in off the ocean, but the weather seems clear.

"Not here," he replies. "Over Texas. It seems there's a strong system moving in, and he says it's not safe to fly at the present moment."

Another dose of nerves dances through my system. "You said I could go home tonight. Are there no other flights?"

"Not at this hour. We use a helicopter to take us from where we are now to the private airport we use for travel. Unfortunately, the nearest commercial airport is three hours away, and they'll likely have the same issue."

His words make sense, but that does nothing to silence the shrieking alarms in my mind.

Pretend, Emma, I remind myself. Pretending is something I became good at over the years. I pretend that seeing Dylan every day doesn't gut me.

I pretend that I don't love him the same now as I did years ago.

Now, I need to pretend that I don't see right through Gio and this entire charade. "Okay. It might be nice to stay another night. Can I call them and make sure someone takes care of my cat?" I ask.

"Of course, of course." Gio nods. "You have the phone; make whatever calls you need."

"Thanks." Nausea sends bile up the back of my throat,

but I take a bite of the strawberries and cream sitting in front of me. "So, where are we? It's beautiful here, but I didn't recognize anything out of the window in my room."

"You said it yourself earlier," he replies with a smile. "Paradise." Gio stands. "I fear I have some business to tend to. Mattheus, come. My love, can you show our daughter back to her room and help her get settled?"

"Of course," Felicity replies with a smile. She stands as well, then lightly kisses Gio as he passes.

As soon as he and Mattheus are out of the room, she reaches out a hand. "Come, Emmaline. I'll walk you back."

I hesitate. Will they lock the door again? Will I be trapped in this place forever? Or will they truly let me go as soon as the plane can land safely?

"Honey, you're safe with me, okay?" she says softly, then takes my hand and gently tugs me to my feet. As soon as I'm standing, she releases me and heads for the door. "I imagine this is all a shock for you," she continues as we move down the hall. "Finding out you were adopted, then coming here."

"I knew I was adopted all along. My parents were always honest with me. So the kidnapping was pretty much the only shock."

"Kidnapping?"

I inwardly wince. "I wasn't supposed to say anything."

"You can be completely open with me," she says softly. She doesn't seem broken. Not in the way they explained. Is that because I'm here? Or was it yet another lie to get me to do what they wanted?

"Mattheus drugged me in my house and brought me here without my consent."

She mutters something under her breath, and her cheeks flush pink with anger. "Come. We're going to take a walk." Instead of going back into the room, she leads me out the back door and into a dimly lit rose garden. The moon is large overhead, and its silvery glow lights our path as we walk among the flowers. "Keep your voice low as we speak, okay?"

"Okay."

"Do not allow your expression to betray what it is we're speaking of."

"Okay," I say again, this time forcing a smile that mimics her own.

"You were never supposed to come here."

I stop moving, shock at her words settling over me. "What did you say?"

"Come, you must keep walking." She smiles when she faces me and loops an arm through mine, then forces me to keep moving. "You mustn't look like something's wrong, Emmaline. He has eyes everywhere. Smile, darling."

I do, but it makes me feel sick.

"Now, what you need to know is that it isn't safe for you here. You need to go home."

"I want to go home."

"He is going to try to keep you here, but if we play our cards right, we can get you out safely. You'll have to move though. Now that he knows where you are—"

"Wait, hang on a second. What's happening? Mattheus says he brought me here because you were suffering."

"Darling, I've been suffering since the moment I uttered my vows. But I never wanted you to suffer the same fate as me."

We reach a bench at the back of the garden, overlooking the ocean as it kisses the shoreline. Felicity sits, so I follow suit, remaining quiet while she thinks through whatever it is she plans on saying.

All the while, my stomach is a pit of knots.

He's going to try to keep you here. Why? I've been alone for over thirty years. Why does Gio want to keep me now?

"I wanted a daughter so badly. A little girl to dress up. The bows, the braids—I wanted it so badly." A tear rolls down her cheek. "Gio and I had a whirlwind romance. It was candles, flowers, stolen kisses—a wonderous proposal. After we were married, I learned who he truly was. By then, I'm ashamed to admit, I loved the lifestyle." She turns to look out over the ocean. "When I found out I was pregnant, I was so happy. Until I realized what it meant. My child, boy or girl, would be wrapped up in his world."

"What world? Who is he?"

Felicity smiles at me, but it doesn't reach her eyes. "A

highly intelligent man who doesn't miss much." She takes a deep breath. "Mattheus came first. I tried so hard to keep him out of it. To convince Gio that Mattheus should be allowed to choose his own path. He was a sweet boy, Emmaline. He really was."

I try to picture Mattheus when he was younger. As one of my kindergarten students—so carefree and happy. But it doesn't come easily, knowing he drugged and kidnapped me.

"He was two when I found out I was pregnant with you." She presses a hand to her stomach. "I was so terrified when I found out you were the daughter that I had once prayed so desperately for." More tears roll down her cheeks. The pain surrounding her is so thick that it presses down around us. Even as she fights against the visible pain with a forced smile. "I knew what a life for you looked like, and I couldn't bear the thought of bringing you into it."

"I don't understand. If it was truly so bad, then why—why did you stay with him?"

"Fear," she replies. "We already had Mattheus, and I knew that I wouldn't be able to get him away safely. I couldn't leave him here, not when there was still a chance I could pull him away from this life."

"Then what happened to me?"

She closes her eyes and takes a deep breath. "I hadn't prayed in years. Truthfully, I pulled away from God and leaned into the life that Gio offered me. But the night I found out you were a girl, I prayed so hard." Her voice cracks. "Harder than I ever had. I prayed for Him to take you away. To give you to someone else."

Her words hit me square in the chest. "You didn't want to have me."

"Oh, darling, no. I wanted you more than anything. But this life is not kind to women. I knew what would happen to you if you stayed. He would have used you as a pawn. You would've ended up married to someone just like him— or worse. When the pregnancy continued, I began to formulate a plan. A way to get you safely out. I befriended a nurse at the hospital, and I paid her to lie to us. To tell us that you—" She pauses a moment and closes her eyes. "That you died. I made her promise to find you a good family. And we parted ways—never speaking about it again."

"He said that you saw a baby. A body."

"A cleverly designed doll," she replies. "Made to look real. We only saw you from a distance, and even as I knew it was fake, my heart broke just the same. Gio never looked too hard at the lie. If he had—" She shudders. "I prayed that he wouldn't, and he didn't."

Shock can't even begin to describe what I'm feeling as I sit here on this bench, listening to what Felicity is telling me. She *knew* that I was alive. This whole time. Hot tears burn in my eyes. I understand her reasoning—she wanted to give me a better life—and she did. But knowing that I was given up for adoption is nothing compared to learning *why*.

"Did you ever check on me?"

She shakes her head. "I knew that if Gio caught wind of it, he'd level the world to get to you, and I would be buried by his wrath, unable to protect you."

"He would have killed you."

"In a heartbeat."

"It's been over thirty years. How did they find me?"

"I don't know." She closes her eyes. "I thought you were safe. I'm so sorry. I'm so sorry, Emmaline." She turns toward me, then reaches up and cups my cheek. "But, my darling daughter, you are oh so beautiful. And as much as I despise the reasons, I am quite glad I got to meet you."

With trembling fingers, I reach up and touch her hand. I never sought out my birth family because, as far as I was concerned, it was Patricia and Emmitt Franklin who raised me, and nothing else mattered. But when Mattheus first showed up, I was intrigued by the idea of discovering the truth about where I came from.

Now, learning what I have, I wish I could go back to when I didn't know.

But that doesn't take away from the overwhelming emotion consuming me as I sit here with the woman who tried to give me my best chance.

"Me too."

"Now. We need to get you out of here. Is there anyone

back home you can think of who can help you? I can't trust anyone here. They're all on Gio's payroll."

Dylan's name is the first one that pops into my head.

And because of that, I shove it back down. "Bradyn Hunt," I say. "He's been a friend of mine for a long time, and he runs a search and rescue business. They're looking for me now."

"Then we need to make sure they find you. Before it's too late."

"What do you mean by that?"

Felicity takes a deep breath. "Let's not worry about that right now, okay? Right now, I want you to focus only on pretending as though you know none of this. They cannot suspect you do."

"Mattheus can't be trusted?" Given that he drugged me, I'm assuming not, but I want to hear it from her.

"No. As much as I hate to admit it, he's worse than his father." Her voice cracks a bit toward the end. Just enough of a waver that I can feel her pain. Her disappointment. That she tried to keep him kind, and he followed the darkness anyway.

"I have the phone." I hold it up. "I can call him."

She shakes her head. "That one is being monitored. Give me the message, and I'll make sure they get it."

"How?"

"I've lived in this prison a long time, darling. I've learned a trick or two about moving in the shadows."

CHAPTER 11
DYLAN

The Bible sitting on my countertop has never been louder than it is right now.

I grew up on God's Word. It was as familiar to me as breathing. Memorizing verses was literally a sport in my house. Yet, I've barely touched it in the past decade. The anger I've carried in my heart ever since I was captured and watched my team slowly fade away in that pit, each of them dying after what they were put through—it made having faith seem impossible.

How could I have faith that God cared when He did nothing to save my brothers-in-arms?

When He didn't break down the prison walls so we could gain our freedom?

Of course, I know the answer. Bad things happen in this world. It's just a part of life. Sin, darkness, evil…it's something everyone in this world faces. But trying to wrap my mind around that when I feel like I'm better off dead is simply not something I've been able to do.

I haven't been able to forgive myself for surviving.

Heart heavy, I pull open a drawer in my kitchen and stare down at the photograph sitting on top. Seven smiling men. The day before they were sentenced to die in a pit, in a country very few knew they were in, where it was unlikely that anyone would ever know what happened to them.

I can still hear their voices.

The crying.

The pleading.

I shove the photo back in and slam the drawer shut. Delta sits up on his bed and eyes me curiously. "I'm good, bud," I tell him, then take a deep breath.

But I'm really not.

Because right now, all I can picture is Emma in that pit. Is she scared right now? Have they hurt her? Will we ever find her?

Will I ever see her again?

"Why her?" I ask aloud to my empty house. "Why did You let them take her?" Resting both hands on my counter, I hang my head low.

"You're not safe. Anyone willing to go to those lengths to get to you is not trustworthy."

"I know."

She'd spoken those words so calmly that it caught me

off guard. I shouldn't be surprised. Not really. Where I struggle to even have faith these days, Emma puts all of hers in God. She trusts Him with everything that she is.

She always has.

Is that what brings her peace now?

And if so, how do I reach that level of peace too? How do I find some kind of normalcy when I'm haunted by everything in my past?

Straightening, I reach out and rest the tips of my fingers on the worn leather book. It's soft beneath the tips of my fingers. Familiar.

So why can't I even bring myself to open it?

Something rubs against my leg, so I glance down. Emma's cat is purring and arching his back as he rubs on my leg.

"I miss her too, buddy," I say as I kneel down and lift the animal. I never considered myself a cat person, but this guy—he's okay. "I need to think of something to call you until she gets back, don't I?" I shift my gaze to Delta. "What do you think, bud? What should we call him?" His tail thumps on his dog bed. I switch my attention back to the cat. "How about Foxtrot? You're fluffy. It fits the theme of animal names around here."

He continues purring and rubs against my chest.

"Foxtrot it is." Taking a deep breath, I set him down onto the floor, then glance back at the Bible. "I'm going to bring her home, okay, bud? Even if it's the last thing I do."

"ANY IDEA WHERE SHE IS?" Freshly showered, I step into Tucker's house around ten o'clock at night.

Bradyn and Riley are already here, both of them standing in the kitchen, alongside Tucker and Alice. All four of them turn to look at me, and I already know the answer: we still have no clue where she is.

"The adoption records are a bust. There were no birth parents listed. The only name in the file was of a nurse who gave a statement that she found the baby in an alleyway behind the hospital where she worked. She couldn't keep the child due to her own circumstances, so Emma was put up for adoption after a search for her parents never turned anything up." Tucker sighs. "I'm sorry, brother."

"What about the names? We get an address with those? We have first and last names."

"Nothing," Tucker replies. "They're ghosts."

"Which means they're probably not upstanding citizens," Riley comments.

I cross my arms. There *has* to be something we can do. "Then let's go talk to the nurse. Maybe she knows—"

"Can't," Riley answers. "She was killed in a hit-and-run last week."

"Last week." I look from Riley to Bradyn. "That can't be coincidence."

"That's what we thought too," Bradyn replies. "But so

far, no digging has turned up any other explanation. According to witnesses, she stepped out into traffic without looking and was hit and killed."

"Then someone is lying."

"There were a dozen people who came forward, claiming they saw the same thing," Tucker says. "I'm sorry, brother, but that's a dead end right now. I'm still digging, but—"

Bradyn's phone begins to ring, the shrill tone cutting through Tucker's words. He withdraws it, and after checking the readout, answers on speakerphone. "Bradyn Hunt," he says.

"My name is Felicity Karver," the woman says. "And I need you to trace this call. Quickly."

Bradyn looks up at me.

Tucker waves us back into his office.

"Are you still there?" she asks.

"Yes. Why am I tracing this call?" Bradyn questions as Tucker takes a seat at his computer, and Alice sits at hers. Both of them begin typing furiously on their keyboards.

"You know why. Emmaline says you run a search and rescue?"

"Emma—is she okay?" I demand.

The woman hesitates. "You're him. The one Gio spoke to."

"Yes. Is Emma okay?" I demand again. Why isn't Emma calling if everything's fine? What happened?

"Right now, she's all right. But if you don't get her out of here, she won't be."

"What do you mean?" Fear tears through me at the mere thought of anything happening to Emma.

Not my Emma.

My ray of sunshine in the dark.

"I can't tell you more than that. We'll be in town tomorrow. That's your only chance of getting to her. There's a boutique near Coral Bay where I like to do most of my trinket shopping. Have you traced the call?"

I look at Tucker, who holds up his thumb.

"Yes."

"Good. You have to keep her hidden until the first of November. After that, there will be no way he can come for her." She trails off a moment. "Save her," she says, her voice cracking. "As I tried to do."

The line goes dead. I stare at Bradyn's phone as though Emma's voice will come through the speakers at any time now.

"What did she mean by that?" Riley asks. "'Save her as I tried to do'?"

"My guess is there's more to this adoption than a baby being abandoned. Where is she?" Bradyn asks Tucker.

"St. John. U.S. Virgin Islands." Tucker points to his computer.

"That's a five-hour direct flight. Can you get Jesper on the phone?" I ask Riley.

"Doing it now." He withdraws his cell phone.

"I think I can answer the whole cryptic 'she's in danger' speak." Alice leans back from her computer, shaking her head slowly. "This is bad."

"Tell me." I move toward her, stopping just short of reading over her shoulder—something I did before, and she chewed me out for exactly that. Apparently, reading over her shoulder is a pet peeve of my sister-in-law's.

"I might have figured out why you couldn't find anything on Mattheus or Gio," she says to Tucker. "I contacted a friend of mine who still works at Web Safe and pulled in a favor." She shakes her head. "Giovanni Karver is the head of the Karver crime family. He's a nasty guy. Big money. The feds have been trying to build a case on him for years but haven't had any luck getting anywhere close to the guy. They've sealed all records of him. Looks like they're trying to keep a close eye on the family."

"Felicity said she tried to save her before. Do you think it's possible that she abandoned her at birth to keep her away from Giovanni? A family like that uses daughters like pawns." I picture a young mother leaving her new baby in an alleyway, abandoning her to the elements in hopes that she would be found because it was a better future than the life laid out before her.

"We won't know until we get more answers. We're wheels up in two hours," Bradyn says. "Elliot and Nova won't be back in time, but we shouldn't need them. If we're grabbing her from in town, we stand a chance at ensuring no bullets fly."

It's half past eleven, so as I step through the never-locked doors of our small town's church sanctuary, I expect to be alone. Instead, Pastor Ford turns to look at me curiously from where he's seated in a middle pew. "Aah, it makes sense now."

I stop in my tracks. "What makes sense?"

"Why I felt like I needed to stick around." He smiles and waves for me to come in farther. "I'm just sitting here absorbing the quiet. Join me."

"I don't want to talk," I say quickly as I take a seat in the pew across the aisle from him.

"That works for me." The pastor who baptized me as an infant closes his eyes and bows his head.

It's one of the reasons why I don't mind coming to church even as I struggle with my own faith. Pastor Ford isn't one to press. He simply waits, biding his time until I'm ready to talk. And there are plenty of times I've come here and chosen not to speak at all.

My gaze drifts to the cross behind the altar. It's lit from behind by a stained-glass representation of Jesus' ascension to heaven. It's an image that used to bring me such hope when I looked at it.

Then everything fell apart, and I lost the ability to believe in anything.

I've been seeking Him ever since. Struggling with the idea that God cares about me at all. There's a voice in my head that tells me He doesn't. That He chose my brothers and Lani but tossed me to the side. I mean, why would I have suffered as I did if He cared?

Grief tightens in my chest.

Why would Emma be taken from me?

Because I'm not sure what else I can do in this moment, I bow my head. I have no idea what to say—I haven't prayed in so long that my thoughts don't want to formulate into a prayer. Should a man like me be praying anyway? What do I have to bring to the table besides a darkened soul and a broken heart?

Those are hardly things fit for a King.

"Lord, we ask that You surround Emmaline with Your light. Please protect her as the boys come to her rescue. Bring her home safely, and shield those who are coming to her rescue. We pray this in the name of Your Holy Son, Jesus Christ. Amen."

I open my eyes and turn to him as Pastor Ford finishes the prayer. "How did you know that was why I was here?"

With a smile, he glances back at the cross. "For one, you're geared up like you're going to war."

I glance down at the tactical gear I'm dressed in. I have

a pistol holstered at my hip, though I did leave the rifle in my truck.

"Then there's the heaviness on your heart. I know that Emmaline is the only one who puts it there quite like that."

I turn away from him and face the front of the church. "I'm that transparent?"

"When it comes to her, you are. I've known you your entire life, Dylan, and I've never seen you look at anyone quite like you look at Emmaline. I've been sitting here most of the day, praying for her." He fixes his gaze on the cross.

"I don't understand why we have to pray for her. The fact that He let her be taken anyway makes me—" I stop speaking just short of letting my anger out.

"God has a plan for everyone under the sun," he says. "But you've heard me preach on that many times before."

I look down at the hands I've white-knuckled together in my lap. "Knowing it doesn't make it any easier to deal with."

"No," he agrees. "It doesn't."

"I have so much anger in my heart. I don't know how to move past it."

"I know you do. Just as you know I'm here when you *do* want to talk about it."

My cell phone dings, so I withdraw it from a pocket on the front of my vest.

Bradyn: *We're leaving the ranch in twenty. Jesper will be landing in about forty-five minutes.*

Me: *I'll be there.*

"I have to go." After shoving the phone back into my pocket, I stand. Pastor Ford does the same and meets me in the aisle.

"Where you're headed has nothing to do with where you've been, Dylan," he says softly. "You aren't ruined because of the things you've suffered. God has a plan for you, and when you seek His light with all of your heart, it will break through that darkness."

His words settle around me like bricks falling onto my head. It's easy to say that I should seek God. I've been trying, but what if, after everything I've seen and done, He doesn't want me to find Him?

CHAPTER 12
EMMA

Darkness surrounds me as I lie in the center of the bed. The only source of light is the sliver beneath the door. It's been on all night, almost like they're trying to make sure I don't ever feel alone enough to try to run.

Not that I could get out if I wanted to. The door is once again locked from the outside, and the window is sealed shut. I wonder if they didn't think I'd notice that I'm sealed in here like a prisoner. Or if they even care. Why try to put up all the family gathering pretenses last night if they planned on holding me hostage all along?

Tears stain my cheeks, and my heart is heavy. I prayed all the prayers I could pray, then climbed beneath the covers in hopes of finding some sleep. Unfortunately, so far, it's eluded me completely.

"Lord, I need help," I whisper into the darkness.

A shadow passes beneath the door, and my heart slams against my ribs just as it has every time someone has walked by. I keep picturing Mattheus coming into the room and drugging me again. Who knows where I'll wake if he manages to knock me out a second time?

What will they do when I continue asking to go home? Will they lock me in this room forever? Put me in shackles? Worse?

And why do all of this? What do they want me here for?

Felicity made it sound as though they had some grand plan for me—marriage to a monster. I shiver as bile burns my throat. Surely I'm past that risk, right? I'm in my thirties. In the movies, forced marriage happens to younger women in their twenties. Not a kindergarten teacher in her thirties.

Things like this only happen in movies, TV shows, or books. They don't happen to ordinary people like me. Right?

Except this isn't fiction.

It's my life.

And it absolutely is happening.

Did my birth family really track me down just to marry me off? Anger and betrayal war within my heart. How could this happen? How could they do this to me? I know I'm a stranger, but I'm still family—right?

Marriage.

"He would have used you as a pawn. You would've ended up married to someone just like him—or worse."

Her words have been on my mind ever since she left me in the hallway, promising that she would do what she could to get me home. But what then? He'll just find me again, won't he?

I curl into my side and grip the cell phone I can't even use because they've apparently tapped into it somehow and will know exactly who I call and what we talk about. If Dylan figured out the message I was trying to give him, or Felicity did as she promised and called them, the last thing I need is Gio and Mattheus finding out and putting a stop to it.

Felicity said he would've killed her if he found out she was the one who orchestrated my fake death.

His own wife.

Forcing me into marriage doesn't seem like too much of a leap when you compare it to that.

A gilded cage. That's what I'm in.

Lord, why? I trust in You, but please get me home. Please, God. I need to be home. For the fall festival, for my students. So I can have a makeup birthday dinner with Talia and Connor. So I can tell Dylan—

The fight we had in the parking lot of the church comes to the front of my mind. I was so angry—furious—at him for leaving the flowers and then pretending not to care. My heartbreak left a fissure where that anger took root, seeding until I couldn't help myself. Because I wasn't clear-headed, I completely ignored the fact that perhaps those flowers *are* his only way of telling me he cares.

Shouldn't I be appreciative of that? Just because he doesn't want to go back to what we were, should I really write him off entirely? It's not as though he cheated on me or purposely broke my heart.

He was held captive and tortured for *months*.

Yet he still chooses to pick me wildflowers for my birthday and leave them in a pretty vase.

That's kindness. And it didn't deserve my reaction.

I wipe tears away from my cheeks, even though more are falling from my eyes right behind them. Right now, I'd give about anything to hear his voice again. To apologize for what I said and how I reacted without thinking.

Will I ever get that chance?

"Emma." His voice fills my mind now. That tortured tone that I've come to know him by ever since he came home.

The tears come faster now, and I hug a pillow against my chest, curling around it and burying my face in it to stifle my sobs.

I want to go home.

To lie in *my* bed, with my pillows and blankets.

I want to cuddle my cat.

Grab breakfast at the diner.

And above all, I desperately want to see Dylan. At least one more time.

———

"GOOD MORNING, EMMALINE," Gio greets as I take a seat at the breakfast table. I set the piece of paper he'd used to summon me down beside me. It had been slid beneath my door right as dawn began to break.

Pretend. I force a smile. "Good morning." The same woman who delivered dinner last night sets a cup of hot coffee in front of me, alongside a small container of cream. It smells amazing, but I eye it warily.

Could it be drugged?

"How did you sleep?" he asks.

"Okay," I reply.

He narrows his gaze. "You didn't sleep at all, did you?"

"No," I admit. "I'm sorry, I'm just homesick." Stick to the truth but pretend.

"Understandable. It has been a relatively stressful time for you since your arrival."

"You mean since I was drugged and abducted from my house?" I ask. Gio talks about it like Mattheus simply lied and manipulated me into coming. Instead, he'd done something that would land him in prison.

"Yes." Gio's tone is harsher now than I've heard it since

I was brought here. "He's been punished for it, I can assure you that."

"Punished? He's in his thirties."

"Does that mean we no longer need direction from our parents?" The way he asks the question slithers beneath my skin, but before I can respond, the door opens. "Ah, yes. Just in time. Please, come in." He holds out his hand, and I turn to see a man walk into the room.

A chill runs up my spine as I watch him stroll into the room like he owns the place. He's tall and muscled, both arms covered in dark ink. A gigantic snake is tattooed up the side of his neck, with the mouth opening right beside his as though it's ready to devour whatever he wills.

Both ears have large black gauges in them, and his blonde hair is slicked back. His eyes are so dark they might as well be black, and when they land on me, my stomach churns in response.

When he takes a seat right beside me—between me and Gio—I shift my focus straight ahead, not missing the pitying expression the woman who brought me my coffee wears when she looks from him to me.

Never in my life have I met a person who managed to instill fear into me by simply being in the same room—until now. And somehow I know, without a doubt, that this is the future Gio has planned for me.

A wife for this monster.

I swallow hard—my heart hammering. *Pretend, Emma. You have to pretend.*

Lord, please help me.

"Heath, this is my daughter, Emmaline." Gio gestures toward me, a proud smile on his face. "Emmaline, this is Heath Slater."

Heath reaches out and takes my hand, then presses it to his lips, eyes on mine the entire time. "Emmaline, you are a rare beauty indeed."

"I—thanks." The area of my hand where his lips pressed burns like his mouth is coated in acid. My skin crawls as he releases me, and I have to fight the urge to gag when bile burns my throat.

"Of course." He turns to Gio. "You did not oversell her, my friend. She is beautiful."

"As I said she was. The spitting image of her mother."

"Yes, yes. You were right."

Nausea churns in my belly, so even though the last thing I want to do is turn my gaze away from this monster of a man, I prep my coffee, hoping I can manage to diffuse this conversation before it takes the turn I fear it will.

I no longer care if it's drugged. Maybe by the time I wake, the Hunts will be here to rescue me.

"Have you heard from your pilot?" I ask Gio, fighting to keep my tone level even as my hand shakes while I stir my coffee. "Has the storm passed?"

"It has," he replies, though he doesn't elaborate.

"Emma has never been married and is a kindergarten teacher."

"You like kids?" Heath questions.

"Yes. I do."

"Why have you never been married?" he asks.

Breathe. I'm honestly shocked neither of them can hear my hammering heart. "Just never met the right man, I suppose."

"Ah. Yes. Well, perhaps that will change."

Unlikely. "I think that I should—"

"Emmaline, Heath is a very powerful man."

"Congratulations." I force another smile, trying to keep my gaze on the man beside me, even though every second I'm looking at him, I'm sure I'm staring at the worst of humanity. How I know that, I'm not sure.

But I do.

Heath continues looking me up and down, like he's willing to sic his tattooed snake on me at any moment.

Every single muscle in my body is tensed. I have to get out of here. I cannot wait for the Hunts to show up. Otherwise, I'll end up shackled to this monster of a man. Of that, I have no doubt.

I start to open my mouth to ask when the pilot will be ready to take off so I can return home, but the door opens. Felicity strolls in, dressed in a white button-down shirt and a pair of loose-fitting red pants the same shade as the lipstick painted on her lips.

"And speaking of beauty," Gio says as he stands. "Look at you, my love."

"Good morning, darling." She kisses him on the cheek, then turns to Heath. "Well, Mr. Slater, this is quite the surprise."

"The surprise is all mine, Mrs. Karver." He stands and kisses her hand just as he did mine, though her smile doesn't falter. Does she feel the same distaste I do? Or is she better at hiding it?

Or—a worse thought—did I place my trust in someone who won't do anything to free me?

She turns to Gio. "Darling, I was hoping to take Emmaline shopping in the village today. Is that all right? I want to show her more of our home."

Gio looks at Heath, who offers the slightest nod, as though giving permission.

Escape. I have to escape. If I'm in a village, then that means I won't be trapped behind these walls. I have to force a smile on my face. "I would love that." I try not to sound too eager. "I'm hoping to get home soon, but if we can make a day out of it before I do, that would be great."

Gio's eyes harden when he turns to me, though his smile stays firmly in place. "Of course, darling Emmaline. Whatever you want."

"Wonderful. Come, darling. I have the car waiting downstairs." Felicity reaches out a hand, and I take it without hesitation. Right now, it's the only lifeline I have.

"You'll take Hector and Jack with you," Gio replies. "They can follow you into town and keep watch. There's been some trouble lately, and I want my girls to be safe."

Felicity turns toward him. "Okay, darling. Whatever you think is best." She kisses him again, then pauses near my chair. "You're going to love this little boutique I favor. They have so many wonderful things, and the cutest clothes."

She loops my arm through hers. "I don't think I have any money. Unless Mattheus brought my purse—"

"Money is no object," Gio calls after us. "Whatever you want is yours."

All I have to do is sell my soul. Or, at least, that's what it feels like.

Felicity and I walk in silence down another set of stairs. The rest of the house is just as immaculate as the parts I've seen, though the second set of stairs opens toward a lower floor that's surrounded by walls of windows. A man carrying a gun stands near the front door. As we approach, he offers a curt nod to Felicity, then pulls the door open.

"Thank you, Hector. You're coming with us?"

"Yes," he replies.

There's a bright red convertible parked in front of the house, with a black Jeep just behind it.

"Fantastic." She opens the door to the passenger side, then waits for me to climb in. As soon as I do, she shuts the door, and Hector follows her around to open the driver's side door. "Thank you, honey," she purrs.

I watch her as she grins at him.

Either she's playing her part well, or she was acting last night.

Trouble is, until I know which one it is, how can I trust her?

"RIGHT THIS WAY, DARLING," Felicity ushers me down the street, a shopping bag in each hand. And that doesn't even count the ones the guards Gio sent with us are lugging around a few paces behind us.

The woman has no shame when it comes to spending money. I lost count two stores back, but I'm pretty sure we're in the neighborhood of four thousand dollars already. Aside from some jewelry, blown glass figurines, and a new pair of shoes for her, she's outfitted me with three new dresses, a big sun hat, and a pair of heels that I would never even consider torturing my feet with.

But I have to admit—kidnapping aside—it's been a fun outing with her. Felicity Karver is a force to be reckoned with, a bright spot on this island that has everyone turning their heads and smiling as they wave. Could be all the money she spends, but I think it's more than that.

I think she cares. Which is a vast difference from the men I sense both Mattheus and Gio to be.

"Ooh! There it is! My favorite boutique on the entire planet." Turning, she hands Hector the two bags in her hands. "I cannot wait to watch you try on everything in here, my darling! They have such cute stuff!"

"We'll be right outside," Hector says, gesturing toward a bench in front of the small boutique.

"You don't want to come and watch the fashion show?"

Hector bares his teeth in a smile. "Not a chance. Though I'm sure she'll look beautiful." I may not know much about men, but I don't miss the way his gaze rakes over me. Nor can I ignore how it makes my skin crawl.

"Okay, fine. Spoilsports. We'll be out in a bit. Feel free to help yourself to some of that chocolate we grabbed at the dessert shop. My treat to you for protecting us." With that, she heads into the boutique, not even bothering to cast them a backward glance.

"I really don't need anything else," I insist. I haven't managed to find a single moment where I can slip away. Either she's been with me, or both Hector and Jack have hovered like shadows.

Felicity heads straight for the counter, but before she speaks to the woman behind it, she casts a glance out the window. Both Hector and Jack are standing outside, their gazes in the dessert bag. "That should hold them a while." She turns to the middle-aged woman with graying hair and tan skin that contrasts beautifully with the canary yellow sundress she's wearing. "Did you get my message?"

"I did. The outfit you'll want her to try on is hanging right by that rack." She points toward a dressing room. "And you need to use that dressing room. It has the most space."

"Thank you."

"Anything for you." The woman reaches over and cups Felicity's hands.

"Okay, darling, we don't have much time." Pulling away from the woman, Felicity ushers me toward a doorway that leads toward the back. After grabbing an outfit that's hanging by the door—a pair of burnt orange shorts and a black one-piece swimsuit—she turns to me. "I want you to know that meeting you was the only joy I have in my life. While I would love to see you again, I know it's not possible. Not for your safety." She leans in and presses a quick kiss to my cheek. "You have to remain hidden until after November 1st, okay? By then, everything will be okay."

"I don't understand. What's happening?"

"Go in there and put this on." She shoves it into my hands. "Then knock on the side door three times, okay? Three times. Remember that." She smiles, tears shimmering in her eyes. "There hasn't been a day of your life where I haven't loved you, my darling daughter."

Tears burn in my eyes now too. "Come in with me."

Felicity smiles at me. "I wish I could. But I have to make sure they can't follow you." She glances over her shoulder again. "Go. There's no more time. That chocolate will only last so long, and then they'll get bored. If you hear me say pineapple, then you know time is up, okay?" She all but shoves me into the room. It's small, consisting of a single chair and one of those full-length mirrors that always seems to add ten pounds.

To the left of the mirror is a door. *Knock three times.*

Pineapple?

I do as she said and quickly change, then slide my feet back into the simple tennis shoes she bought me at the last store we were in.

"How is it going in there, darling?" she asks.

"Good. I just finished getting dressed."

The bell dings, signaling another customer entering the building.

"Oh, good! I fear that shawl might look like a pineapple on you, but I just had to see. You boys are just in time," she adds.

Pineapple. I eye the door. "It looks—okay. I'm just adjusting; then I'll come out."

"Sounds great. I can't wait to see."

Quickly, I rush over toward the door and raise my fist. *Won't they hear, though?* I clear my throat and knock once. Twice. Before I get to the third knock, the door opens and someone yanks me through, then closes it quietly again.

I start to scream, but a strong hand clamps over my mouth, and I'm yanked against a hard chest.

"It's me," a familiar voice whispers. "Quiet though, okay?"

I nod. *Can it be?* My eyes fill with tears again, and I breathe in deeply, recognizing the citrus-and-mint body wash he's used for as long as I can remember.

Slowly, his hand moves down from my mouth, trailing over my cheek and shoulder before dropping. It's pitch-black in here until a sliver of light appears from a crack in a doorway leading outside.

It's then that I see him.

Dylan.

My heart leaps with joy as hope spreads through me like wildfire. He's here—and that means I'm okay.

"We have to move fast." He takes my hand and pulls me out onto the street. Instead of his normal tactical gear for missions, he's wearing a pair of board shorts and a white T-shirt. A baseball cap is pulled low over his face.

We begin walking, and he reaches into his pocket to withdraw a pair of dark sunglasses. "Put these on."

I do.

"And this." He pulls a rolled-up floppy hat from his back pocket and offers it to me. "Scoop your hair up and hide it beneath."

Once again, I do as he says while he guides me toward the beach.

"Shouldn't we be running?" I ask frantically.

"Don't look behind you," he says sharply. "Running is what they'll be looking for. In order for the diversion to work, we need to hide in plain sight."

"What div—" Before I can even finish speaking, a shrill scream rips through the afternoon. I start to whirl toward the shop, my thoughts on Felicity. What if they discovered she helped me? What if—

"Stay focused," he says as he slings an arm around my shoulders. It's casual. Something he did countless times back when we were dating. But the shiver it sends through my body is entirely new.

It's the most contact we've had since he came home.

"We have to go back for her."

"We can't."

"Dylan, she's my mother."

"I know. But that's not the plan she came up with, okay?"

Please, Lord, let her be okay. Please don't let me lose her too. Her face swims into view, the tears in her eyes. She was saying goodbye—but for how long?

Dylan tugs me toward the water.

"I-I can't swim, Dylan." I begin to panic, the one incident at a lake when I was fourteen and nearly drowned pushing the fear of everything else aside.

"Emma," he says softly, coming around to face me. "I won't let you go, okay?" His hazel gaze pins me, and in those gorgeous eyes I know so well, I see the promise of his protection.

Lord, please be with us.

Instead of responding verbally, I kick my shoes off, and Dylan strips out of his T-shirt, abandoning it on the ground. I suck in a breath at the sight of the scars marring his muscled chest. I know what they did to him, but to see it—

Focus, Emma. Running for your life here.

I start to remove the hat, but he stills me with a hand on my arm. "Leave it on until we're in the water, okay?"

Unable to draw breath when my fear is at war with my desire to be close to him, I simply nod.

Dylan takes my hand and leads me into the water. He smiles at me, and the sight of it steals my breath yet again. For a moment, he's the happy teen I knew all those years ago. A young man excited to go off and serve his country.

The darkness in his eyes has ebbed, and for that same moment, I forget why we're out here, wading into the surf. Behind me, there's commotion, running and yelling, but in front of me is the man I've loved all my life.

A man who risked his life to come for me.

CHAPTER 13
DYLAN

As adrenaline pumps through my veins, it's all I can do to remain focused. Because right now, in this moment, Emma is *all* I can see. On the beach behind us, there are at least a dozen armed men swarming the crowds, searching for her. We're far enough out and cloaked by bright sunlight that they'd have to strain to see us…but it would only take one moment, and they'd be on us.

With her life in the balance, I shove all of the darkness down and fight against the fire spreading through my veins because her hand is in mine. Fire that threatens to consume us both if I let it.

Another few paces, and then we'll be there.

Waves crash into us, but I maintain my stance as I slowly back farther into the water. We can't look like we're in a hurry, or that will set them on us sooner rather than later. *Stay calm.* One step after the other, I guide Emma past the breaking of the waves until we're out far enough that I can tell she's barely standing.

A woman on the beach screams as she's ripped up from where she was lounging on a beach chair. One of the armed guards who'd been following Emma flips her around to face him, then shoves her to the ground when he sees she's not Emma.

"I need you to slowly begin to lower into the water, okay?"

"I can't swim," she says again. Her face is pale, and I imagine her eyes are wide with terror behind the dark sunglasses still covering them.

"I know you can't, but I can, okay? I won't let you drown, Emma."

She hesitates just a moment but then begins to lower herself farther into the water, until only her head is sticking above the surface, the hat covering her sheen of blonde hair. I shrink down too, slowly taking steps back. Until— my foot brushes against something hard.

Yes. Finally.

"I'm going to go under, and I need you to stay right here for just a minute, okay?"

"You said you wouldn't let me go," she says frantically. Her breathing is rapid, her body trembling.

"I won't let you go. But I need to get something."

More yelling on the beach.

They're getting more frantic.

Won't be long before they turn their attention to us.

"We have to hurry," I urge.

She closes her eyes and nods. "Lord, please be with us. Please be with us," she begins to pray.

I take a breath and drop down below the surface. With one hand on hers, I use my other to raise the long knife I drove into the sandy ground earlier today. Attached to it is a bag with our rescue. As soon as I have them in hand, I break the surface and take her hand to place it on my shoulder. Nausea churns in my stomach in response to the contact, but I beat it down.

I'm with Emma. This is Emma. We're in an ocean, not a prison cell.

"Hold on here, okay?"

"Okay." She grips me. I struggle against my own demons that are trying to claw to the surface because right now, Emma's life is all that matters. Not mine. Not my pain or the panic trying to shove out all rationality.

Just her.

Please don't let me lose myself.

I take the long knife I'd used to hold the bag in place and slide it back into the leather holster at my back. Then I reach into the bag and withdraw a pair of goggles, quickly sliding them over my head. I don't pull them down over my eyes and nose just yet though. They'll dull my vision above the water, and I need to be able to keep track of the men currently searching shops along the shoreline.

Reaching forward, I remove the sunglasses from her face. Her pupils are so dilated that I can barely see the blue of her eyes.

"We're swimming?" The hand gripping my shoulder begins to tremble even worse, so I pause a moment and reach up to touch it with my own. Darkness swirls around the edges of my vision.

No. Please no.

"Do you trust me, Emma?" I whisper the words, almost afraid to hear her answer. After all, with everything I've put her through…how could she?

"Yes," she replies without hesitation.

"Then trust that I won't let you drown, okay?"

Emma nods, so I continue withdrawing items from the bag. First, I slide one flipper onto my foot, then do the same with the other. As soon as they're secure, I withdraw two mini oxygen tanks fitted with mouthpieces from the bag.

I hand her one and point to the mouthpiece. "You're going to bite down around this and breathe slowly, okay? You need to be calm so you don't run out of oxygen too fast."

Another yell on the beach.

I look up and see the men hassling people closer to the shore now.

Another hit of adrenaline kicks my system into overdrive.

"Okay," she replies.

Reaching into the bag one final time, I remove another pair of goggles and quickly pull her hat off her head to slide them over her face. All while I keep an eye on the shoreline.

One glance this way, and they'll make us.

"I'll have a hold on you the entire time, okay? Just gently kick your feet. And if you feel you can, close your eyes. It will help." After sliding my goggles down and shoving the bag, her hat, and sunglasses into the Velcro pocket of my swim trunks, I bite down around the mouthpiece of my tank and take her hand off of my shoulder to weave her fingers through mine.

Emma follows suit, biting down on the mouthpiece. With her eyes locked on mine, we slip beneath the surface of the water.

It surrounds us, enveloping our bodies as it silences the sounds from the shoreline. My hammering heart is all I can hear. But the water pressing in around me helps to mute the feeling of her hand in mine. Which helps me pretend that no one is touching me.

We're far enough out that the waves aren't pushing us back to shore, but we still have a long way to go before we're safe. I stay focused on that simple fact, and doing so manages to help keep everything else at bay.

These waters and this island will be *crawling* with Karvers people if we wait too much longer. I have mere minutes to get us to the pickup location. So, keeping a tight grip on her hand, I kick my feet and push us out further.

We need to be out far enough that the boat won't seem suspicious to anyone on the shoreline. My hope is that they'll turn their attention to the island rather than the waters, but I can't take any chances.

My muscles burn from exertion, but I keep pushing forward. *Not too much farther now.* We're far enough out that the ground below has fallen away and made way for the dark abyss below. I glance back at Emma again, hoping she still has her eyes closed.

For someone who can't swim, being unable to see the ground below will feel an awful lot like torture. Thankfully, her eyes are still closed. I pull her forward a bit more, swimming with one arm and both feet.

I've never been more thankful for my special forces training. Specifically, the two months we spent training with SEALs.

Ahead, I glimpse a red weight dangling down in the water. *Bingo.*

I pull her forward and keep swimming until we've reached it; then I squeeze her hand tightly. She opens her eyes, and I point up.

With wide eyes, she frantically kicks her feet, and I

push her to the surface. We break free beneath the bright sun, and Riley reaches down to pull her into the boat.

"Hey there, Emma."

Bradyn and Tucker pull me up, and I drop the breathing apparatus onto the floor of the boat, then slide the flippers off and set them beside it too.

"You good?" Tucker asks, his gaze dark.

He wants to know if I'm stable. Or if I'm struggling with the forced proximity I shared with Emma. More likely, he wants to know if I'm myself or the monster they made me. "I'm good."

"Yeah?"

"Yeah." But it's a lie. Because every second I sit here, every breath that passes, I can feel the hands of my torturers on me. It's not Emma's hand that was in mine—it was theirs.

It wasn't her hand on my shoulder.

It's a blade driving into my body.

No. No. Desperate for distraction, I push to my feet and cross over toward the bench where Emma's sitting. Riley has draped a towel around her shoulders, and her eyes are closed, her breathing ragged. I take a seat near the bow, leaving some distance between me and Emma.

With the immediate threat past us, those voices in my head grow louder. I close my eyes and lower my head into my hands as Bradyn starts the motor and heads out farther into the ocean. The loud rumble of the engine isn't enough to drown out the voices, but it is loud enough that no one can hear the hammering of my heart—and for that, I'm grateful.

I STEP into the front door of my house, then move aside so Emma can walk in after me. Thanks to the flight home, she's dry and wearing a pair of clothes Lani packed for her before we left to get her.

Delta sprints over to greet us, his tail wagging.

"Hey, handsome." Emma leans down and pats him gently. She barely spoke the entire flight back, burdened by all that happened, but now she seems lighter. A bit more like herself.

"I'm going to check in with Kennedy and get the guest room set up; then I'll be back," Bradyn says before leaving the house. He's coming back for Emma since she'll be staying with him and Kennedy in their spare bedroom. She's close to Kennedy, so I know she'll feel comfortable there.

It's what's best, but I'd be lying if I said I didn't wish she could remain here. With me. So I can protect her. Except that has the chance of being more dangerous than anything she's faced so far.

"Ash! There you are!" Emma squeals when her cat comes trotting out to see what's going on. His back goes up, and she sinks to her knees. Within seconds, the cat is rolling around in front of her while she loves on him. "Oh, it's so good to see you, baby." She looks up at me. "Thank you for taking care of my cat."

"There were drugs in your place. It didn't seem right to leave him there just in case he got sick."

"Thank you," she says with a smile.

"Yeah." I run a hand over the back of my neck, then head into the kitchen to feed Delta. With it being a quick rescue mission, we'd left the dogs here, so my mom fed him breakfast this morning, but he's already acting like he hasn't eaten in days rather than hours.

After filling the bowl with kibble, I wash my hands.

"His name is Ash?"

She smiles and nods as she cradles the cat. "My sweet boy."

"I—uh—was calling him Foxtrot."

She arches a brow. "Foxtrot?"

I shrug. "He's fluffy. Fluffy starts with 'F'. I was sticking with the phonetic alphabet naming convention…so Foxtrot."

Emma laughs. "Foxtrot. I really like that. How about you? Ash Foxtrot Franklin?"

Desperate to do something to keep my focus off of her, I reach into the fridge for a bottle of water. "Want one?"

She nods and sets the cat aside to stand. Because I'm so afraid our fingers will brush and set off the charge inside of me, I put the water on the counter rather than hand it to her.

"Thanks."

"Yeah." I lean back against the counter and take a deep breath. As I do, Emma comes around into the kitchen and stops in front of me—keeping enough space that I don't feel smothered, yet close enough that my heart rate increases.

Keep it together.

"I'm sorry, Dylan."

"For what?"

"The fight. I had no right to blow up on you like that."

"The figh—" And then I remember the day at the church. In reality, it was only a couple of days ago, yet it feels like lifetimes. "It's fine."

"No, it's not." She has yet to open her bottle, gripping it with both hands. "You were being kind by leaving those flowers, and I threw it in your face—literally."

"I messed up. I should have just let you move on. I'm the one who should be saying sorry."

"Move on." She lets out a laugh, but there's no humor in it. "When are you going to get it?"

I clench my teeth together, doing what I can to keep myself grounded in the reality that is here. Because when she takes a step closer, it's all I can do to keep breathing. The intense reaction I'm having now is due to all the closeness over the past few hours. Knowing that doesn't help though. Not when I'm a volcano about to erupt.

"I know that you're different now. I'm different. But—" Emma takes a deep breath. "I don't want to push you, Dylan, but I want you to know that, if I haven't moved on already, I doubt I ever will."

"You need to," I choke out.

"Why? You leave me flowers; you risk your life for me; why can't you just admit how you feel?"

"It's never been about how I feel," I snap, anger raging inside me. I drop the bottle of water and grip both sides of the countertop. "I can hardly stomach being touched—do you know that? Do you know that whenever I feel hands on me, I'm thrown back into that cage? Every tiny contact leaves acid on my skin." Tears burn the back of my throat.

"But you held on to me in the water."

"Because if I didn't, you would've drowned. I'm paying the price for it now, believe me." The voices scream louder.

Delta trots over and leans against me. Absently, I reach down and bury my fingers in his fur.

"I saw your scars," she whispers. "I saw what they did to you. But you didn't die, Dylan. You came back. You deserve a chance to live."

"No, I don't," I choke out. "I should have died back there. Everyone else did." The panic has its jaws around me now, biting down and squeezing the life right out of me with jagged teeth as sharp as broken glass. My chest is so tight I can barely breathe, and as the edges of my vision begin to darken, I know I'm about to teeter right over the edge.

Releasing the countertop, I take a step back to put distance between us.

Space. I need space. So I don't hurt her.

"I can't do this, Emma. Please—" The farther back I get, the colder I grow, even as tension snaps around us like lightning.

She's my storm.

My perfect storm.

"Okay." She moves away from me, tears rolling down her cheeks as she wraps both arms around herself. "I'm sorry, Dylan."

CHAPTER 14

EMMA

"Thanks for letting me stay here," I tell Kennedy as she pours hot water into two mugs to steep some tea. My throat is raw from crying, my body sore from swimming who knows how far. Even if I wasn't the one doing most of the work, the ache is still there.

As is the nightmare of opening my eyes and looking down into an abyss ready to swallow me whole. After making that mistake, I'd kept my eyes shut until Dylan squeezed my hand to tell me we could surface.

I've never been so happy to be on a boat in my life.

"Of course. Don't even mention it." She takes a seat on the couch beside me. Ash is cuddled up on my chest, purring and kneading biscuits into the shirt Kennedy let me borrow after my shower.

Even though I should be overjoyed that I escaped the

fate Gio had laid out for me—at least for now—my heart is heavy. My soul worn.

I saw Dylan differently tonight than I have before.

I used to think he'd just changed so much that he didn't feel the same for me anymore. But now I see the truth: he's too broken to consider himself worthy of love. And that is so much worse.

"I can hardly stomach being touched—do you know that? Do you know that whenever I feel hands on me, I'm thrown back into that cage? Every tiny contact leaves acid on my skin."

I blink rapidly to try and keep the tears from forming in my eyes.

What a horrible existence, to be surrounded by people yet feel so alone.

"Are you okay?" Kennedy asks, tilting her head to the side to study me.

"Yes," I reply quickly; then the guilt over my lie has me shaking my head. "No. I'm not."

"Let's talk about it."

Bradyn is back in their bedroom, likely getting himself cleaned up after the long day, but I glance around anyway to make sure he's not near. Not that I wouldn't want to share anything with him, but when it comes to Dylan—I just can't. I know they struggle with who came back from that deployment too.

"It's just a lot," I tell her. "I wish I knew what happened to Felicity after she helped me escape. Then there's—"

"Dylan," she finishes.

"Yes."

"Bradyn said that he's the one who went after you. Tucker tried, but Dylan insisted that it had to be him."

I nod. "He told me that he can't stomach being touched. Is that true?" The tears fill my eyes now, and my throat constricts. "Did everyone know that but me?"

"It's true," she says sadly. "The occasional hug from his mom or his brothers seems to be okay, but aside from that —it costs him in ways we can't understand."

"Doesn't that break your heart?" A tear slips down my cheek.

"Absolutely," Kennedy replies. "But God is the only one who can help him, and Dylan seems pretty set against going to Him for help."

It's honestly a surprise to me that he's struggling with his faith. "Why? He's in church on Sundays."

"Sure. But he doesn't go because he's seeking God. He goes because he knows it'll break his mother's heart if he doesn't."

Which is so completely Dylan. He would never want to do anything to hurt her.

"I just wish—even if it's not with me—he could find happiness. He deserves it, and he doesn't think he does."

"I feel the same." Kennedy covers my hand with hers. "We all do. But you can't make someone surrender and seek peace. He has to want it for himself. And right now, Dylan's familiarity is in the pain. He doesn't see a way out."

AFTER A NIGHT of sleep riddled with nightmares, I'm sitting at Ruth and Tommy's dining room table, a steaming mug of coffee in my hands. My stomach is full, thanks to the delicious breakfast Ruth made for all of us, but all the pancakes in the world can't fill the hole in my chest.

Especially in those moments when I'd glance over at Dylan, only to find him staring down at the plate of food he barely even touched. Did he sleep at all last night? Or was he troubled too?

"Okay, it's time for me to head into town." Mrs. Hunt dries her hands on a towel, then hangs it back up before crossing over to me and kissing me gently on top of the head. "I cannot tell you how happy it makes me to see you sitting here at this table."

Forcing a smile, I look up at her. "Me too."

She smiles happily, then leaves the kitchen. With her gone, it's the brothers and me, along with Nova and their dad, Tommy. I know what they want from me, and I'm prepared to tell them everything. Especially if it means I get to go back to my normal life as soon as possible.

"Any idea about when I can go back to life as usual?" I ask Bradyn, hopeful that they already have a plan.

According to what Bradyn told me last night, we still can't let the town know I'm back. Gibson is the *only* one who is privy to the truth. Everyone else has to believe that I'm still missing so that, if Gio comes looking, he finds nothing. It hurts my heart to know that my friends are going to suffer, thinking I'm still missing, but if it keeps everyone safe, then I'll do it for as long as necessary.

"I'm not sure," he replies. "Felicity Karver said something about keeping you safe until the first of November. I'm not entirely sure what that means, but she made it sound as though the threat to you will be over by then."

"She said the same thing to me," I tell them.

"How could she know that?" Nova asks.

Bradyn shrugs. "There seems to be a timeline on whatever plans Gio had for Emma."

A timeline? And then it hits me, along with stomach-churning nausea. "The wedding."

"What wedding?" Dylan demands. It's the first time he's spoken all morning. His attention is no longer on his plate but firmly fixed on me.

Since I'd still been pretty shaken even on the plane ride home, no one pressed me for information. I spent the entire time wrapped up in my own thoughts and praying my way out of the dark corners of what could have happened to me.

So I haven't had the chance to fill them in on what happened while I was being held.

"Felicity told me that she paid a nurse to tell them I died after birth, then put me up for adoption to keep me away from Gio."

"Oh my." Nova shakes her head sadly. "She gave you up to protect you."

I take a deep breath. "Yes. She had no idea they'd brought me there until Gio paraded me into the dining room for dinner. He played off the fact that his son—my brother—drugged and kidnapped me. He just told me that Mattheus got a little ahead of himself in his excitement to bring me home."

Dylan emits a low growl. He pushes to his feet and leans back against the kitchen counter. *More space. Always more space.*

"Because drugging and kidnapping is an entirely logical reaction to wanting to meet your sibling." Riley rolls his eyes. "Unbelievable."

"Based on what I read, in that family, it's typical." Tucker crosses his arms. "The Karvers are bad people. Sorry," he adds to me. "I know they're your birth parents and all."

I shrug. "Patricia and Emmit are my parents. Felicity and Gio are simply the people who brought me into the world. They didn't raise me. I appreciate what Felicity did for me, and I pray she's okay, but that doesn't mean I look at her as anything more than a kind woman trapped in a terrible circumstance."

"Good logic to have," Elliot says with a smile.

"Thanks." I clear my throat, then continue, "Felicity warned me that they were watching the cell phone they gave me. She told me that she would deliver a message for me, so I gave her Bradyn's name." I briefly look over at Dylan, whose expression has hardened further.

Where's the man who smiled at me yesterday? Who held my hand as he swam us to safety?

"Since you run the search and rescue company, I figured you'd be the easiest to get in contact with."

He nods. "She did call. Told us that you were safe, but if we didn't get to you in time, then you wouldn't be. Right after that, she told us we needed to hide you until after November 1st. That once it passed, there would be no more threat to your life."

"I don't understand what that means though. Wedding dates can be changed, so there must be something else."

"Okay, expand on the wedding," Tucker says. "Whose wedding?"

I glance at Dylan a moment, only to find myself staring into his troubled hazel eyes, unable to look away. He clearly can though because he breaks the eye contact first, freeing me from the hold he had on me.

"She didn't say a wedding exactly. She said that my fate would be to marry someone like him—or worse—

and she couldn't stomach it, which is why she gave me up."

"An arranged marriage is common in crime families," Elliot says, shaking his head.

"But I'm in my thirties. I hardly fit the bill for that. I'm not a wide-eyed nineteen-year-old with no life experience." I scoff. "I'm basically an old maid at this point."

"Hardly," Dylan says, his tone low and gruff.

I have to fight the urge to look at him. "She promised to get me out and told me I had to play the part until then. Which was easy until Gio introduced me to Heath Slater the next morning."

"Heath Slater?" Tucker questions as he writes his name down on his notepad.

"Yes. I've never seen a man more intimidating." A shiver runs through me just thinking of him. "He managed to suck all the light out of the room just by entering it. I could feel the darkness rolling off him. I've never experienced anything like it before."

Nova reaches over and gently takes my hand. "You're safe now."

"I know." He haunted the nightmares that plagued me last night. Every time I closed my eyes, I saw Dylan die at his hand before the snake tattooed on his face devoured me whole. Is it my mind playing out my worst fear? Or what is coming my way?

"What do you believe Gio's intentions were by introducing you to him?"

"It seemed an awful lot like—" I trail off, trying to find the right words. "Like Gio was putting me on display for purchase. But it was done so subtly that, if Felicity hadn't told me what she did, I probably wouldn't have noticed."

"He was going to *sell* you?" Nova's eyes go wide. "His own flesh and blood."

"We've seen people do far worse than that," Elliot says softly.

"That's horrifically true," his wife replies. He snakes an arm around the back of her chair and rubs her back softly.

"They didn't say anything that confirmed it, but when Felicity came in and asked me to go shopping, Gio looked at Heath before giving permission. And it was only *after* Heath nodded that Gio said we could leave."

"I'll figure out who Heath Slater is and what we're dealing with," Tucker says. "We need to know what that timeline is. Maybe Felicity went to the cops and they're planning on moving in on Gio? We know he's being watched and someone scraped everything about the family offline. It could be in preparation for making a move on him."

Bradyn nods. "I'll call Frank and ask him to see if he can poke around a bit. He has more contact with the feds than we do. Until then, you need to stay here on the ranch. And honestly, it's better if you're inside more than not. We have to keep you shielded from view on the off chance they manage to track you here and send someone to get eyes on you. Since you called us—"

"It's not a far reach to believe I'd come here," I finish.

"Exactly."

I take a deep breath. "Okay. I can stay inside."

"I'll bring you books," Riley offers. "We need to avoid your house since they'll probably be watching it. But you can borrow mine."

"Thank you." I smile at him, grateful for the kindness.

"And I have clothes you can use. I'll grab you some other necessities from town," Nova adds.

"I'll see what I can find out about your betrothed." Tucker stands. "What, too soon?" he asks after Dylan storms out of the kitchen, moving so furiously I'm surprised the floor didn't catch fire in his wake.

"He's already having a hard time," Nova scolds Tucker. "You could have been more delicate."

Tucker shrugs. "Sometimes, you need to give someone a good, angry jolt before they wake up."

CHAPTER 15
DYLAN

Music blasts through the speakers as I slam my fist into the heavy bag. I stripped out of my shirt at least half an hour ago, when it became so hot in here that I could hardly breathe. Not that it helped. I'm still suffocating.

I've been beating this thing up for nearly two hours now, and the edge I came here to burn off is still not gone. Honestly, it's worse.

Because I looked up Heath Slater myself.

I may not have access to the systems Tucker does, but Google does a fine job of pulling up old news articles about the drug dealer who built himself an empire on the blood of innocents. Given he hasn't been arrested in over a decade, I'm assuming he's managed to bring some law enforcement under his wing too.

Which is going to make him even harder to stop.

Marriage.

Gio Karver intended to sell his daughter to a monster like Heath Slater—and for what? What could Gio possibly have to gain by doing that? Is it all about the name? Connecting the two men by marriage?

Why did he believe Emma would ever go along with it? Surely he knew she'd push back. That she wouldn't go willingly. She didn't even know him three days ago.

What if we hadn't gotten there in time?

Except I know what would've happened. Men like Slater love the thrill of breaking someone down. He would have destroyed her.

That thought drops me to my knees. Ragged breath after ragged breath, I try to fight the intrusive thoughts. The images of Emma being forced into marriage—raped, beaten, whatever else Heath Slater felt he could do to her before finally snuffing out the light in her eyes.

I fall forward and brace my hands on the floor.

They're bruised and bloody because I hadn't even bothered to wrap them before moving in on the bag.

I thought the pain might help numb me.

"Dude, you're going to kill yourself." Lani comes rushing in and sinks to her knees beside me. Gently, she touches my sweat-slicked shoulder. I jolt at the contact, lightning in my blood. "Dylan, you're trembling. Where's Delta?"

"House," I choke out.

"He can't be a service dog if you don't have him around to provide service," she scolds, then gets to her feet. I know she's still in the gym, but she's out of eyesight until she brings a bottle of water over toward me, along with a clean hand towel.

Without asking, she dumps the water onto my knuckles, washing away blood and sweat. It stings, but I lean in to the pain, letting it distract me from the agony I'm feeling inside.

"You should have wrapped your knuckles."

"I didn't have time." I sit back on my heels while Lani crosses her legs in front of me.

"Talk to me."

I shake my head.

"Dylan Hunt, you can't keep doing this. Not to us and certainly not to yourself. You can't keep shutting down."

"Don't you see?" I demand, anger burning in my chest. "I don't know how to be anything else! I can't quiet the voices! I'm not strong enough to beat back the demons!"

"That's a whole lot of horse poo and you know it. You're the strongest man I've ever met, and if you tell anyone I said that, I'll deny it." She's trying to lighten the mood, but it doesn't touch the ache in my chest.

The tightness constricting my lungs.

Drip. Drip. Drip.

I place both bloodied hands on either side of my head and fight the urge to scream.

"Dylan, breathe," she says. "Come on."

I shake my head and drop my hands. "The things that could have happened to her, Lani. He would have destroyed her."

"Who?" she asks. "Oh, that Slater guy? Tucker filled me in earlier," she adds.

"He would've torn her apart."

"But he didn't get the chance because you guys got to her in time."

"I should've been a better man. Then she would've been here with me, and Mattheus couldn't have gotten close to her. I could have protected her." I clench my hands into fists, and the blood begins to ooze from the cracks in my skin.

"Stop beating yourself up." Lani takes my hand. The simple contact is enough to have my stomach churning—even though it's my sister.

I pull away, too far gone to risk it. I could lose my head and hurt her. "You need to go," I choke out. "I'm not safe."

"And I'm not leaving."

"Lani—"

"Lord, please be with Dylan. Please help him see that You have a plan for him, even though he can't see it. Please, God, help him battle the darkness clinging to him. Help him focus on You, Lord. When he can't see past his own pain, let him see You. In the name of Jesus, I pray. Amen."

I can't even find my voice to murmur an "Amen." And why should I? Does God even care about me?

"Dylan, you need help. And you have to stop trying to do it all yourself."

"No one can help me."

"That's not true. But you have to want to help yourself."

"I do."

"Do you?" she asks. "Because I think you're so guilt-ridden about what happened to your friends that you hate yourself for surviving. I think you're angry with God because you don't understand why He kept you alive. Over and over again. All those times you ran face-first into danger, ready to die, He kept you protected. It's the same reason you were so distraught when Tucker nearly died."

"He did die," I growl. "I watched the light leave his eyes."

"But God brought him back. Are you mad at Him for bringing Tucker back?"

"Of course not."

"Then why can't you understand how we feel? How grateful we are that God brought you back too?" Tears stream down her cheeks. "Everyone walks on eggshells around you, afraid that they'll set you off, but maybe it's time someone does. Maybe, Dylan Hunt, you need a wake-up call. Because if you had seen all of us when they told us you were gone, that we would never see you again—" She trails off and takes a deep breath. "Well, then you would start seeing just how much you're loved. And our love is nothing compared to what God feels for you."

"I'm so mad, Lani," I choke out, a strangled sound that can barely be called speech. The panic begins to fade away, and I come down from the attack. Slowly, but enough that I can breathe again.

"I know you are, big brother. And those demons you carry? They'll latch onto that anger and drag you straight to hell if you let them. Don't let them. You want to be angry? Be angry at them. You've always fought for those who can't fight for themselves. But now you need to fight for *you*."

"Two times in the same week? Three if you count Sunday. It's good to see you, Dylan." Pastor Ford takes a seat in the pew across the aisle from me.

I'd called him shortly after Lani bandaged my hands.

"Thank you for meeting me."

"Thank you for calling." He studies me but doesn't mention my wrapped knuckles. Given he's a man who doesn't miss much, I know he sees them and is likely just waiting for me to open up. For me to explain how it happened and if it was what drove me to finally show up here, ready to talk.

Maybe not ready, but if not now—then when?

Because Lani is right. My demons want me to keep suffering. They want to drag me back into hell, and I'm so tired of fighting them alone. So very tired.

"I wanted to die." I toy with the phone in my trembling hands. "And not just when I was in that cell, but after too. After I was home. If I weren't so afraid, I probably would have taken it into my own hands a long time ago." The confession is one I haven't ever spoken out loud—to anyone.

They'll never know how close I came to finishing what no one else seemed to be able to do.

He's silent for a moment, and I can't tell if it's because I caught him off guard or he's choosing his words carefully. "Do you still feel that way?" he asks.

"Yes," I reply honestly. "Not all the time, but more times than I care to admit." Emotion burns in my chest, and even as I've reached the point where I want to desperately turn back, I keep going. "I don't understand why God saved me and not them. Or why He let me go through that in the first place. The things they did to me—" I trail off, tears burning in the corners of my eyes. My chest tightens, heart hammering. "I'll never talk about it, but the memories are there. And even the slightest brush of contact takes me back to that place. Why would He save me so I can live in hell?"

"God isn't the one who's put you in a living hell, Dylan."

"It feels that way. He could make it stop. So why doesn't He?"

Pastor Ford falls silent as he stares forward at the cross. "You know the story of Job, right?"

I nod.

"Then you know that he was a blameless man who trusted in God completely. Yet he lost everything. His children, livestock, health, friends—even his wife tried to get him to curse God and die. Yet he continued to worship God because he knew that we shouldn't only accept the good things. That in this world, both good and bad people will suffer, yet those of us who have put our faith in Him have the promise that one day, our suffering will end."

"So I should slap on a smile and pretend I'm not dying inside? Is that the trick? I just act okay, and one day I'll feel that way?"

"No." He takes a deep breath. "Dylan, you can't face this alone. He is the only hope you have of finding the peace you desperately seek. In every moment, especially the darkest ones, you have to lean on God for strength. Pray —even if you're doing so with tears running down your cheeks. Even if you can't find the words. Kneel, and surrender to Him. He doesn't care how you come to Him, just that you do. Stop living in the guilt you carry for surviving, and accept the gift He granted you because you did."

I lean forward and bury my face in both hands as I fight the urge to get up and sprint out of here. Lani's words are the only thing keeping me here.

"You've always fought for those who can't fight for themselves. But now you need to fight for you.*"*

I *want* to fight for myself. I *want* to be better. To find at least some semblance of the man I was before. But I fear he died back in that pit and the rest of me was just too rotten to go with him.

"It doesn't feel like a gift, Pastor. It feels like a curse. A weight around my ankles. I'm living half a life. Watching my brothers start their own families while knowing I could never have that. Lani will eventually settle down too, and then I'll be alone. It's torture."

"There is not a thing God can't do, Dylan. Saying you'll never have that just because you're struggling now is like saying it'll never rain again in the middle of a drought. You have to choose to face what happened and move through it with God. He can bring you through it, just as He brought you from that cave."

I can't speak, my throat tight as I fight to hold back tears.

"God didn't hand David a crown to make him king," he says softly. "He sent him Goliath. He didn't keep Shadrach, Meshach, and Abednego from going into the furnace, but

He remained with them in the flames. God doesn't promise we won't face trials, but we are never going through them alone, Dylan."

I clutch my fists together and rest my forehead on them.

"One day, when you're on the other side of this, you'll have a wonderous testimony to share. Of the suffering you went through and how God brought you through it. Don't you see how you can reach those who are struggling with the same questions? God can use each and every one of us for His Kingdom."

"I'm not nearly clean enough to be used, Pastor. If you knew what I'd seen—what I lived through—"

He gets up and comes to sit beside me. Far away enough that the panic doesn't begin, but closer than he's sat to me since I got home over a decade ago.

"Dylan," he says softly. "Jesus didn't die only for those who come to Him dressed in their Sunday best. He died for the addict, the murderer, the gossip, the liar, the adulterer—everyone. He was sent here for us. So that we could be made clean when we stand before God. We only need to repent and follow Him. Even when that path gets impossible to walk, we do as Job did and lean on Him through all of it."

"I don't even know where to start," I whisper, feeling a breath of hope as I sit here in the pew. Is it possible that I can find relief? Is it possible that some day, I'll wake up and not wish I was six feet in the ground?

"You start with God's Word. And a lot of prayer. Friday is Good because Sunday is coming," he adds. "Just because today is dark doesn't mean tomorrow will be too. Your story isn't done, Dylan. Put your faith in Him, and fight against the darkness trying to steal you away from the light."

<hr>

"Hey, where you been?" Tucker questions as soon as I step into the barn we remodeled and repurposed to serve as the office for Hunt Brothers Search & Rescue. After speaking to Pastor Ford, I went for a run near the creek, using the silence to talk to God. While I don't have any answers, I can admit that I feel a bit lighter.

And that's something.

"Around." I cross my arms. "What was so urgent?"

Bradyn is leaning back against the wall, his arms crossed, his expression stern. Riley is popping bubble gum —a habit he partakes in whenever things get a tad stressful. Elliot's hat is backward as usual, his mouth flattened into a tight line.

Then there's Tucker. Who's currently looking at me like I'm a bomb about to go off.

They only see a monster. That voice echoes through my mind, sending a wave of fresh anger through me. How am I supposed to change if the ones around me only ever see me one way?

"Can someone fill me in here?" I demand. "Or are we just going to sit around staring at each other?"

Tucker sighs and turns his laptop around to face me.

I lean in, noting a photograph of Emma's birth mother, smiling, beside an image of the boutique owner who'd shown me where to hide in that fitting room.

"Local Woman and Boutique Business Owner Murdered in Robbery, Then Assailant Burned Boutique to the Ground." Clenching my hands into fists, I stare down at the headline, reading it four different times, hoping to see a different outcome each time. Did Gio have his own wife and an innocent woman murdered? Or was this Heath Slater? Retaliation for Emma's escape?

Emma. How do I tell Emma that another one of her parents is dead? I know she told us last night that she sees Felicity as a kind stranger who helped her, but I know her well enough to know that's not entirely true. It's going to break her heart.

"Does she know?"

"No." Bradyn runs a hand over the back of his neck. "We wanted to make you aware first."

"I'll tell her."

"Dylan, I can—"

"No," I interrupt Tucker. "I will tell her." I cross my arms. "What's our next move?"

"What do you mean 'our next move'?" Riley asks. "We did our job. We searched, we rescued. Emma is here and safe."

"But for how long? Karver or Slater could come for her at any moment. Given Karver is clearly not above murdering family members, what's going to stop him from simply deciding she's not worth the trouble and taking her out?"

"This." Tucker turns the computer back around, clicks some keys on the keyboard in rapid succession, then turns it to face me again. "We believe it's a text thread between Felicity and a woman named Harlow Slater. Heath Slater's mother."

Felicity: When will the flowers be delivered?

Harlow: January first. Black roses are preferred. Though if you go with white roses, those have better longevity. Ranunculus is always an option.

Felicity: They're too fragile. Black roses are what fit better at this point. We're past the white roses, don't you think?

Harlow: I don't want to agree.

Felicity: I know, my friend, but I know flowers, and they're the only legitimate option.

"How did you get this?"

"The number she called Bradyn from was a burner. But I was able to hack into it and make a copy of the data on it.

I'm guessing they didn't find the phone when they took her."

"Okay, but what does this mean? Black roses? White roses? Are you thinking wedding?"

"We're thinking bigger than that," Elliot says. "Black roses used to be sent as an omen of death by those who ordered hits on large crime families. White roses are a symbol of purity, and it could also mean—"

"Surrender," I reply. "A white flag."

"Yes, when compared to the black roses. We believe that they were trying to speak in code just in case the messages were intercepted."

"Ranunculus is one of the most popular wedding flowers," Riley explains. When my brothers turn to him, he simply shrugs. "Read a book once in a while."

I study the message, trying to restructure the conversation between the lines. "So death was headed her way unless she surrendered to the wedding."

"That's what we think."

"Emma's marriage to Heath Slater." Just saying the words makes my stomach churn. "Does it say anything else about that boutique owner?" I question. "About how she was killed?"

"You're thinking torture." Elliot shakes his head. "Knowing what we do, I wouldn't put it past Gio to carry that out. But how's he hiding it? Surely someone saw something."

"How does one control anyone? Money and the threat of violence. Both of which Gio has in spades. Is Harlow still alive?" I step back from the computer.

All of my brothers exchange looks with each other. It's one I know well—they agree on something I don't. More than likely, they think going after Gio Karver is the wrong answer. But from where I'm standing, it looks like the *only* chance we have at ensuring Emma gets to live a life without constantly looking over her shoulder.

"We need to let the feds take this one," Bradyn says. "We spoke to Frank, and he said he'd get with his contacts."

"All you'll do is tip Gio and Heath off. Do you really think neither of them has dirty cops on their payroll? And if it gets traced back that we've been snooping, they'll figure out she's here."

"Dylan, we're not cops. We're not even military anymore."

"And has that stopped us before?" I demand, turning to Tucker. "You went on the run with a wanted fugitive when Alice was being framed. And you"—I turn to Elliot—"hid vital information from the police because you were afraid it would implicate Nova."

"This is a crime family the feds have been after for decades," Bradyn reminds me. "If they haven't been successful, what makes you think we can find something to pin on him?"

I clench my hands into fists. "Because, for me, this is personal. He went after Emma. Grabbed her from her house with the intent to traffic her to another crime family in exchange for who knows what. They came into *our* house. Pine Creek. How does that not bother you?"

"Dylan's right," Elliot says. "And you all know he is. If we stand a chance at finding the truth, then we need to do it."

"Who knows what resources Gio has." Bradyn clenches his jaw. "This could be a suicide mission for all of us if we press too hard."

"Then don't. I can do it alone." I turn to leave, but Riley steps in my path.

"You're not alone, Dylan. But we have to be smart about it. This guy isn't playing by anyone's rules but his own. We have no idea why Gio made the agreement to exchange Emma, or why there's a deadline on it."

"Then we talk to Harlow. Because *she* does. And after what happened to her friend, I imagine she's pretty terrified."

CHAPTER 16
EMMA

Frustrated, I turn off the television and toss the remote onto the cushion beside me. Ash glances over, annoyed at the noise, as he's lying on the back of the couch. Apparently, I'm the only one who can't stand being in one place for too long.

There's so much to do. So many things I needed to get prepped for the fall festival I'm likely not even going to be able to attend.

I miss my students.

My house.

"Sorry, bud," I say to Ash as he lays his head back down. "One can only watch so much television before it drives them mad." Which, unfortunately, is about where I'm at. It's only been two days, and I'm already so bored I'm ready to risk them finding me again.

Okay, maybe not *that* bored, but I'm getting there.

Pushing to my feet, I head over toward the large picture window that overlooks the front of Bradyn's house and the property in front of it. It's gorgeous, the hills covered with tall grass that dances in the slight breeze.

I may be bored stuck inside, but I can't doubt the beauty of my view from this gilded cage.

Dylan crests the hill just in front of Bradyn's house. Without knowing that I'm watching, his expression is far less guarded, and he even smiles at Delta, who trots beside him, tongue hanging out of his mouth, ears perked.

He's wearing dark jeans, cowboy boots, and a sweat-stained white T-shirt. A dusty cowboy hat sits atop his light brown hair, shielding his hazel eyes from the sun. *Gorgeous.* The man is gorgeous.

From a distance, you'd never know just how haunted he really is.

I haven't seen him since yesterday when he'd stormed out of his parents' kitchen. He hasn't called, come by—it's been no-contact, and I've hated every minute of it. At least before, I stood a chance of running into him in town.

Of catching sight of him from a distance. Whether it was going into the diner, the post office, or the feed store—which he typically does on Thursday. Trying to see him from time to time, even if it meant going out of my way, was how I coped with losing him.

He was all I had after my parents died.

And then I didn't even have him anymore.

His gaze lifts to the window, and he stops walking. For what feels like hours, we stand there, staring at each other. Two people unable to have even a simple conversation without it turning into a fight.

Dylan raises his hand.

I raise mine.

Then he continues toward the house, so I cross the living room and pull the door open right as he steps up onto the wooden porch and removes his hat.

"Can I talk to you?" he asks, tension squaring his shoulders.

"Yeah." I step aside to let him into the house, but he shakes his head.

"Out here."

"I'm allowed outside?" I ask with added theatrics.

It brings a smirk to Dylan's face, which catches me entirely off guard. "Right now, I think it's fine. And I can't —" He trails off. "It's better if we're out here."

Closing the door behind me, I take a seat on the porch swing. Dylan keeps his distance, opting to lean back against the porch railing instead. He sets his hat aside and crosses his arms.

"Why are we better out here?"

"So we're not alone." He gestures toward the pasture, and I see Elliot restringing some fence alongside Riley.

"You don't trust me?"

He starts to respond, to say something, but then pauses

for a moment. "I'm the one I don't trust." He swallows hard. Delta trots over and leans against his leg. Dylan drops his hand, and he threads his fingers through his dog's thick fur. "I tried to kill Riley."

"What?" I ask. Surely, I heard him wrong. Right?

"Back when he and Tucker pulled me out of the pit. I was so far gone mentally that I attacked him. If I hadn't been so weak from starvation and dehydration, I probably would have killed him."

"I didn't know that." I try to imagine how Dylan must have felt when he'd slipped free of the nightmare and realized what he'd nearly done. The guy who wouldn't even kill a spider when we were growing up, nearly murdering his brother.

It must have destroyed him.

"They kept me shackled until I could be sedated."

"Dylan." I cover my mouth with my hand as that scene plays out before me, as though I were watching it happen right now. I'd seen him shortly after he got back, emaciated and dirty, so it's not that hard to picture.

I wish it were.

"Do you remember when you came to see me at the hospital? After I got home."

"Yeah."

"When I grabbed your arm?"

"I remember." Tucker told me I was lucky, but I don't believe I was ever in any real danger. That's just not Dylan.

"I knew who you were when you came in, but the moment you got too close—" He closes his eyes and takes a deep breath. "It threw me back into that cave."

I don't want to risk saying the wrong thing and stopping him, so I try to remember to breathe as he tells me more than he ever has.

"That's how it was for the first year. I couldn't be left alone, just in case I lost my head and ran away, so I lived with Tucker and Riley. Anytime someone touched me, whether it was an accidental brushing of their hand on me or a simple handshake, I would get so sick to my stomach I'd either throw up or lose my head. Every second of closeness cost me another piece of myself." Dylan doesn't make eye contact with me, nor does he move from where he's leaning against the railing. "Then, it got a little bit easier. I was able to finally hug my mom three years after I got home."

A tear slips down my cheek. *Three* years? "I had no idea."

"You wouldn't have. In moments of lucidity, I begged my family not to tell anyone. I thought it was because I didn't want the town to know, but I think—on some level— it was about you."

"Me?"

He looks at me now, and there are tears glistening in his hazel eyes. "You always saw me as this strong, capable man, and I'd been beaten down to the point where I didn't want to live anymore. I didn't want you to remember me like that."

"I would have understood."

He nods. "That's what made it harder. For me, it was better if you were angry at me than to know you pitied what I'd become."

I cross over to stand in front of him, though I keep my distance. "Dylan, I wouldn't have pitied you. I would have tried to help. I would have done anything you needed because I loved you."

A tear slips down his cheek. "In the ocean, I asked you if you trusted me, and you said yes immediately."

"I do."

"Then trust me when I tell you that it was the best choice. The distance between us kept you safe."

"I didn't care about safety. I only cared about you."

He takes a step closer to me now. "Do you know what it would have done to me if I'd hurt you? There would've been no coming back for me, Emma. You were *all* I thought about when I was being held. You were my only light in that pit, and I *lived* in our memories during my darkest moments." Another step closer. "When I got home, and I saw you, I thought—"

"That I wasn't really there. That you were living in another memory." I cover my mouth with a shaking hand as my heart breaks for him all over again. And not just for him —but for me too.

For what we were.

What we could have been.

"I'm sorry," he says. "For all of the pain I caused you. For being too weak to face you when I should have."

"You're not weak, Dylan. You're the strongest man I've ever known."

"If you'd seen me then, you wouldn't think that."

"I saw you in that hospital bed, and I *still* think that. There's nothing you could've done that would make me feel any different."

"Emma, I wanted to die. I begged God to take me. To put me out of my misery, and when He didn't respond, I began to believe He'd just forgotten about me."

His words shatter what pieces of my heart remain. Dylan had been so lost—so broken. He'd needed me, and I stopped trying to reach him because it was easiest for me. Because I was hurt by believing he'd just decided I wasn't who he wanted to be with.

How naïve I was.

How sheltered.

"God doesn't forget people. People forget how to pray."

Dylan takes another step toward me, putting us closer than we've been since that ocean. "You saw the scars I carry. That's only a small piece of what they put me through. I was forever changed in that prison, Emma. Soiled. Damaged. And I still don't think I'm clean enough to even breathe the same air as you."

"Clean enough? Is that what you think? That I'm too clean for you?"

He closes his eyes and takes a deep breath. "You deserve better than half a man."

"I don't see half a man when I look at you, Dylan Hunt. Do you know what I do see?"

His gaze levels on mine.

"I see a man who's seen the vilest parts of humanity yet still chooses to dedicate his life to saving it. I see a man who—despite his own pain—came for me when he could've sent any one of his brothers." The tears continue rolling down my cheeks, but I make no move to wipe them away. "I see *you,* Dylan. Not your pain."

A shudder runs through him, and he starts to move back but stops. "I don't know how to be the guy you knew."

"Good. Because I'm not the same either."

Dylan nods, then closes his eyes and bows his head slightly. With trembling fingers, he reaches up and gently touches the side of my face.

I go completely still, afraid that if I don't, then he'll pull away.

After a few heartbeats, he does anyway, then takes a step back.

"There's something I have to tell you. It's why I came down here."

"More? I feel like we just had the best conversation we've had in years." I try to smile in order to somewhat defuse the tension between us, but Dylan doesn't react. "What is it?"

He takes a deep breath. "Felicity is dead."

"What?" His words hit me, shattering what little happiness I had over this breakthrough with Dylan. "What do you mean *she's dead*?"

"She and the boutique owner were murdered. Local police are calling it a burglary gone wrong."

I stumble back a step, the guilt over their deaths like a dagger to the heart. "It's my fault they're dead."

"No, it's not," Dylan says, his tone level.

"Yes, it is. Felicity snuck me out; that woman at the boutique helped her. Dylan—" Eyes wide, I stare up at him in horror. "They're dead because of me."

"They're dead because of the man who killed them— not you."

"I can't believe he killed them. Gio did this. Or Mattheus. Maybe Heath. Any of them could have been responsible. They're all monsters."

"I'm going to figure it out, okay?"

"You?" I look up at him. "No. You can't go anywhere near them. The cops—"

"Labeled it a robbery. Emma, he's going to come for you again, and I won't risk sitting around and waiting for some fictitious timer to run out. I want this over. I *need* this over."

"Why?" That small voice at the back of my mind tells

me it's because he wants his space back. I'm here, and it's hard for him with me this close. Didn't he just tell me as much? But as much as I want to go back to my normal life, I'm also afraid that, once I leave this ranch, things will go back to the way they were between us.

Distant. Cold.

"Because I need you safe," he replies, tone soft. "You deserve to be safe. To not spend your life looking over your shoulder. So I'm going to do whatever it takes to finish this."

"And if he catches you?"

"He won't."

"You can't know that for sure."

"Maybe not, but I do know that I won't sit here and wait for him to make a move. Not when there are leads to follow."

CHAPTER 17

DYLAN

"What's the mission then, boss man?" Jesper asks as I place both hands on the sides of the cockpit and lean in a bit. It's far louder up here than in the seated section I just vacated, but Tucker is napping, and the voices in my head are drowning me.

"We're meeting Harlow Slater," I reply.

He glances over at me and arches a brow. As usual, his blond hair is shoved beneath a baseball cap. He's wearing headphones over one ear while the other is slid off to the side so he can hear me. "Slater. As in the Slater crime family based out of the deepest bellies of New York City?"

"You've heard of them?"

"Oh yeah, I've heard of them. Or, more accurately, what they do to the people who work for them." He shakes his head angrily. "They're a bad bunch."

"That much I do know. But she has information that could prove valuable to me, and I need to get to her before they realize she's a threat to them. What do you know about them?"

"Just what I've heard through the grapevine. You know, when I was flying stuffy, no-morals rich people around before I met you Hunts."

I can't help but smile. Jesper is a highly decorated Air Force fighter pilot. He's flown more missions than anyone will ever know. Which is what makes him perfect for what we use him for. The guy has gotten us in and out of some tight spots on more than one occasion. He's fast, efficient, and discreet—three things that are desperately needed when you're dealing with high-profile targets such as well-known traffickers.

You can't risk tipping them off, or the risk of those they've taken is put into even more jeopardy than it already is.

"Just what did you hear through the grapevine?"

"Carl Slater—the patriarch before he met his own untimely death—loved to throw people out of planes."

I wish I could say I was surprised—but the evilness human beings are capable of is something I'm quite familiar with. "Disturbing."

"Yeah. And the son, Heath? Has a fondness for drowning people."

Emma is terrified of water.

What would he have done to torment her if the marriage had gone through and he'd discovered that?

"Fantastic," I respond dryly. *Another reason to stop him.*

"As I said, bad people. Be careful. Let me know if you want additional boots on the ground on this one. I'm happy to come and watch your back."

I consider it. Most of the time, he stays back at the airport hangar and watches the plane, but if we're walking into a trap, it might be a good plan to have someone no one knows on our side. "You know, I think that might be a good idea."

THE SMALL CAFÉ nestled near the beach, in Point Pleasant, New Jersey, is relatively quiet as Tucker and I step inside. The aroma of fresh coffee and baked goods drifts outside, but coffee is the last thing on my mind.

Especially when I see a blonde woman in the corner, large dark sunglasses covering her eyes. The white blouse she's wearing has embroidered flowers all over the front of it like an explosion of color. Her hair is pulled back into a tight bun—not a strand out of place.

Even if I hadn't seen her picture, I'd have known she's Harlow Slater. It's just that obvious. As I wait for her to acknowledge me, I try to bury my desire to simply force her to tell me where I can find her son so I can stop this whole thing right now.

"Hi, can I help you?" the barista greets happily.

"I'll grab the coffee," Tucker offers, then heads toward the counter.

I note Jesper sitting at a table near the corner, his gaze trained intently on a book in his hands. He'd gone in thirty minutes before us. That way, he was here and settled before we came in. No one should suspect we're here together.

Harlow finally shifts her attention to me and offers a single, tight nod, so I cross the shop and head to the small round table. As I sit across from her, Delta lies down at my side, and Harlow removes her glasses. She's in her early sixties, but thanks to what must be multiple plastic surgeries, no one could tell. Her brown eyes are red-rimmed, and her lips tremble just a bit as she takes a deep breath. Is this fear or grief over the loss of her friend?

"Dylan Hunt, I presume?" she asks, offering me her hand.

"Yes." I don't take her hand, so she drops it. "Thank you for meeting with me."

"Yeah, well, you didn't leave me much choice."

Since I threatened to turn the text messages over to her son in exchange for Emma's safety, I can't exactly blame her for the frustration in her tone. But when she refused to meet with us, I had to do something. Right now, she might be the only person who can give us the answers we need.

"Would you like something?" Tucker asks her as he sets two paper cups of coffee down.

She points to the one already in front of her. "I'm fine."

"We're sorry about your loss," Tucker starts. "Felicity Karver was your friend?"

"My best friend," she replies. "Since college."

"It must have been rough—marrying men from rival families."

She glares at me. "We fell apart for a time but grew close again over the last few years."

"Since the death of your husband?" I press. It can't be coincidence that he died six months ago and now his son is trying to marry Emma.

"What can I say? As soon as his thumb was ripped off of me, I was desperate for my roots. Is this why I'm here? To talk about the loveless marriage I spent most of my life in?"

"No."

"Then let's just get this over with, shall we? I don't have all day, and the longer I'm away, the more suspicious it looks."

Fine. "Why does your son need to marry Gio Karver's daughter?"

"*Need* to marry her?" She shakes her head. "You have it all wrong. Gio needs Heath to marry the girl."

"Why?"

"A few months ago, Gio got into some trouble. He was

having an affair, and that twisted son of his learned about it. He put the woman in the ground, and her husband came forward with evidence that would have proven the Karvers were responsible. Heath stepped in and quieted the matter."

"Meaning he murdered the woman's husband and paid off anyone who would've talked," I surmise.

"Exactly." Harlow leans back in her seat.

"Why didn't Gio just take care of it?"

"Because he's so broke he can't see straight. What he does have is currently being monitored by the feds," she sneers.

Interesting. "Then explain to us why your son agreed to marry her? If he doesn't need to, why settle down into marriage with a woman who has no interest in it?"

Harlow eyes me, then shifts her attention to Tucker before returning it to me. "You two are in over your heads. This is so far beyond what you can even begin to wrap your mind around."

"Try me," I growl, ignoring the insult. It's not the first time I've been underestimated, and it won't be the last.

"Your dear Emmaline—or Gwendolyn, as Felicity called her—will be the sole heir to the Karver family once the rest of them are out of the way."

"I thought you said Gio is broke," Tucker counters.

"He is—on paper. But the man has his sticky fingers in millions of dollars' worth of real estate, as well as connections to high-power drug manufacturers. Heath wants to take full control of the entire empire. Emmaline allows him the opportunity to do that. Once the rest of the Karvers are out of the way, she's the last living blood relative. Which means—"

"She gets full control of it. She can liquidate the assets," Tucker says. "It would only take a DNA test to prove she's their biological daughter."

"Exactly." Harlow crosses her arms.

"Then explain the text messages. Why did it read like you were working with Felicity to keep this deal from happening?"

Harlow is quiet for a moment. She purses her lips, and her gaze darts from side to side. "Because I want my son to pay for all of the evil he's committed. I want the legacy my husband was so determined to protect to be burned down until it's nothing but ash," she growls. "Felicity felt the same. Neither one of us signed up for this when we got married."

"You expect us to believe that you both accidentally married the heads of separate crime families? Those odds don't quite add up," Tucker says.

Harlow glares at him. "I found out after the fact that the only reason he married me was because he knew I was friends with Felicity, and he was hoping to have me pump her for information on Gio. So no, Mr. Hunt, I suppose the marriages weren't by accident. However, I never would have married him had I known the type of man he was."

I almost feel bad for her.

"Then why didn't you leave?"

She turns to me. "I had a son. And despite everything, I wanted him to know his father. I thought that I could keep him from following along in his footsteps, but by the time I realized I was wrong, it was too late." Her eyes fill, but she blinks the tears away.

"Did you help Felicity rescue Emma?"

She swallows hard. "I had a hand in making sure Gio let her leave the house. He was intent on keeping her there up until the wedding, but when I spoke to Heath that morning, I told him he needed to make sure he could get Gio alone so they could discuss the parameters of the deal. I also made sure to mention that the woman would likely be less of a headache if she had another reason for wanting to stay around."

"Such as a relationship with her mother," Tucker finishes.

"Exactly."

"But how could you know it would work?" I ask.

"I didn't. I merely started the dominoes so Felicity could get her out." She dabs at her eyes with a small paper napkin. "Then they killed her for it."

"And here I thought it was a robbery," I say, my attempt to gauge her reaction.

She glares at me. "We both know that's not true. Gio had her and that boutique owner killed for rescuing your

Emmaline. And instead of staying in hiding so that Felicity's death wasn't for nothing, what do you do? You go poking your nose into places it shouldn't be."

I ignore her. Pretending there isn't a threat doesn't make it go away. It only makes it harder to react when the predator finally strikes. And he *will* strike. "Felicity told us that we needed to keep Emma safe until after November 1st. Why?"

Harlow lets out a heavy breath and takes a drink of her coffee. "As I told you, I want to see both organizations leveled to nothing but ash. So Felicity and I started a chain of events that will—" Delta lets out a warning bark seconds before glass shatters, and I dive to the ground, taking Tucker with me.

Without hesitation, I crawl over and tug Harlow down to the ground. She lands on her back, blood saturating the front of her blouse. "Tucker, she's been hit!"

"On it." Tucker presses both hands to her chest while I crawl toward the window ledge to peer out. Jesper stays where he is, weapon in hand, watching the back door just in case they flank us.

"What is happening?" the barista screams.

"Stay down!" I order. With adrenaline surging through my system like molten lava, I scan the street, looking for our shooter. It doesn't take me long to see him because he's not even trying to hide. A man dressed in black waves at me from the top of a building across the street. "He's there!" I yell as he ducks back out of view.

Delta snarls, ready for a fight.

I turn back around as Tucker raises one blood-stained hand to remove some gauze from the tactical backpack at his side. My gaze drops to Harlow and the blood pooling beneath her. And when I see Tucker's bloody hand retrieve more gauze, I'm thrown back to the server room with him, watching the life drain from his eyes.

I'm thrust into the past. Back even before I nearly lost my twin.

Flashbacks slam into me—one after the other.

Blood dripping onto concrete. Deafening screams. Excruciating pain.

It's all there, firing one right after the other in rapid succession.

Delta whimpers and rests his head against me, but I barely feel him.

My heart is hammering—yet everything is moving slowly at the same time. The walls begin to close in, suffocating me with memories I desperately want to keep buried forever. Why can't they just stay buried?

Lean on Me.

Those three words silence everything else. And Emma's words follow. *"God doesn't forget people. People forget to pray."*

As I close my eyes, my breathing begins to steady.

Lord, please don't let me lose myself. Not now. Keep me in the moment. Help me, Lord. Please.

The world begins to come back into focus as a sense of calm washes over me—a peace that makes no sense, given our current circumstances.

"Dylan, you good?" Tucker questions, half yelling in a way that makes me wonder if he hadn't been trying to get my attention while I was teetering on the edge.

"Yes." I come to Harlow's side and kneel down.

Her eyes are wide and full of tears. "He's going to kill all of you," she says. "Anyone who tries to stop him will die." Her bottom lip trembles.

"We're not easy men to kill," Tucker tells her. "Save your energy."

"Ambulance is on the way," Jesper says.

"Just let me die," she says.

"No," Tucker and I reply in unison.

"You get a look at the guy?" Jesper calls out.

"Not really. Wore black. Arrogant enough that he waved at me."

"He waved at you?" Tucker asks.

"Yeah." Sirens blare as police and paramedics come to a halt in front of the coffee shop. "We can't leave her here in Jersey," I tell him as I look down at Harlow. I think she's still alert, though her eyes are closed and her breathing ragged. "If she lives, we need to get her back to Pine Creek."

CHAPTER 18

EMMA

"Hey," Kennedy greets as she steps into the house and slips off her boots. She looks exhausted—something I can more than understand since I was privy to her and Bradyn's conversation this morning about everything that needed to be done today. Their to-do list put all of mine to shame.

Meanwhile, I'm in nearly the exact same spot I was in this morning. Though I did scrub every inch of this place and bake three kinds of cookies before settling down with my Bible and a cup of hot tea. "Hey. Good day?"

She surveys the house, then inhales deeply. "From the look and smell of things, it's about to be one. You didn't have to clean. Or cook. You're our guest, Emma."

"I know, but I'm going crazy over here, and it seemed like the only way to regain some of my sanity. I'm a big stress cleaner." I set my Bible aside and get to my feet to stretch. Thankfully, they'd gone to my place and grabbed a few of my things. Though not enough to alert any suspicion should people be sent there to look for me. "Oddly, it helps me relax."

"Fair enough." Kennedy smiles and hangs her baseball cap on a hook near the front door. "Bradyn will be in shortly. Elliot stopped him and said he had some news, so they went to their office."

"News? Is everything okay?" *Did something else come up?* I haven't spoken to Dylan since our conversation yesterday, when he told me that my birth mother had been killed and promised to help me find answers.

No matter how many times I told him I didn't want them at the risk of his life, he wouldn't listen. I assumed he wasn't coming around because he's been busy. But—did something happen? Surely he wouldn't have made a move without telling me, right?

"Everything's fine." She retrieves a glass from the cabinet and starts to fill it with water; instead, she turns off the water, sets the glass on the counter, and turns to me. She chews on her bottom lip and places a hand on her hip.

"What happened, Kennedy?" I ask again, already imagining one horrible scenario after the other.

"Dylan and Tucker have been in New Jersey all day."

"New Jersey?" I cross my arms. "Why?"

She hesitates just a moment. "To meet with Harlow Slater."

"Harlow Slater," I repeat the name. "*Wait*, as in Heath Slater? I'm assuming the same last name isn't a coincidence."

"It's not," she says. "Harlow is his mother. She and Felicity were close friends, and the boys thought they could get some answers from her since Tucker hacked into a text thread between them."

My face grows cold, my stomach plummeting. "Then what's the news? Is everything okay?" All I can picture is Heath attacking Dylan. Of him falling back and Heath standing over his body, only it's not Heath I see—it's a snake. Just like the one tattooed on his face.

"I'm sure they're fine, okay? Bradyn probably had to go because they were checking in. They do that sometimes, all gather for the check-in. If it were an emergency, he would've looked a lot more worried."

"So he looked worried?"

"No. I mean, a little concerned, but that's just Bradyn. He worries until he doesn't have to."

"Kennedy—"

"Emma, it'll be fine. Okay? I didn't want to worry you, but I thought you should know just in case."

"Just in case something goes wrong and they get themselves killed." I shake my head. "I begged him to leave it alone."

"Let's just hold off and see what Bradyn has to say, okay? He'll be in any minute."

I clench my fists and fight the urge to track Bradyn down myself. Surely we would've all gotten the call if it were something more serious, right? They wouldn't leave all of us in the dark.

Still, something is wrong. I know it is. I uncross my arms and clench both hands into fists.

Lord, please let them be okay. Please let them be okay, I repeat.

How could they walk into a den of vipers like that and *not* have something go wrong? Gio is a bad man…but Heath Slater is so much worse. Thankfully, I don't have to wait much longer because the front door opens and Bradyn strolls in.

"Are they okay?" I blurt.

He glances over at Kennedy, who shrugs. "She deserved to know. You know it, and I know it."

Bradyn sighs. "I know. I told Dylan to tell you," he adds to me.

I cross my arms. "Yeah, well, Dylan doesn't have the greatest communication skills. What happened?"

"There was a shooting at the café they met Harlow Slater at."

"A shooting?" I choke on the word and have to reach out to steady myself on the wall behind me. "Are they—did they—"

"They're both fine," he says quickly. "Harlow Slater was hit, but the bullet missed anything vital and went straight through. She's been in the hospital all day, and they've been dealing with local PD."

They're okay. I take a deep breath, but the helpless twisting in my gut remains.

"Who shot her?" Kennedy asks.

"We don't know. But Dylan and Tucker are staying with her for protection until she's able to leave the hospital."

"Then what?" I demand. "If she was the target, they'll just keep coming after her." I think about Felicity. I may not have known her well, but that didn't keep me from crying most of the night, thinking about the little time I had with her.

How unfair it was that she was killed all because she helped me.

Will Harlow meet the same fate? And why?

How many more people have to die before this is all over? Ice water in my veins, I redirect my attention to the conversation.

"We're not sure who pulled the trigger yet."

"But you have your suspicions," I say.

Bradyn nods. "Both Gio and Heath have motive to want her dead if she helped Felicity in the way we think she did."

"Helped her with what?"

Bradyn crosses his arms and leans back against the door. "She told Dylan and Tucker that she wanted to see her husband's legacy crumble. That she and Felicity had that in common. She also helped organize your escape with the boutique manager."

I press a fist to my chest, just above my heart. "She's okay?"

He nods. "For now."

"When will they be back?"

Bradyn shrugs. "I'm not sure about that either. Tucker said as soon as possible, but they have to wait until she can be released from the hospital."

"They're at risk just being there," I say.

"They are, but that's the job."

"Except the job was finding me, not stopping two major crime families. I'm right here. The job is done." My heart is pounding. Head spinning. He's going to get himself killed. Someone else is going to die for me before this is all over.

Is that why Dylan is doing it? Because it's a risk? I shove the thought aside even as it crosses my mind. *No.* He wouldn't be risking his brothers this way. Even if he doesn't value his own life, he values theirs.

"You know Dylan. He's not going to let this go until the threat is over."

I look up at Bradyn. "Then make him stop. You're in charge, right? You're the one who officially runs the team."

"Emma—"

"Tell him to stop. That it's not worth his life."

"He doesn't see it that way."

"He doesn't have to. If you order him to—"

"Emma. We don't operate that way. Yes, I started the company. Yes, I technically run it, but we all work together. We all decide which missions we take, and I'm not going to tell him to not risk everything for your safety when I did the exact same thing to protect Kennedy."

I glance over at Kennedy now, who's been silent during our exchange.

"That was different," I insist.

"No," Bradyn replies. "It really wasn't."

"Yes. You two were together."

Bradyn's expression softens just a bit. "You might not be in a relationship anymore, but make no mistake—my brother never stopped loving you, Emma. Even if I did try to convince him that we couldn't be involved in this, he'd go do it alone. He's not backing down from this. Not until the threat is eliminated—or he is."

Tears fill my eyes, and I wrap both arms around myself. "That's what I'm afraid of."

"WHAT DO you think the future looks like for us?" I ask as I tilt my face up to stare at the stars.

Dylan's arm is around my shoulders as I lean against him on the porch swing while we wait for my mom to come pick me up. "What do you want it to look like?" he asks.

I turn my head to look at him. "I asked you first."

He grins. "But I want everything you want, Emma Franklin. Which means you already know what I want."

I smile, my heart fluttering in my chest just like it always does whenever he says ridiculously adorable things. Which happens relatively frequently. Even at seventeen, I know what I want.

I know exactly *how I want the rest of my life to go.*

"Let me think," I say as I sit up and tap my finger to my chin. "I want a cat. And a dog. Maybe some chickens."

He laughs. "All doable."

"And I want wildflowers everywhere. A house surrounded by them."

His smile widens. "Again, doable."

"And I want you. Forever. A family. I want to teach our children the way your mother taught you guys, and I want to raise them with you."

Dylan leans in and presses his lips to my forehead. My skin sizzles where his lips linger. "I can give you all of that and so much more."

"Good." I smile, my entire world right here on this swing with me.

"I love you, Emma."

"I love you too, Dylan." As he pulls away, I lay my head against his shoulder again, soaking in every second of this moment. It doesn't matter that we're young. Dylan and

I were made for each other. Both of us placed in each other's lives by God.

And I'll spend every day of my life thanking Him for that.

WITH ASH CURLED up beside me and my Bible open in my lap, I wipe tears from my eyes as the memory of that peaceful night lingers in my mind. We were so young—so naïve to believe that we had a future ahead of us.

Yet here I sit at three o'clock in the morning, propped up against the headboard, chasing sleep that continues to outrun me.

I've cried until my eyes hurt, prayed until I had no words left, and now I sit here, staring at the wall, wishing that I could at least talk to him. But since Tucker told me that Gio and Heath could be monitoring my cell phone and email, I have to avoid using either.

Groaning, I set my Bible aside and lay back in the bed. Ash yawns and stretches before moving toward the foot of the bed and curling up again.

"Lord, why is this happening to me?" I whisper aloud to the empty room.

I've never been much for confrontation. It just never felt worth it to me. By the time a situation has escalated to the point of an argument, both sides are typically so rooted in their reason for the argument that there's no chance of trying to rationally get a point across.

But I'd welcome a confrontation with Dylan right now because it means he'd be *here* to fight. Maybe if he were, I could convince him that he needs to let the authorities handle this so that he can stay safe.

Maybe I could convince him that my life means nothing if he's not in it—even from a distance. That him being killed would be worse than any fate Gio or Heath Slater have in store for me.

Would he care then?

If he knew that losing him would cost me everything?

CHAPTER 19
DYLAN

"You're wasting your time trying to protect me," Harlow says from her bed. She's sitting up and thumbing through a magazine as if she didn't nearly die yesterday. It's been like this ever since she woke up from the anesthesia. She's barely spoken unless it's to tell us that we're wasting our time on her.

Thankfully, as soon as the nurses finish the discharge paperwork, we're headed back to the ranch. And whether she likes it or not, Harlow is coming with us. Something she's been pretending isn't going to happen.

But even if I have to throw her over my shoulder to get her there, she *will* be in Pine Creek by the end of the day.

Even Tucker got tired of her arguing, so he headed downstairs to get us both coffee while the nurses work on her paperwork. We're mere hours away from going home, and I can't wait. Emma's been on my mind all day.

Just as she was on my mind all night.

"It wouldn't be a waste of time if you'd tell me what I want to know," I counter.

"I can't give you anything else."

"You're lying." I continue staring out the window at the bright afternoon sun. We'd checked Harlow in as Jane Doe, only after a phone call from a federal agent—courtesy of Frank Loyotta—convinced local PD and the hospital staff to keep her anonymous.

Though I doubt it'll stay that way for long.

The door opens, and two armed men step in ahead of a third.

Adrenaline pulses through my system, and Delta growls at my side, his hackles standing on edge. "*Sitz*," I order him. *Sit.*

Dressed in black leather, a snake tattoo climbing up the side of his neck and ending on his cheek, Heath Slater is everything Emma described. Though I don't find him intimidating. No, I've stared monsters like him in the face before and lived to tell the tale.

So, as far as I'm concerned, Heath is merely another monster in need of slaying.

A criminal I plan to help put behind bars.

"Heath," Harlow greets, her tone sharp and lacking all emotion. "Nice of you to visit."

"Of course, Mother," he replies with a savage smile as he moves farther into the room.

My hand instinctively goes to my lower back, where a firearm is holstered. "You can stop right there, Slater."

He stops and turns his attention to me. "Well, well, if it isn't the cowboy. Dylan Hunt, I presume?"

I'm not surprised that he knows who I am. I tighten my hands into fists, fighting the urge to end things right here. Right now. "Yes."

"Good. I've been wanting to have a sit-down with you for a couple of days now." He leans back against the counter near the needle disposal unit.

"What a coincidence, so have I."

Heath smiles. "Look at that, then. What a coincidence that my mother happened to get shot in your vicinity. And how kind it was of you to bring her here so she could be tended to."

It was planned, then. "That why she's not dead? Because you wanted me to bring her here?"

"Are you insinuating that I had something to do with my mother being shot?"

"I'm not insinuating anything," I reply. "Merely making an observation based on facts." I cross my arms.

Heath stares at me for a moment, clearly sizing me up. He'll likely underestimate me. They always do. But the most venomous creatures on this planet appear unassuming at first. Until they strike. I may not have the height of Bradyn, nor the same bulky muscle mass of Elliot, but even combined, they don't match my lethality.

"Where is my wife?" he asks, tone level, voice calm.

"I wasn't aware you were married."

He grins. "Emmaline. Where is she? I won't ask again." He doesn't even try to coat the threat in his voice. Too bad he's trying to go toe-to-toe with a man who's had a death wish for over a decade.

"I have no idea what you're talking about."

He chuckles, but there's no humor in it. The façade he's had since stepping into the room begins to crack, showing his frustration lingering beneath the surface. Heath straightens and takes a step closer.

Delta growls in warning, but Heath pays him no attention as he crosses his arms right in front of me. We're nearly a match for height and mass, but I'm not worried.

Not even a little.

"You're out of your league, cowboy," he warns. "If you're not careful, you and every member of your family are going to end up at the wrong end of a tragic accident."

"Similar to the one Felicity Karver faced in that boutique?"

His arrogant grin spreads. "What a tragedy that was. Does Emmaline know what happened to her? Or did you hide it so she'd be unaware of what happened to her mother? All because she couldn't remain where she was supposed to." He clicks his tongue. "Naughty girl."

My muscles are trembling in response to the shackles I've placed around the fury pumping through my veins. I want to lay him out on the floor right now. Watch as that arrogant smile fades from his face.

But that would only land me in jail for assault, and who knows how many cops he has on his payroll. I'll likely never make it out of the cell they throw me in. So, I control myself—for now.

"I bet you hid it from her because you know she'd blame you too. See, I know you're the one who took her from me. I watched the security tapes and saw you enter the boutique. Saw you leave too." He moves closer, and I drop a hand to Delta's head to keep him in place. "If you knew what happens to people who steal from me, then you'd never have touched her."

"She's not *yours,*" I growl, taking my own step closer. We're nose to nose. So close I can feel the heat of his breath on my face.

My stomach churns as my mind tries to throw me back into that pit. Hot breath fanning over my face. My neck. *Lord, don't let me lose it now.*

"You're a bug compared to me, cowboy. And the sooner you realize that, the easier it will be for everyone involved. I will find Emmaline. And when I do, no one in her vicinity will be spared. I'll lay waste to everything."

"Whoa, looks like I missed a party invite," Tucker announces as he steps into the room.

Heath continues glaring at me for a moment, waiting for me to break eye contact first, but I don't even blink. Not until he tears his gaze away and turns toward my twin. "Tucker Hunt. Tell me, how is Alice?"

Tucker's expression goes from cool to ice-cold in a second. He squeezes a cup of coffee so hard that it collapses in his grip, and hot coffee spills out, coating his hand and the ground. He doesn't even flinch at the heat.

I drop my arms and clench my hands into fists as a fresh wave of anger pulses through me.

"I thought so," Heath adds, then turns back to me. "I'll be seeing you really soon, cowboy." With one final glare in my direction, he steps back and heads toward the door. "You too, Mother."

The door closes as the last of his armed bodyguards leaves the room.

"We need to get back to the ranch," I tell Tucker.

He nods. "And prepare for war."

STEPPING out of my truck and making my way up toward my house should feel far better than it does now. But when I see my dad sitting on the porch, a familiar look on his face, I groan.

"I'm tired, Dad," I say quickly, seriously hoping to avoid a conversation I'm really not in the mood to have.

"Not too tired for this. Sit with me, please," he adds, then gestures toward the rocking chair beside the one he's in. Delta wags his tail and plops down at my dad's feet, and Dad pets him while he waits for me to take a seat.

I set my bag down near the door, then sit in the chair.

"That woman you brought back with you, is she dangerous?" he asks.

"She's not."

"But someone associated with her is."

"She's Heath Slater's mother."

He turns toward me, eyes wide. "As in the Heath Slater who intends to marry Emma?"

"One and the same."

"Why is she here? You're not using her as bait, are you?"

"I'm not stupid, Dad."

"No," he agrees. "But you've been known to be a bit reckless from time to time."

I wish I could argue, but he's not wrong. "With my life. But never with any of yours."

My dad nods. "Then why bring her here?"

"Heath would've killed her. And she's the only one who can give us all the answers."

"She hasn't already?"

I shake my head. "But I think that will change."

My dad eyes me curiously. "Because Emma's here. You believe she'll open up to her?"

"It's worth a shot. Felicity was her best friend, and Emma looks just like her. I'm hoping that will be enough."

"And if it's not?"

"Then we keep her safe until he's no longer a threat."

"He's her son."

"It's not like that, Dad. Their family isn't like ours. Blood doesn't equal loyalty. Her son has had her under his thumb ever since her husband died and he took over. She hates him, and he tried to kill her."

My dad whistles. "I'm glad I'll never understand what she's going through then."

"We set her up in the vacant cabin. She'll have twenty-four-hour surveillance on the entire exterior of the house. Windows and doors have sensors. No one's getting in or out without us knowing about it."

"That makes me feel a bit better then." He sighs. "I don't mean to doubt your reasoning, son, but I just want to make sure—"

"I know, Dad." I take a deep breath. *Now is as good a time as any.* Nervousness replaces my frustration for not being able to head straight in and shower. "I've—uh—started reading my Bible again."

He turns toward me, joy reflected in his familiar gaze as a smile spreads over his face. "You have?"

"I don't want to feel like this anymore. And I figure, if anything can help, it's Him."

My dad's been trying to get me to open up ever since I got back. Sometimes, he'll just come over and sit on the porch with me in complete silence. Waiting for me to rip open the wounds of my past and bare my soul so he can help me pick up the pieces.

He's always been like that. A superhero in this world. At least, he is to us.

"You're on the right path. He's the only one who can."

"It's a process."

"You're starting, though, and that's what matters."

We fall into familiar silence as the world around us moves slowly. Birds chirp in the distance, and cows graze in the field across from my house. I've always felt like time stood still here. Even right after I got home, when the world was at its loudest, there was a sort of peace that settled over me whenever my feet would touch the bare ground of this place.

More than once, I'd woken up from a nightmare, covered in sweat, and run outside barefoot. Something—anything—to ground me back into reality.

"How are you doing with Emma being so close?"

"Fine. She's—uh—actually going to come stay in my guest room."

My dad turns to face me again, this time his eyes wide with surprise and concern. "Are you sure that's a good idea?"

"She'll have a lock on her door," I say, frustrated because it's the same argument I had with Bradyn when I informed him that she needs to be staying with me. But after Heath's clear threat, I won't risk my brothers' wives getting caught in the crossfire. Not when I'm the one who kept instigating a fight they wanted to leave alone. "It's safer if she's with me."

"Is it safe for *you* if she's with you?"

I glance over at him, and fresh irritation bubbles to the surface. My dad has never been afraid to ask difficult questions. He's kind, God-fearing, and would do anything for us. But right now, I wish he'd just let it go. I wish they all would. "I'll be fine."

Truth is, I'm not entirely sure. But she can't stay there. Not if it means risking the lives of the families my brothers are building. If Slater or the Karvers come for her, they won't be going through my brothers to get to her. No, they'll come straight to me.

And no amount of preparation will help them when they do.

"How's Alice?" Heath's threat was clear as day. He might as well have spelled it out: *"I know your family, and they aren't safe."*

"Are you sure?" he presses.

"Positive, Dad." I push to my feet. "I need to shower and get fresh sheets on the guest room bed before she gets here."

"You get in the shower," he says as he stands. "I'll handle the guest room."

"It's okay."

"I don't mind, son. I'll even make you a fresh pot of coffee."

I grin, seeing an opening to ease the tension a bit. "Doesn't Mom usually make the coffee?"

"Hey, I know how to use a coffeepot."

"I believe you," I say, holding up both hands, then bending down to retrieve my bag. "But if you set off the fire alarms, I'll never let you live it down."

CHAPTER 20

EMMA

"Look, if you aren't comfortable with this, you *can* stay here," Kennedy insists as I finish packing my clothes into a duffel bag she let me borrow. "It's totally okay. I don't care what Dylan's reasoning is, I'm not scared of this Slater guy."

"I'm okay." It's not entirely the truth—but not a lie, either. The idea of being so close to Dylan is actually the first bit of true joy I've felt since this entire nightmare started. It'll be the one bright side. Except there is a part of me that is also afraid I'll do or say something that will push him further away and undo all of the progress we've made.

Then again, maybe being in close proximity to each other will push us past the rest of the walls he's placed between us.

Maybe, at the very least, I can get my friend back. Even if it can't go any further than that.

"Are you though?" Kennedy asks. "I love Dylan, but sometimes he's not the most comfortable person to be around."

"He used to be," I tell her sadly.

She winces. "I shouldn't have said it like that. I'm sorry, I didn't mean—"

I pause what I'm doing so I can focus fully on her. "I know what you meant, and it's okay. Dylan was the love of my life. Even before we were in a relationship, he was my best friend. I believe that part of him still exists."

"I believe it does too," she replies. "I just want to make sure you're *both* okay."

"I know," I reply, smiling at her. "We'll be fine."

The door pushes open the rest of the way, and Bradyn steps inside. "You about ready? I can drive you and Ash over. Dylan just texted and said things are good to go over there."

I zip up the bag, then turn to face him. "Your charge is ready to go."

He laughs and, in true Hunt brother fashion, reaches out and takes my bag from me. These guys have always had legendary manners. Their parents wouldn't settle for less. "Let's get going then."

Bradyn sets my bag into the backseat of his truck, then opens the front passenger side door so I can climb in with Ash in hand. The litter box and all of Ash's food is already in the backseat since he'd loaded it for me earlier.

After kissing Kennedy goodbye, he climbs behind the wheel and starts down the road that leads to Dylan's house. My stomach is a pit of nerves that grows deeper with every inch we travel closer.

"If you decide this isn't what you want to do, you can call, okay? I love my brother, but you know he didn't come back the same man. The last thing I want is for this to hurt either one of you."

"I know. But we'll be fine. It's not like we're strangers. And I'm not nearly as fragile as you guys seem to think."

"I know you're not. But you're kind of like our second little sister," he says as he turns down Dylan's drive. "So we're all a bit protective of you." He grins at me, and I smile right back. Since I never had siblings, I always felt like the Hunts were mine too. With them, I had four brothers and a sister.

Dylan was never a sibling connection for me though. With him—even before I knew what it meant—there was always something more. A jolt of electricity that shoots through me anytime we're together.

Almost as though part of my soul recognizes his.

We come to a stop in front of Dylan's expansive wildflower garden. Bright, beautiful blooms that make me smile just looking at them. I'd barely been able to see them the last time I was here since it was dark.

All the shades of yellow, gold, red, orange, green—it's stunning. A rainbow of color right in front of his house.

"I want a house surrounded by wildflowers."

The memory hits me square in the chest. Is it possible? Did he plant those for me? Before I can fully process the thought, Dylan steps out onto the porch alongside Delta. His hands are in his pockets, his hair still wet from his shower.

Why must I love him so much? My heart rate quickens as he comes down the porch steps and opens the door for me.

"Thanks," I say as I climb out of the truck with Ash in my arms. The cat is completely unbothered by the travel, likely because he was so sick when he was a kitten that I took him everywhere. He's just used to it by now.

He offers me a nod and closes the door behind me before opening the back passenger door and retrieving Ash's litter box and food. After closing that, he heads up onto the porch, still completely silent.

Which, of course, only makes me more nervous.

"Harlow get settled in?" Bradyn asks as he carries my duffel into the house.

"She did," he replies. "Acted like she wasn't happy about the house arrest rules, but she honestly looked a bit relieved."

"I trust your judgment over what she says," Bradyn replies.

Dylan sets the litter box down onto the floor near the kitchen—right beside a bag of fresh litter and a stack of wet cat food cans. I smile, unable to fight the joy I feel that he thought about my cat. I know it's silly, but it's the little things.

Dylan was always good at the little things.

Like flowers every year on my birthday.

Guilt spreads through me all over again when I remember that day in the church parking lot. It was less than a week ago, but it feels like forever, given everything we've faced over the past few days. How I wish I had handled that differently.

Delta trots over to me and sniffs at Ash, who wiggles in my grasp. Since I know they got along when Ash was here before, I don't stress as I let him free. He and Delta sniff each other for a moment before Ash trots over toward the water bowl and takes a drink like he owns the place.

It makes me smile.

He's comfortable here, and that's good. Now I just need to find comfort in it too.

"Any word from Tucker on Slater's movements?" Bradyn asks.

Dylan shakes his head. "I'll check in with him later, but so far, it doesn't look like he's doing anything."

"Sounds good. Keep me updated if you hear anything before I do. I'll do the same." Bradyn turns toward me. "If you forgot anything, just let me know. I'm around if you need me."

"Thanks so much, Bradyn. For everything."

"Anytime." As he steps out onto the porch, Dylan goes with him and closes the door behind them.

Since I'm not really sure what else to do, or which room Dylan will have me staying in, I don't attempt to move my stuff. Instead, I take a closer look at his space. Aside from that brief time a few days ago, I've never been in his house.

It's sparsely decorated, with no pictures on the walls. Curtain rods hang over each window, holding long, slate-colored curtains that nearly brush the hardwood floor. The kitchen has quartz countertops, dark veins weaving through the bright white stone.

The kitchen opens into the living room where there's a TV hanging on the wall across from a leather three-seater couch.

That's it.

No photos. Throw pillows. Nothing.

Which is so unlike the Dylan I always knew. He had such a personality. Growing up, his room was always deco-rated with bright colors. A neon green comforter, bright blue curtains—he loved color.

And now everything seems to be shades of gray. Is that how he sees his life? Lacking all color? Or does it remind him of who he used to be?

The door opens, so I turn to face him as he steps inside. Lingering near the door, he shoves both hands into his pockets. "Sorry about this. I know it's probably not what you wanted, but I think it's what's safest for everyone."

"I'm okay. I don't mind. If you show me where I'm supposed to be, I can put my stuff away and get Ash's litter box set up."

"I'll handle the litter box. When he was here before, I just had it in the laundry room. Is that okay?"

"Yeah. Of course." It warms my heart that he doesn't want to lock it in a bedroom. Instead, he wants Ash to feel like part of the family too.

"Great." Dylan gestures toward the hallway. "This way." He starts walking, pausing near a door closest to the kitchen. "This is the bathroom." After turning on the light, he pushes the door open to reveal a bathroom decorated in similar colors to the living room.

Lots of gray. No color.

"There are fresh towels under the sink." He turns off the light, then moves down the hall a bit more, opening a door on the opposite side of the bathroom. "Here's the guest room where you'll be staying."

I step around him and move inside, smiling when I see a patchwork quilt on the bed. This one has plenty of color. Blue, green, yellow, red—it's an explosion of personality, and I know just who made it. "Your mom?"

He smiles. "Yeah. My dad brought it over from their house right before you got here. He said your room could use some color. Apparently—in his words—my guest bedding was far too boring."

My own smile spreads. That is so Tommy Hunt. "That's so sweet."

"That's Dad." He runs a hand over the back of his head. "There's room in the drawers for your stuff and empty hangers in the closet. There's a lock on the back of the door." He partially closes it and gestures toward the handle then the slide lock toward the top of the door. That one looks freshly installed, the wood still bare around where he drilled into the frame.

"I'm not worried, Dylan. I trust you not to come bursting in here unannounced."

"Don't." His tone turns serious, his expression darkening. "At night, you lock both of these, okay? And you don't come out—no matter what you hear."

"Dylan—" My stomach twists. "I'm not afraid of you."

"You should be," he says. "I told you, I nearly killed Riley. Would have if given the opportunity. I don't trust myself around anyone because, in those moments, it's not me in the driver's seat, Emma. I become the monster they created, and I cannot be trusted."

My chest aches, a vise around my heart squeezing until I can barely breathe. How can he see himself as a monster? All I see is a beautiful, broken man who desperately needs to forgive himself.

"Please, Emma. Promise me. This doesn't work unless you promise me that you'll lock these and stay inside."

"I promise," I whisper. "I'll keep the door locked at night."

"And you won't come out."

"I won't," I agree. I don't tell him that I still don't fear him. That even when he was in that hospital bed with a death grip on my arm, it wasn't anger I saw in his gaze. Or even confusion. It was brokenness.

I don't believe for a second that he would've hurt me. And maybe that's me being naïve, but I'll choose to live that truth until the very end of my life.

"Thank you."

Tears burning in the corners of my eyes, I nod.

"I'm making burgers for dinner. I hope that's okay."

I clear my throat. "That sounds amazing."

"Good." He smiles just a bit, a slight lift in the corners of his lips. "They should be ready to go in about thirty minutes or so. We're far enough from the edge of the property that you can come outside if you'd like. Once you're settled. I have fresh sweet tea and lemonade."

"Arnold Palmer. My favorite."

He smiles now, a full, heart-stopping grin that momentarily erases the darkness in his gaze. "I remember."

CHAPTER 21
DYLAN

"*What if you lose it?*"

Tucker's words have been echoing through my head since I told him on the plane that I planned on bringing Emma here. He was adamant that he knows I wouldn't do it on purpose, but that it's still a risk.

As if I didn't know it was.

As if I forgot that I'll never be able to have a family of my own because I can be a threat to anyone at any moment. All it takes is a trigger, and I'm off like a bullet, tearing through anyone in my path.

Delta glances over at me, so in tune that he can sense when I start to teeter on the edge of that cliff. "I'm good, bud," I tell him, then do my best to shift my attention away from the dark thoughts that never stray too far away.

Burgers sizzle on the grill, the hearty aroma filling my

nose. A glass of sweet tea in my hand, I stand on the back porch overlooking the pool I had installed last year. It's long and rectangular—the length perfect for swimming laps. Which is one of the ways I cool off in the middle of the night when the nightmares hit.

The deep side is fifteen feet down, and there are moments where I'll cling to a weight so I can completely submerge myself just to block out the screams echoing in my head.

The torturous *drip, drip, drip* that still haunts me.

Cold showers stopped working a long time ago. I need cold and exertion. Which isn't great, come summertime when the water is nearly as warm as the air outside. Still, it's something, and I'll use whatever I can to regain myself during one of those attacks.

"This is so beautiful."

I turn as Emma steps out onto the porch, wearing leggings and an oversized blue T-shirt that falls to her mid-thigh. She's swept her hair off of her neck and into a high bun on top of her head, and her cheeks are tinged with pink, though there's no makeup on her beautiful face.

She steals my breath. I flex the fingers of my free hand, wishing I could reach out and touch her. Run my fingers over the soft skin of her cheekbone as I brush strands of hair the color of sunlight behind her ear.

And then I hate myself a bit more for knowing that I can't.

"Thanks." I turn toward the pool. "The burgers will be ready in about fifteen minutes. Fries are in the oven."

"Burger and fries? Mr. Hunt, you are spoiling me." She leans forward, placing her forearms on the porch railing. "I always loved being here on the ranch. Growing up, it felt like this magical wonderland where anything was possible."

"It's a great place."

"It really is." She straightens, then makes her way down the back steps toward the pool. "When did you have this put in? Is it original to the house?"

I shake my head. "I added it last year. Same thing with my shop." I point to the building to the right of the pool. It has its own porch with some chairs and a bathroom inside for anyone using the pool. I don't have many visitors, but my family will occasionally come swim.

"It's really nice. You should plant some more flowers out here," she says, gesturing over toward the bare right side of the pool. There's a decent-sized grassy area between the pool and a road that leads toward Tucker's place. "Wildflowers," she says softly, as if I don't already know. "Similar to the ones you have in front of your house."

A house surrounded by wildflowers. Does she remember? Does she know that I planted those for her? As a way to bring a part of her here with me?

"I'll look into doing that."

"I can. If you like. Get the plants, and I'll put them in

the ground for you." She beams at me. "It's not like I have much else to do. And you said it was safe for me to be outside here, right?"

I nod. "We're far enough from any accessible roads and surrounded on three sides by the shop, tree line, and house. It shouldn't be an issue. Besides, he already knows you're here with us. Not exactly a secret anymore."

She smiles. "This is true." Turning her attention back to the pool, she slips out of her sandals and steps onto the small ledge where the water is only a few inches deep, staying close to the edge of the pool.

Even though she's in a place where she can stand, my stomach still lurches at the thought of her falling in.

"That feels amazing." Closing her eyes, she tilts her face up to the sky and lets out a heavy sigh.

Warmth spreads through my chest as I watch her. Emma has *always* just fit. Even when I was an awkward kid with a crush on the girl who sat next to me in class. There wasn't a day in our teenage years when I didn't think we'd end up together. Married with kids, living here on the ranch.

Now she's here, but it's nothing like that. And it's certainly not for forever.

"I would never want to leave this place." Stepping out of the water, she retrieves her sandals. "I love that it's not deep. It's the only kind of water I want to be around."

"You really need to learn to swim."

"I'm too old now," she jokes. "I would look ridiculous with floaties on."

The mental image hits me fast, and I chuckle, imagining her wearing floaties on either arm. "Nah, I think you'd look adorable."

"Adorable?" she grins.

My stomach flips. "Something like that." The cell phone in my back pocket buzzes, so I withdraw it and check the readout. Lani's name flashes on the screen. I tap to answer, then press the cell up to my ear. "Hey."

"Hey there yourself, big brother," Lani greets happily.

"How's it going?"

"Not bad. Just left the clinic and wanted to check in on you."

"I'm fine. Making dinner."

"For yourself?"

I snort. "I'm assuming you know Emma is here?"

"A birdie told me."

"That birdie named Riley?"

"You know he's not great with secrets. The guy could be his own telegram company. Are you okay?"

"I'm fine."

"I know you will be, I'm asking if *you* are okay. After our talk?"

I shift my gaze to Emma, who's standing near the grassy area and studying it like she's picking out a plot for every single flower she plans to plant. Flowers I have every intention of going out and buying the first chance I get. "I'm doing good, sis, thanks for checking."

"Anytime. All right, you know where I am if you need me. Love you."

"Love you too." After ending the call, I shove the phone back into my pocket and check the burgers. Since they're ready to flip, I grab my spatula and flip both patties.

"Those smell delicious." Emma walks up onto the porch and leans in closer to the grill, inhaling as she does. "I am so hungry."

My vision swims, heart rate increasing in an instant. Sweat beads on the back of my neck, and I have to physically take a step back as that familiar panic begins to set in at her closeness. From the look on her face—she notices.

"I'm sorry," she says as she quickly moves farther away.

I take three deep breaths to steady myself. Embarrassment heats my cheeks. Pathetic. I'm pathetic. "It's okay."

"I just forget sometimes." She crosses her arms, gripping each elbow with the opposite hand. It's her way of closing herself off, of trying to appear smaller than she is so I don't lose my head.

How ridiculous is it that she has to?

"It's okay," I say again, this time a bit sterner. Not because I'm angry at her but because I hate myself for how I respond. She didn't even touch me, and my body reacted as though I was facing down an armed assault. "I need to go grab something to carry these in on."

She nods, so I head into the house, pausing in the kitchen a moment to catch my breath. Tears burn in my eyes. I want *so badly* to be normal. To be a man who deserves Emma. Will I ever be that man?

Or will she find someone else and move on before I am?

My gaze lands on the Bible on my counter.

On the ribbon bookmark hanging out from the bottom of it.

"If you look for Me wholeheartedly, you will find Me." I read that in Jeremiah 29 just this evening. Right before Emma got here.

I'm looking. Why haven't I found Him yet? Why hasn't He taken this pain from me? Made me whole again? Will He ever?

"THANKS SO MUCH FOR THIS," Emma says, holding up the now-empty bowl of popcorn in her lap. She's seated on my couch, all the way against the edge, while I'm on a hard dining room chair, practically on the opposite side of the living room. *Man, I'm pathetic.*

Even Delta and Ash seem to be doing better than I am. My giant dog has curled himself onto the corner of his dog bed, while the feline is stretched out in the center, clearly at ease in his new environment.

"You're welcome." I shift my gaze back toward the television, where reruns of Scooby Doo have been playing since we sat down to eat dinner three hours ago. I'm not even entirely sure what's happening in the episode since all of my mental focus has been on trying to figure out how to survive the night.

She'll be going to bed soon.

I need to go to bed soon.

But how am I supposed to sleep?

I've tried sedatives—they only make me more dangerous because I'm harder to snap out of the nightmare. Maybe I should have her tie me up? I glance over at her, trying to picture Emma zip-tying me to my bed frame.

Yeah, that won't happen.

I could call Tucker and ask him, but on the off chance a threat really does arrive, I'd be helpless. Either way, I'm risking her life. I just need to trust she'll lock the door and hope it's strong enough to keep me out.

Emma yawns and stands. "I think I'm going to go to sleep."

"Okay." I stand and head into the kitchen as she does. "I'll wash that; you can just leave it in the sink."

"I don't mind, Dylan." She squeezes some soap onto the sponge, then turns on the water before she starts washing out the bowl.

She'd insisted on washing the dishes from dinner too.

Seeing her in my kitchen is driving me crazy. Because all I can think about is making her stay here. Of giving her a reason to take a chance on me again. Tightening my hands into fists at my sides, I try to beat back the voices in my head.

The ones laughing at me for even wishing for such a thing.

"You're too broken," they say.

"That's why God hasn't helped you yet. He knows you're a lost cause." They scream those things in my mind on repeat.

"'Lord, have mercy on me. Make me well again.'" I chant the two lines from Psalm 41 over and over again as I try to silence those voices. They're the enemy. They're not real. It's Him I want to hear.

Only Him.

Lord, protect me from the wicked.

I draw in a deep breath. "Tomorrow, I'd like to go see Harlow together if you're up for it."

Emma looks over the sink at me. "Why?"

"I think she'll talk to you."

"Because her son wants to marry me?"

"Because your birth mother was her best friend. You look like her, and she died protecting you. Harlow strikes me as a woman with a hard exterior but a gentle disposition once you get past it."

"She's the wife of a criminal. How soft can she be?"

"According to her, she didn't know who he was until she was too far in to get out. Same with Felicity."

Emma's expression darkens as she sets the bowl in the drying rack and turns off the water. "I'll think about it."

Her answer honestly surprises me. "You don't want to talk to her?"

"I don't know if I do."

"She knew your mother."

"Felicity may have given birth to me, but she was not my mother."

I sense her pain. She likely doesn't even realize how bad she's hurting, but it's there. Something I recognize because I, too, like to bury my pain. It's much easier than dealing with it. Except I know from experience, no matter how deep down you bury those personal demons, they always find a way to claw themselves to the surface.

The only true way to get rid of them is to face them and take away their power by reminding them—and yourself—that you serve a God who has already won the battle.

Something I'm working on. And God willing, I'll figure it out sooner rather than later.

"I know that you're hurting, Emma. But we need answers, and Harlow is the only one who can give them to us. She's refusing to say anything else to me and Tucker, but I hope she'll talk to you. If you're not up for it, I understand, but I think it's the only move we have right now. The clock is ticking, and we need information sooner rather than later."

Emma crosses her arms. "Why?"

"What do you mean, why?"

"Why do you have to keep looking into this? I'm here —and safe. Felicity said that, if you just keep me safe until after the first of November, then the threat is over. That's less than two weeks away. Why not just let that clock run out?"

I stare at her. *Is she serious?*

How could she not want to know the truth?

"What makes you think this deadline means anything? That whatever they did will work?"

"Because she was adamant about it."

"Emma, I won't have you living your life looking over your shoulder. It's a horrible reality to be in."

"But it's *my* reality," she replies, pressing a hand to her chest. "Mine. Shouldn't I get a say in it? If I have to choose between living without you or looking over my shoulder for the rest of my life, I choose the latter. I can live like that. I can't live if something happens to you."

"Nothing is going to happen to me."

"You can't know that."

"I do know that. Just like I know we need to figure this out. He's not going to stop. And I'm not betting your life on some fictitious timer put in place by a dead woman and her friend." I wish I could take back the harshness of my words as soon as I say them.

But they're there. Lingering between us.

Her gaze hardens further, and she pales slightly.

"I'm sorry. That was callous."

She glares at me, though now I see that it's not anger on her face. It's fear. "I'm afraid, Dylan."

"I know you are." I don't tell her that she shouldn't be afraid, that there's no reason for her to be with me around. But the truth is, she has every right to be afraid. Heath Slater is a monster just as she described, and after staring him in the eyes, I'm not sure anything short of a wooden box will stop him from getting to her.

Honestly? As long as he's no longer a threat, I couldn't care less whether he's in a box or a cage.

"I don't want to lose you again," she whispers, her heartbreak hanging on every single word.

It makes my chest ache.

"Emma," I say softly, "I've been lost since they put me in that pit. I'm trying to find my way back, but I don't know if I ever will. Let me do this for you. Let me finish this fight so you can live a life of peace. The life you deserve."

She stares at me, tears shimmering in her eyes. "And if I say no? If I tell you to drop it?"

I grind my teeth together. "Then I'll walk away. But I think it's the wrong move."

She continues staring at me. Is she trying to read me? To see if I really would do as she asks and walk away? "I don't want anything to happen to you."

"Are you asking me to let this go?"

"No," she says. "But I'm asking you to prioritize your life just as you do mine."

She might as well have asked me to hand her the moon on a silver spoon. Honestly, that feels like it's a greater possibility than what she's really asking for. But I need her to let me keep looking into this, and if that's what it takes, then— "I'll try."

She nods. "Then I accept that. But I don't want to be in the dark anymore. You didn't tell me you were going to New Jersey, and that made me angry. I deserve to know."

"Deal. Will you talk to Harlow tomorrow?"

She nods. "I can try. But I can't promise anything will come of it."

CHAPTER 22

EMMA

Harlow Slater is not who I pictured.

In my head, I'd compared her to Heath. Painting her as a Morticia type from the Addams Family. Instead, she's petite, with streaks of silver in her blonde hair. Her eyes are not nearly as full of malice as her son's, and her features are far softer than his too.

She looks like any normal woman.

Yet, she had a hand in raising a monster. Just like Felicity did.

She's seated on the front porch of the cabin, a mug of coffee in her hand. Dylan remains near his truck while I'm sitting next to her, waiting for the woman to speak. Which she hasn't done since we were introduced.

Though. every now and then, I catch her staring at me. Is she seeing Felicity when she does? Or the woman her son intends to marry?

"You look like her," Harlow finally says. "Like Felicity. The spitting image of her when she was younger. Before Gio put her through the Botox injections and plastic surgery."

"She had plastic surgery?"

She nods. "He thought her nose was a bit too sharp. That was just the start of it too. He molded her like clay. Top to bottom, even though she was beautiful before—like you are."

"Did your husband do that to you?"

"They all do it," she says. "There's an expectation of women married to dangerous men. We must look as beautiful as they consider themselves lethal." The way she says it makes the ache in my chest grow.

The fear I've been trying to bury threatens to surface again. Is that what will happen to me if Heath gets his hands on me? Will he change me? Stripping away everything God blessed me with until he's not only destroyed my heart and soul but my body as well?

I glance over at Dylan.

Heath won't get to me.

"How long did you know my mother?" I ask, hoping to gently steer the conversation away from Heath—for now.

"Since college," she replies. "But that's not what you really want to know." Harlow turns to me. "How about you ask me what you really want so I can go back to the solitude I've been placed in?" She looks so sad—so broken. What was she like before? Back when she and Felicity were college girls with their entire lives ahead of them?

"Why does Heath want to marry me?"

"It's not about the marriage," she says. "Truthfully, the only thing Heath wants to do is destroy. The Karvers are in to him for a lot of money, and he told them they have until the new year to pay up, or he's going to wipe their entire line from the face of the earth."

If it's a New Year deadline, then why did Felicity insist on November 1st?

"How did I end up getting offered as payment?"

She sighs. "I wasn't supposed to be privy to that conversation, but I overheard Heath on the phone with your fath—Gio," she corrects. "He said that he had a daughter who grew up in a tiny town with no outside corruption. Asked Heath if that would buy him some additional time to get the money together."

My stomach twists. I was a pawn to be sacrificed for the betterment of the king. A story as old as time, but never easy to digest. "No outside corruption, what does that mean?"

"You're a good girl," she replies. "And Heath loves to play with his food. You would be an innocent flower he got to crush just for the fun of it."

Bile burns the back of my throat. "Seriously?"

"My son is a terrible man, Emma. And I refuse to pull

any punches. You want information from me? You have to be strong enough to stomach it."

"I am."

"Are you?" she asks, eyeing the floral dress I'm wearing.

I know that I probably look exactly like the innocent flower she's describing. But inside, I'm far stronger.

"Yes." I tighten my hands into fists in my lap. "So he accepted me as a partial payment."

"Yes. But only because he had no intention of letting Gio live past the wedding. Heath had every intention of ensuring the entire Karver line—except for you—died the moment you said 'I do.'"

"Why?"

"Because then you would be the sole heir to everything they had. With your background, no one would suspect you had anything to do with his dealings. And since they never got anything actually concrete enough to freeze his assets entirely, they would all be yours. And by proxy—"

"They'd belong to Heath."

"Yes. And not just the money or real estate holdings. The drug manufacturers Gio used would be fair game too. By eliminating the Karvers, Heath is putting himself at the top of the food chain."

"What was he planning to do with me?"

"He would've broken you down. Made you wish for death. And then he would've granted you that mercy."

"Death is not a mercy."

"Oh, honey, sometimes death is just that." She shifts her attention to where Dylan is standing. "Ask your soldier; I'm sure he'd agree with me."

I swallow hard, recalling Dylan's words from the other day. *"I wanted to die."* Could Heath have truly pushed me to that point? Somehow, I have no doubt that he could. That before he was done with me, I'd be begging for God to take me from this life.

Dark thoughts breed darker ones, though, so I shove those to the side. "Why did Felicity tell them to keep me hidden until November 1st? That I would be safe after that?"

Harlow takes a deep breath. "She called me the night they brought you into that dining room. She was panicked and told me that this couldn't happen. That we had to save you. So we took all of the evidence we have on both Gio and Heath, compiled it into one envelope, and set it on a time delay with a messenger service to send to the authorities."

"Why a time delay? Why not just send it immediately?"

"To give us time to get out of the way when their empires came crashing down around them. By then, Felicity had already contacted your soldier and started those dominoes."

"Can you remove the time delay? Send it now?"

She continues staring off into the distance, tears in the

corners of her eyes. "The night Felicity was murdered, Heath managed to get the information out of her. He broke her, and she gave him the name of the messenger service. He made me watch as he burned the documents. I literally watched my freedom go up in flames, and I had to pretend like I didn't know anything about it and that I didn't care." She turns to me. "There is no hope, Emma."

"There is always hope."

"No. Not this time. Heath is coming for you, and he will destroy *everything* in his path. There is no stopping him."

I swallow hard, trying to absorb everything she's telling me. There is no countdown. At least, not in the way we thought. Instead, Heath is coming for me—and Dylan was right. We have to stop him.

"He has to have a weakness. Something else we can use to stop him."

"All of the evidence is gone," she says. "It was too risky to keep digital copies, so we relied on those papers."

"There are no copies?"

She shakes her head. "I'm sorry, Emma, but there's nothing. I truly hate that this is your fate, but it's time to accept it." She nods toward Dylan. "He's going to die because he won't let this go. But the rest of these people?" She gestures toward the ranch. "They stand a chance at surviving if you just accept what's coming."

"Dylan won't die."

"Honey, he signed his death warrant the day he came for you on that beach. Heath won't stop until he's dead too."

"YOU'RE QUIET."

I look over at Dylan as he comes out onto the porch with me. I've been sitting out here for hours, ever since we got back from meeting with Harlow. The rest of the conversation was just the same information over and over again.

I'm going to be taken.

Dylan will be killed.

And there's nothing we can do to stop it.

All we can do is damage control, making sure no one else gets hurt.

"You know, when I asked her why he hasn't come for her yet, she told me that he knows she's too afraid to do anything. That she's not really a threat, and if he wanted her dead, that sniper wouldn't have missed. She said he likes to play with his food first."

"I would agree with that."

I glance over at him, shocked and disgusted that Harlow wasn't exaggerating. "Really?"

He nods. "She was used as a lure. To draw us out into that shop so he could challenge me in that hospital room. It was a strategy. He just thinks I'm too stupid to play chess."

I smile, though inside I feel anything but happy. Dylan was always good at chess. Competed for a while too. "Remember when you tried to teach me how to play?" I ask, resting my cheek on my knees as I look at him.

He smirks. "I remember you were terrible."

"You let me win once."

"I did. And the smile on your face when you did is still something I think about."

Tears burn in my eyes, the emotion hitting me out of nowhere. "She said you're going to die. That you signed your death warrant when you came for me on that beach. Why did you come?"

"Do you think there was ever an option for me?" he asks, tone low. He moves closer to me. "Emma, I would rather go back into that cage and live the nightmare of my captivity over and over again—for the rest of my life—than watch you suffer."

The tears begin to flow now, and I turn my head to rest my forehead on top of my knees so he can't see them. "I can't watch you die. I already went through that once. I can't do it again."

The swing moves just a bit as Dylan takes a seat beside me. "Emma."

I open my eyes and turn my face toward him. He's trembling, his eyes dark and his body tense, but he remains there, seated beside me. So close that our thighs are brushing. "You shouldn't be this close if it's so hard," I tell him. "It's okay. You can move away."

"Not until you understand." He takes a deep breath. "I didn't walk away from you because I wanted to. Or because I'd changed so much that I didn't love you anymore. I walked away because I was terrified of hurting you. I *am* terrified of hurting you. You were the only light I was able to hang on to, Emma. I'm trying to find my way back to God, trying to understand why He saved me. And now I'm thinking that maybe He didn't let me die in that cave so that, when it was time, I could save you." With trembling fingers, Dylan reaches over and takes my hand in his. He threads his fingers through mine and sits as still as a statue. "If that's all I do with this second chance He granted me, then I'll consider it a life well-lived."

"I love you too, Dylan," I whisper. "I never stopped."

"It's a lot to ask, but I need you to be patient with me. I need you to trust that I'm trying."

"I do trust you," I tell him.

Even though I want to squeeze my hand and offer him some reassurance, I don't because I sense that it might be enough to push him over the edge. A suspicion that's confirmed when Delta trots over and rests his head on Dylan's lap. With his free hand, Dylan strokes his dog, and I can feel him relaxing just slightly as he does.

"The countdown isn't real. At least, not anymore," I

say, hoping that returning focus to our current predicament will help distract him.

"What do you mean?"

"Harlow told me that she and Felicity had documents. Physical evidence of Gio and Heath's criminal dealings. They submitted it to a delivery service for November 1st. They planned to have it handed over to the authorities so that they would have what they needed on both crime organizations to finally be able to dismantle them for good."

"Where's the evidence?"

I can see hope on his face, and I hate that I'm going to have to destroy it. "It doesn't exist anymore. Before they killed Felicity, Heath got the name of the messenger company out of her. Harlow said she watched as he burned the documents."

His hope vanishes, and his cheeks flush with anger. "So even if we were to wait, it wouldn't matter."

"No. She says there's no way to stop him. But there has to be."

"There is," he replies. "And we'll find it."

CHAPTER 23
DYLAN

"Delivery for you." Tucker steps up onto my back porch, a wide smile on his face, and tosses me the keys to my truck.

"Thanks for doing that." Since I didn't want to leave Emma here alone, he went and picked up the flowers I ordered from the local garden center. Flowers that I hope will help bring some light back into her eyes, now that we know that keeping her safe until November 1st no longer guarantees she won't be in danger.

"Not a problem, brother." He takes a seat on the chair next to mine and stares out at the pool. "You doing okay?"

"Yeah. I'm managing."

"You can talk to me, Dylan."

"What do you want me to say?" I demand. "That I'm spiraling because I can't see a way out of this without bloodshed? That I'm battling with the part of me that wants to hunt him down and eliminate the threat rather than work through the logistics of trying to put him behind bars? Because that's where I'm at, Tucker. Convincing myself that, although the world would be a better place without the Karvers and Slaters in it, it's not my job to track them down and put them in the ground. All it would take is a squeeze of a trigger, and this could be over."

More than a dozen times, I've opened the safe in my closet and stared at my rifle. I could do it—I've taken lives before. Then, it had been war. Is this really any different? Different location, same fight.

At least, that's what I'm telling myself.

"Justice isn't ours to deal out," he says. "And when you start blurring those lines is when you really begin to lose yourself. You become a murderer just like they are."

"He's going to kill her, Tucker. Harlow told her as much. As soon as he has his hands on the wreckage left behind after he eliminates the Karvers, he's going to do the same to her." My throat constricts. "She told Emma that Heath likes to play with his food. And that Emma is an innocent flower Heath will get to crush just for the fun of it." I turn to my twin. "Tell me that's a man who deserves to live."

"That's not for us to decide. That's God's wheelhouse, Dylan." Tucker's expression is serious, and I can see that he's worried I won't listen. That I'll go off and handle things.

"I've pulled a trigger before. What's three more?"
Heath. Gio. And Mattheus.

One, two, three.

Drip, drip, drip.

I shake my head, trying to clear the lines that continue to blur.

"This is murder, Dylan. Not self-defense. If they come here and you have to use lethal force to stop them, that's self-defense. You go after them, that's premeditated murder."

"They're coming anyway."

"But they're not here yet."

I close my eyes, my heart rate steadily increasing the more frustrated I get. I hate feeling helpless. This inability to take action is killing me. Because, even though I *know* Tucker is right, I desperately want to eliminate the threat my way.

"Dylan, we'll get him."

"According to Harlow, there's no stopping him. He's a predator who is coming for her one way or another. Me too, apparently."

"Then maybe you need to change up the game."

"I tried; you said no."

He snorts. "I'm not saying take your rifle and put them in the ground; I'm saying get her out of the way. Take her somewhere he can't find her. Until November—"

"There's no November countdown," I tell him. Because

I've been processing for the last couple of hours since Emma told me everything, I haven't had the chance to tell him—or anyone—what all she said.

Mainly because I know how I *want* to handle it, and I didn't want to be talked out of it. However, Tucker's right. If I hunt them down and put them in the ground, I become what I always feared those men made me in that cage: a murderer.

And Emma deserves more than a murderer.

"What do you mean?" he questions.

"When Felicity realized they'd found Emma and brought her in, she contacted Harlow, and the two of them put together all of the paper evidence they had against Gio and Heath. The documents would have given the feds everything they needed to put them both away for good." I take a deep breath to quell my frustration as best I can. "Harlow delivered it to a messenger service the next day— right after Felicity called you—and told them to delay delivery until November 1st."

"Which explains why Felicity said they wouldn't be a threat after then."

I nod. "Only, Heath tortured Felicity before he killed her, and she gave up the messenger service to him. Those documents are gone. Harlow watched him burn them."

Tucker groans. "There's no digital signature? Nothing to trace?"

"Emma asked her that, and she said both Gio and Heath

only do business the old-fashioned way. She said it took years of secretly photocopying stuff to build the collection they had. They didn't keep digital copies of any of it because it was too risky."

"Why didn't they turn it in sooner? Why wait so long?" His tone is frustrated, his gaze dark. He's mad too. Mad that they didn't take into account what could happen if things went wrong.

"They wanted to be far away when the feds got the information. They'd planned on fleeing beforehand. It was foolish."

"They're not professionals," Tucker says. "They were scared women who were looking for an out."

"And their mistake may cost Emma her life."

"It did cost Felicity hers," he says.

"So that means it's okay for Emma to be on the chopping block?" I snarl.

"Not at all." Tucker leans forward and turns his body to face me. "I love Emma too. Not in the same way as you, obviously, but she's family to me."

"You didn't consider the morality of it when you laid waste to that camp I was being held in." I turn toward him, mentioning the one thing I never wanted to bring up again. "How is this any different?"

Tucker clenches his jaw. "We needed to ensure that what happened to you *never* happened again. To anyone."

"Which is what I need to do. I need to know that Emma

is safe, Tucker. How many more lives is this guy going to be allowed to take before we stop him? What about Alice? The baby? What if he comes here and she's caught in the crossfire?" It's a low blow but one that's been on my mind right alongside the risk to Emma.

Tucker's glare darkens further. He's battling with it too. "Nothing is going to happen to Alice or the baby," he growls. "As for our rescue of you, this isn't some militia base in the middle of a third world country, Dylan. These are high-profile criminals who likely have police in their pockets. You go after them on American soil, and you're likely to end up dead too."

"It's a sacrifice I'll make for her."

"Is that one she'd want you to make?"

"Value your life like you value mine." Emma's words echo in my head.

"Exactly," he continues. "Let's do this right. Trust the process. Trust me. I'm watching his financials like a hawk. If he so much as buys a new keychain, I'll know."

I take a deep breath.

Trust.

"Fine. For now." I turn toward him. "But if things escalate much further, I can't promise I won't sacrifice the humanity left in me to ensure she's safe."

"Then I'll be right with you, brother. At your side until the very end."

"Emma?" I call out as I step into the house thirty minutes later. Tucker left nearly twenty minutes ago, and I'd spent the time since then unloading my truck and pondering his words. *"I'll be right with you, brother. Until the very end."*

I don't think he realizes those words brought me back to reality more than anything else he said. Because I know he's telling the truth. Tucker would throw his life away for me in an instant—all of my brothers would—just as I would for them.

And that's something I can't let happen—ever.

No matter what happens, I can't go after Slater. Not if it'll put my brothers at risk too. So I'll do as Tucker asked, and I'll trust the process.

I'll put my faith in God showing us the way out of this mess. Because, even if I may worry that He's forgotten about me, He hasn't forgotten my brother. Or Emma.

Emma opens the door to her bedroom and steps out. Her face is red from crying, but she smiles in an attempt to hide it from me. "Hey, what's up?"

I wish I could hug her.

Wish I could wrap my arms around her and pull her against my chest, soothing the ache I know we're both feeling. But even just thinking about it sets off a chain reaction in my body. My heart rate increases, and my stomach churns, so I shove my hands into my pockets. "I have something to show you."

"Oh?" She leaves her bedroom door open and heads down the hall. "What is it?"

"Outside." I turn and head back through the house and onto the back porch.

The moment she steps outside, Emma gasps. "Dylan. They're beautiful!" She rushes down the porch and toward the collection of still-potted flowers I placed near the bags of mulch and rolls of landscape fabric waiting beside that grassy area she said would be perfect for flowers.

"I also grabbed some wildflower seeds. Figured we could sprinkle those between the planted flowers, that way we get color now too."

Emma turns toward me, a bright, happy smile on her face. "We?"

I shrug. "Ranch chores are being handled by my brothers right now, so I have a lot more time on my hands than I'm used to. Might be good to put them to work."

She starts toward me, clearly ready to hug me, but stops, expression faltering just a little. "Thank you, Dylan."

Try.

Trust.

Lord, please don't forsake me in this moment. Please give me strength.

I close the distance between us, the air so thick that I can barely move. When I stop in front of her, Emma stares up at me with wide blue eyes. *Lord, please,* I pray again, then take her hand in mine and raise it, pressing it to my chest before covering it with mine.

I have to close my eyes as the edges of my vision begin to darken, but I still can't find my breath. Sweat beads on the back of my neck.

My entire body is trembling, my heart racing, but I'm trying. Maybe if I keep trying, I'll be able to heal. Delta leans against my leg, his attempt to help ground me in this moment. I hadn't even heard him get up, but that's not surprising.

He's always there when I need him.

"Your heart is racing," she whispers.

I nod, knowing I can't find words right now.

"Thank you, Dylan."

Once again, I nod. Her touch is heaven and hell at the same time. Sweet escape and brutal torture. Because I want more, but I know I can't have it without risking losing my head in the PTSD that won't seem to relinquish me.

God, please help me.

Emma pulls her hand away but doesn't release mine. Instead, she presses my palm against her cheek.

Her skin is soft beneath my trembling fingers.

"How about we get these flowers planted?" she asks. I can feel her smile against my hand.

Opening my eyes, I stare into hers and feel some of the panic slowly slip away. *I'm in my backyard with Emma.*

Not in a prison cell, facing down an enemy.

I take a deep, steadying breath, and although my heart doesn't stop racing, the dark edges of my vision clear. It's progress. And I'll take every single inch of progress I can get.

"Let's do it."

She releases my hand, so I drop it and draw in a deep breath as I reach down to pat Delta. That's how he knows I'm okay. A single pat will let him know I'm fine, whereas if I rest my hand on him, he knows I'm still deep in the struggle.

The fact that I was able to have that casual contact and didn't go into a spiral is a miracle in and of itself. Even if it does seem like such a slight thing, for me, it's a shift of my world. A crack in the walls I placed around myself.

She turns away from me and starts looking at the flowers.

All while my heart rate returns to normal, and I'm hit with a level of peace I haven't had in as long as I can remember. Emotion wells up within me, an overwhelming avalanche of feelings that have nothing to do with my fear and everything to do with the feeling of her hand on my chest, of mine cradling her cheek.

A miracle.

That's what it is.

And that can only mean one thing…right?

God, is that You?

CHAPTER 24

EMMA

"You want to leave?" With a glass of Arnold Palmer in my hand, I shift my gaze away from the flowers we spent the afternoon planting so I can focus entirely on Dylan. I can still feel his hand on my cheek, just as I can still feel the hammering of his heart beneath my palm.

But he'd been himself the entire time. Proof that the monster he's created in his mind doesn't exist. That he may struggle, but he's not lost.

Thank You, Lord. I smile, feeling God present with us right now. He's always there, and that brings me calm in the midst of this storm we're facing.

"I think it's probably for the best," Dylan replies, then takes a sip of his sweet tea. "Get some distance between us and this place. He won't know where to find you then."

"What about stopping him?"

"We can do that from a distance—we're already doing it that way. And I'm no computer whiz like Tucker, or a strategist like Bradyn and Elliot. I'm the brute force that comes in behind them," he says with absolute conviction and no arrogance. It's a simple fact. "The skills I offer aren't needed just yet."

A shiver runs through me as his words settle in. Just what skills is he talking about? "What about Riley? Where does he fall in the skills category?"

Dylan smirks. "Riley has a bit of everything. He's actually been to see Harlow and managed to get her talking a bit more. Nothing much, but he's trying to make her comfortable in hopes she'll have something else to offer."

"Really? I don't know why I'm surprised. I still remember him sweet-talking his way out of trouble when he accidentally drove his truck through Mrs. Perry's flower bed in the eleventh grade."

Dylan laughs. "Yeah, he's got a gift, for sure. The point is, I think it's best if we go. At least for a little while."

"What about my cat?"

"My mom actually offered to take him in. If that doesn't work, we can try to bring him too. It's just a long trip."

"Where are we going?"

"Better if I don't say that just yet." He sets his tea down and crosses his arms. "But it'll be somewhere safe."

I consider. "We just planted all those flowers."

"They'll be here when we get back. Automatic sprinklers," he explains with a smile. "They'll be fine."

"What about Harlow?"

"She'll remain here. I don't think he's after her—at least, not yet."

"What makes you think that? He tried to kill her."

Dylan shakes his head. "That shot was specifically meant to not kill her. The weather was good, clear line of sight—the sniper shouldn't have had any issue killing her."

"That's so twisted to think about." I take a drink from my glass, hoping it'll somehow settle my churning stomach.

"I agree. Point is, I don't think he wants her dead. He'll come for her, sure, but it'll be at the same time he comes for you, or after."

"So if I'm gone—"

"It makes it even safer for her here."

I nod. "That makes sense. If your mom can keep Ash, that would be great. He's a tolerant cat, but shifting around too much might stress him out. What about Delta?"

"He'll come with us. I need him."

"Good. I'm glad he'll be with us." Leaning down, I pet Delta, who immediately rolls onto his back and shows his belly. "He's a good boy, aren't you, buddy?"

"He really likes you."

"I like him too." I give him one more big pet, then lean back in my chair. "When will we leave?"

"First thing in the morning," he says. "I've already let Bradyn, Tucker, Elliot, and Riley know, and they've agreed to keep us in the loop if anything is found out. But I think putting some distance between me and this case is the smart move. At least, for now."

"Can I ask why?"

Dylan's jaw clenches. "Because I wanted to track down and kill everyone who's a threat to you."

I'm not sure what I expected, but it wasn't his candid response. I know that I'm naïve to the troubles of this world. I've lived happily in my bubble here in Pine Creek, recent kidnapping aside, but the idea of Dylan staring a man in the face and pulling the trigger is such a hard thing to picture.

"The skills I offer aren't needed just yet." Killing? Is that the skill set he's referring to?

He's always been so sensitive. So kind-hearted, and the idea of hurting anything never even crossed his mind. Was it the training he went through that hardened him? Or his time being held captive?

Both?

He turns to me. "Not pretty, right? It's true though. I've eliminated dangerous men before, and in my head, this would be no different."

It's the closest I've ever gotten to learning what he did for the special forces. "This isn't war."

"It is," he counters. "But I also recognize it's not the

same caliber, and while I wouldn't hesitate to put him down if he came for you, tracking and killing him isn't right." Dylan sighs. "It makes me no better than he is."

I reach over and take his hand, hesitating only a moment before my fingers close around his.

He stiffens beneath my touch, and I nearly pull my hand away, but then he turns his and links his fingers with mine. My heart flips in my chest, and warmth spreads through me, starting at my hand and traveling up my arm.

"We'll go first thing in the morning," I say. "And all of this will work out. You'll see." I smile at him, hoping it'll reassure him that he's making the right choice.

"I've been praying more lately." He pulls his hand away. "Trying to find peace."

My smile widens so far that my cheeks hurt. "That's great."

"I think I'm finding a little bit at a time. But it's a work in progress."

"That's okay," I tell him. "I'm proud of you for trying."

"I want more than I have now." He turns to me. "I thought I was okay with being alone. Of watching my brothers start families and have children. But the past few days, I'm realizing I don't want that existence."

I have to remind myself to *breathe* as I listen to him. Is he saying what I think he's saying?

"I want to heal because I want a family too. And I want a chance with you. If you think you could see me that way after everything I've put you through. I know it hasn't been easy—or fair."

The smile that spreads over my face is so beyond wide that it hurts—but I don't care. "Dylan, you're the only man I've ever loved. I would wait forever for you."

He smiles, relief evident in the softening of his expression. "Let's hope it doesn't take that long."

***

GLASS SHATTERS, ripping me from sleep.

Still exhausted, I shoot up out of bed and stare toward the door. Silence. *Did I imagine it?*

A man lets out a broken cry, and more glass crashes to the ground. I jump out of bed. *Dylan!* Adrenaline surges through my system, making my limbs shake as I rush toward the door.

As I'm reaching for the top lock, though, his warning comes back to me. Just as the promise I made to him two days ago does.

"At night, you lock both of these, okay? And you don't come out—no matter what you hear."

Delta barks.

I promised him I would stay in here. But what if he's hurt? What if he needs me?

Another bark.

I throw my promises to the side. I will *not* sit here and

wait for him to self-destruct or get hurt because I'm afraid. So, with trembling fingers and another hit of adrenaline surging through my system, I unlock the door and step out into the dark hallway. Slowly, I make my way down the hall and toward the living room.

The moment I step inside, I see the source of the broken glass is the vase he'd had on his end table. It's shattered on the floor, flowers trampled. The table it had been sitting on is tipped on its side.

A new fear ices through me. Did Heath come? Did he take Dylan?

I slip into the kitchen and retrieve a knife from the block on Dylan's countertop. Pain shoots up through my foot, and I hiss through clenched teeth as I raise it and pluck a chunk of glass out of my heel. *Come on.*

The glass is all over the kitchen, so I backtrack out, a trail of blood following me as I make my way around the counter and toward the open back door. I can bandage my foot once I know that Dylan's okay.

It can wait. He can't.

As soon as I reach the door, the fear that Heath found us vanishes. There's no one else in sight—just Dylan. Kneeling right at the edge of his pool. Both hands are planted on the concrete ledge, and Delta whimpers beside him, nuzzling him with his snout.

"Dylan?" I call out.

He doesn't answer, so I limp down the porch steps and

cross the ground toward him, going slow so I don't startle him.

"Dylan? Are you okay?"

Still, he doesn't answer. Moonlight shines down on top of his bare back, and as I get closer, I get a horrific view of what looks like whipping scars across his back. Jagged and raised, they cover every inch of his skin.

How did I not see those before? When we were in the ocean?

I'd seen the ones on his chest, but these— How much more did he suffer?

How much pain did he have to live through before they rescued him?

What wounds did they inflict that cannot be seen?

Tears stream down my cheeks as I reach Dylan. "Dylan?" I whisper, but he still doesn't say anything. When he doesn't even look at me, I reach forward and gently touch his arm.

He explodes like a bomb, his entire body erupting as he lunges to his feet. I jump away, trying to get out of the way, but lose my footing and fall backward—knife still in my hand.

"Help!" I scream right before I hit the water.

It surrounds me, closing in around me like a vise. I panic, heart racing as I kick my feet and thrash in the water. Water fills my lungs when I try to scream. My chest burns. Something hits the water, and strong arms come around me.

I'm hauled against a hard body and all but thrown out of the water and onto the side of the pool. I cough, water spewing from my burning lungs.

"I'm so sorry, Emma. I'm so sorry." Dylan is there, rolling me onto my side and gently patting my back. "I'm so sorry," he says again, tone panicked. Water drips from his hair onto my face while I suck oxygen into my lungs.

"It's okay," I choke out. "Wasn't your fault."

"It was my fault. Why didn't you stay in your room?"

"I heard the glass break and Delta bark. I thought Heath was here, that you were hurt." I roll over onto my hands and knees, then push up to sitting. My entire body is shaking violently from the rush of adrenaline and the chill of the pool.

Dylan is staring at me—a tortured look on his face. His eyes are dark, his bottom lip trembling. "I'm so sorry," he whispers. "This was a mistake. I should have known better."

"No." I crawl over toward him, then place both hands on his muscled shoulders. Tremors rack through his body. "Growth has setbacks. Don't pull away from me because of this. Please, Dylan."

"I nearly killed you."

"No, you didn't. I fell into the pool. You came after me. If I knew how to swim, this wouldn't have even been an issue."

"I pushed you."

"No, you didn't. I jumped backward." I run my hands up onto his cheeks, shoving my own fear aside because I see the terror in his hazel gaze, and it breaks my heart. Unsure what else to do, I close my eyes and bow my head. "God, please be with us in this moment. Please take this fear from Dylan, let him see that he doesn't need to be afraid. God, please. Please," I add with a whisper. "Let him see that I'm okay. That You're here. In Jesus' name, I pray. Amen."

Dylan's hands come to my wrists, and he squeezes gently as he lowers his head to mine.

We sit there, foreheads touching, water dripping down around us, bodies trembling. Mine from the adrenaline, his from fear. Together, we remain there, kneeling for who knows how long.

But with every second that passes, Dylan's body grows steadier. Until he pulls away from me and leans back, sitting on his heels.

"You could have died, Emma." His voice is steadier now, his tone sharp.

"But I didn't. Next time, I'll avoid the deep end of the swimming pool." I glance over my shoulder, and a shudder runs through me. "Maybe I should learn to swim. Even if I'll need to special order floaties in my size."

Dylan plants both hands on the concrete and shakes his head. "You amaze me."

"How so?"

He looks up at me, expression dark but less tortured. "You're cracking jokes."

"What else is there to do? I'm alive, and you're yourself again."

His expression darkens further. "I told you to stay in that room. You shouldn't have come out."

"I'm not going to hide from you. Maybe that's the problem, Dylan. Maybe you've been hiding for so long that you forgot how to live."

"I won't find myself at the risk of losing you."

"I'm not going anywhere, Dylan. We're not going back to what we were before, with you avoiding me every chance you get. I hope you know that. When this is all over, if you try to hide from me again, I'll track you down." I smile, hoping to ease some of the tension.

"I can't go back to the way we were either," he says. "But this isn't safe."

"We'll figure it out together." I try to stand and suffer a painful reminder of the injury to my foot. Hissing, I lift the foot. "Ow!"

Dylan's eyes go wide. "You're hurt. What happened?" he crawls over toward me, remaining on his knees. As he lifts my foot, I plant my hand on his shoulder for support. Something I do without thinking. Thankfully, he seems so focused on my foot that he's unbothered. "This is bad, Emma."

"I stepped on some glass."

"You're going to need stitches." Standing, he lifts me into his arms and carries me into the house. "*Blieb,* Delta," he orders his dog, who takes a seat near the door.

As he flips on the light, I note the blood trail I left behind. There's a significant amount of it smeared all over his floor, and I'm surprised I didn't realize how badly I was bleeding. Then again, with how dark it was, I couldn't really see much.

He sets me on the counter, then grabs a clean kitchen towel from a cabinet and presses it against my foot. "Hold this here. Keep pressure."

"I'm okay, Dylan."

"No, you're not," he snaps. "Stay there." Carefully stepping around the glass, he disappears into the hallway. Delta remains near the door, watching me.

"I'm good, bud."

He wags his tail but doesn't move.

Moments later, Dylan emerges, a shirt and towel in his hand, already on the phone. "Get here. Fast," he orders, then ends the call.

"Who did you call?"

"Lani."

"She's not going to appreciate being woken up in the middle of the night," I joke as my teeth start to chatter, the chill of his air conditioner icing my still-wet body.

"It's not the first time," he says. When I don't press, he slips a towel around me, wrapping it tightly. "I've ended up hurting myself before during an episode, and Lani's who I call. She's here more times than you'd think."

His confession makes my heart ache even more. "Oh."

Dylan slips into his shirt, then retrieves a broom from his laundry room. Carefully, he sweeps the broken glass, mindful not to step on any himself or smear the trail of blood.

"I'm sorry about that; I didn't realize I was bleeding so badly."

"It's not your fault. It's okay." But I can see that it's anything but okay. He's genuinely troubled by the sight of my blood, so much so that Delta whimpers from the doorway, clearly desperate to get to him. "*Blieb,*" he orders again, taking a deep breath before kneeling and sweeping the glass into a dustpan and then depositing it into the trash.

As he straightens and comes back into the kitchen, his gaze lands on the knife block—with one missing.

"Oh no. I am so sorry! It must be in the pool."

"You took a knife outside?"

"I thought Heath was here. I thought he was hurting you."

Dylan stares at me; then a whisper of a smile lifts the corners of his lips. "You were going to take him on with my chopping knife?"

"Whatever I could find," I tell him.

His amusement falters. "You're lucky I didn't see it. I

didn't even see you until you were falling back into the water."

"You wouldn't have hurt me."

"You're wrong."

"No," I reply without hesitation. "I'm not. And I'll bet my life on that every single time."

"THERE YOU GO. ALL DONE." Lani strips her gloves off and sets them on the coffee table beside her. "Feel better?"

"Much. Thanks." The ache is still there, but thanks to the local anesthetic she gave me, the sharpness of the pain is gone.

"Anytime." She smiles, then lifts her gaze to the back patio where Dylan has been frantically scrubbing the concrete ever since she got here. "He okay?" she asks, keeping her tone low. I love that she asks me about him, rather than asking how I'm doing.

I'm sure his brothers feel the same, but being protectors themselves, they seem more worried about me. When they should be concerned for him. "I think he's getting there." I wrap the thick blanket Dylan draped around my shoulders after carrying me to the couch more tightly around me. "He didn't mean to knock me into the pool. Honestly, it was my own misstep that had me in that water. And he didn't hesitate to jump in after me."

"I know he didn't mean to. Dylan's not as dangerous as he thinks he is. Somehow, he managed to convince himself that *he's* the monster, not the men who tortured him for three months."

"I wish I could make him see what I do."

Lani squeezes my hand. "If anyone who walks this earth can, it's you."

"He told me that he wants to try again. When he's ready."

Lani's expression lights up despite the clear exhaustion on her face. "That's huge."

"I know." I glance over my shoulder. "It's what I've wanted ever since we ended."

"He comes with baggage. And plenty of demons frothing at the mouth to drag him into the pit."

"I won't let them," I reply. "Even if I have to wear God's armor for the both of us for now, I'll stand with him."

Lani smiles. "I know you will. Now, how about you? You've had a pretty large number of stressors in your life. Are you sleeping okay?"

"Not too bad, tonight excluded," I reply. "I mean, I'm not doing fantastic. There are definitely some things I'm dealing with, but I have God on my side. No matter how bad things get, He's always there and always good."

"Amen to that." Lani stands. "All right, brother, Emma is all good," she says, loud enough for him to hear. "She'll need to avoid any weight-bearing movement on that foot for the next twenty-four to seventy-two hours. After that, limited movement," she says, eyeing me. "The stitches can come out in ten days as long as it's healing well."

"Thank you."

"No problem." She glances at her watch and yawns. "If you're offering coffee, I would love some. I have to be at the clinic in two hours."

"Coffee it is." He smirks at her, though it doesn't fully reach his eyes. *He's pretending he's okay. Why does he feel like he has to hide his pain?* "Emma?" he asks.

"Yes, please. Coffee would be great."

CHAPTER 25
DYLAN

"That a new way of fishing?" Tucker asks as I climb out of the pool with my knife in hand. "Or were you practicing risky escapes again?"

"Emma dropped it in here last night. I was retrieving it."

Tucker narrows his gaze, then notices the blood-stained concrete I still haven't managed to fully clean. "Is she okay?"

"She's fine. Cut her foot on broken glass. Lani stitched it up."

"Dylan, what happened?" Tucker crosses his arms, and I set the knife on the table, then dry my face with a towel.

"What do you think happened? You're certainly looking at me like I attacked her, so why don't you just ask that?"

"Did you?"

"No." I pause and lower the defenses I put up the

moment I realized he was here. I don't need to be told how close we were to Emma truly getting hurt. I've gone over every second of it ever since it happened. "I had an episode, and she surprised me. I jumped up, and she jumped back, slipped, and fell into the pool. I jumped in, pulled her out, and called Lani."

"Broken glass?"

"Happened in the kitchen." I leave out the fact that it broke because I was trying to get a glass of water, and my hands were shaking so bad, I dropped it. I'm so angry. I thought I was getting better, took too many risks, and Emma got hurt because of it.

It was a stark reminder of who I truly am and how dangerous I can be. Last night wasn't even the worst it's been, either. What could've happened if it *was* the worst? If I hadn't been snapped out of it so quickly?

"I'm glad you're both okay."

"You're trying really hard not to tell me 'I told you so.'"

"Absolutely not. Dylan, I *want* you to find happiness. I want things to work out because you deserve some joy in this tortured existence you've been living in."

"You didn't make it a secret that you thought her staying here was a bad idea."

"Sure, but not because of you. I know that, if anything happened to her, minor or otherwise, you'd let it eat you alive. I'm tired of watching things eat you alive."

My anger deflates. "I'm doing surprisingly okay. Mad at myself, but what else is new?"

Tucker is quiet for a moment. "Where is she?"

"Inside, taking a nap. We'll be leaving as soon as she wakes up."

"You probably should up that timeline."

"Why?"

"One of Slater's known aliases just boarded a private plane to Dallas. That's why I'm here."

"He's coming here?"

Tucker nods. "Looks that way."

"Then we need to stay. I need to help prepare the ranch." My mind starts racing. We need to set proximity alarms, get everyone who can't fight to the barn on the far side of the property. Where they'll be out of sight and safe.

"We're already on that. And it won't matter if you can get Emma out. I'll send you Slater's number. When you're away from the ranch, call him. Let them trace it. He'll know you're not here anymore. Trash the phone, then use a burner."

"If he comes here anyway?"

Tucker smiles. "Then we'll call you when the problem has worked itself out. As far as I'm concerned, if he sets foot onto our property, he's a threat, and we'll treat him as such. Don't worry about us. My gut says he won't risk coming here if she's not here."

"His mother?"

"We'll make sure Harlow is safe too."

"You're sure you'll be okay?" It seemed like a good plan before, but now that I'm facing the reality of it, I hate the idea of leaving my family alone while I run. But Tucker is right—if Emma isn't here, then Heath won't want to chance it. It would be a stupid thing to do. An unnecessary risk. And he doesn't strike me as a man who makes those often.

"We'll be fine. You did the same for me, remember?"

"Those were cops coming for Alice, Tucker, not a crime boss."

"You still risked your lives to make sure I got her to safety. Let us do the same for you, okay? Get her out, and we'll handle the rest."

EMMA'S BEEN silent ever since we hit the road. We're about two hours away from the ranch now, so I guide my truck into a gas station, park next to a pump, and pull out my phone. "You know what to do?"

Nodding, she takes my phone and taps on the number Tucker texted me. Then, she places it on speakerphone. It rings twice before he answers.

"I expected this call," he says. "Did you decide to hand her over to me?"

"No one is handing me over to anyone," Emma says.

Her voice is level, but her hand holding the phone is shaking.

Heath is silent a moment. "Ah, Miss Emmaline. How lovely it is to hear your voice."

She shuts her eyes tightly. "I'm only calling to let you know that you're headed in the wrong direction."

Again, he's silent a few beats. His way of trying to maintain control, likely as they trace the call. "Is that right?"

"Yes. You won't find me this time."

"I assume lover boy's ranch is still standing—for now. Maybe I'll still pay them a visit."

"Go ahead. But you should know that local police have been alerted and are right there, ready to take you in the moment your tire tread crosses onto their property."

"Is that so? I've dealt with the police before. Maybe I just took a wrong turn. Needed to turn around."

"Or maybe we handed over your photograph to every single person in town so they know to turn you in the moment they see you."

"And just what am I being turned in for?"

"Kidnapping. Murder. Pick one."

"I didn't kidnap anyone. Your brother handled that."

"Mattheus also has his own fan club here in town since no less than a dozen people in town saw me with him at the diner right before I was kidnapped. See, my town isn't like your big city. People here care about one another, and they'll stand on the side of what's right. So go ahead, show up. It'll be the last thing you do, and frankly, it'll make my life a lot easier."

"I will find you, little dove, and when I do, you will pay for every minute you made me wait." The call ends, so she hands the phone back to me. I get out and walk around to the passenger side, then place it into a plastic bag, set it on the ground, and smash it with the heel of my boot.

As soon as I do, I toss it into the trash bin and get back inside, pulling out the burner phone I grabbed before leaving the house. "Are you okay?"

"Yeah." She runs both hands over her face. "Even his voice makes my skin crawl. I only met him once, but I can picture him clear as day. You know?"

"I know."

She's quiet for a moment as she gathers herself. "Do you think it worked?"

"I'll be surprised if it didn't. He's too smart to risk getting caught trespassing."

"What if he doesn't think he'll get caught?"

"You just let him know the entire Pine Creek police force is looking for him. He doesn't have to know how small it is." I smile at her, hoping it will disarm some of the nerves I see reflected on her face.

"Yeah, well, I'm going to pray anyway."

"Then let's pray." I reach over and wait for her to take my offered hand.

Her eyes widen in surprise, but she slides her slender hand into mine and bows her head.

I take a deep breath. I haven't prayed out loud in years. What if I mess it up?

You won't. Two words. Clear as day in my mind. They ease the rest of my nerves.

I clear my throat. "Lord, please be with our family and friends. Please surround them with Your protection and keep them safe in the name of Your Son, Jesus Christ. Amen."

"Amen." Emma gently squeezes my hand; then I pull away. "Thank you," she says.

I nod, feeling a bit lighter than I have in years. "We're headed to a private airstrip in Tulsa; then Jesper is going to pick us up from there."

"Where are we headed?"

I grin at her. "You'll see."

"WE'VE ARRIVED AT YOUR DESTINATION," Jesper announces as soon as the plane touches down on the runway.

The nerves I've felt this entire plane ride were enough to have me craving the fresh sea air I'll get the moment we step off this plane. I haven't been able to have any contact with Tucker or the others, so I have no way of knowing whether or not Slater left them alone in our absence.

I've been praying, though. Pretty much constantly.

Which is new for me.

"You ready?" I ask her.

"To find out where you brought me? Absolutely." She stands, using the crutches Lani brought her before we took off. Carefully, she makes her way down the aisle, right behind me.

"*Hier,* Delta," I order, and my pup hops up and trots over toward the door.

Jesper comes out of the cockpit and smiles at us as we pause in front of the door.

"It has been a true honor to be your pilot of choice," he says.

"Same. I'll call when we're ready to head back."

"Sounds good," he replies as I grip the handle and turn. But before I can even push it open, the door is ripped out of my grasp.

The barrel of a gun is shoved in my face, and a large hand grips the front of my shirt.

I spin and slam out with my boot, hitting the attacker square in the chest. He falls backward—down the steps and onto the concrete.

Delta growls.

But I don't send him out because, standing at the base of the stairs, alongside the furious-looking armed man I just sent down to the bottom, are Heath Slater, Mattheus

Karver, and about a dozen more men—all with guns aimed in our direction.

I whirl on Jesper, who's drawn his own firearm and is pointing it at Emma's head. She's silent, tears in her eyes.

I start toward him, fury in my veins, ready to tear him apart where he stands, but he clicks his tongue and presses the barrel closer. "I said I'd deliver. She doesn't have to be whole for me to get my payment."

"You betrayed us," I snarl, my hands clenching into fists. I could go for the gun at my back, but if I do that, Emma will likely get hit in the crossfire.

Since flying a plane isn't something I've ever done, and shooting our way out isn't an option, I have to play my cards right.

For now.

But I *will* make him pay. One way or another. He won't get away with this. "We trusted you."

"It wasn't personal," he deadpans. "I had debts that were owed."

"Go ahead and come on out of there," Heath orders. "And tell your mutt to stand down, or I'll put a bullet in him."

"You hurt my dog, and I will rip you to pieces," I snarl as I turn toward him. "*Fuss,* Delta," I order anyway. *Heel.*

"Good boy," Heath says with a smile. "German commands, right? I'll have to remember that. Always wanted a dog, and here you go, bringing me one already so expertly trained."

With thirteen guns pointed at us, I don't taunt him. I may be fast and lethal, but I'm not bulletproof. Neither are Delta and Emma. Our best chance is if I bide my time and wait for the perfect opportunity.

On legs heavy as lead, I walk down the steps.

"Go ahead and place your hands on the back of your head there, cowboy. Not trying to have a Wild West shootout once you get down here."

My stomach twists as I do as he says. Darkness edges into my vision, and if I weren't so concerned for Emma's safety, I might not care if the monster comes out. But she is here. And the monster won't stop with just the enemies.

Lord, please be with us. I trust You. I trust that You have a plan. Please don't let it be for us to lose.

"Good boy. I told you he could follow directions," Heath tells Mattheus.

"Yeah. Good. Shoot him and be done with it."

"Nah, not yet. I have something fun planned for him." He grins at me as I reach the bottom, and it's all I can do to keep my temper reined in. I *have* to play this smart. Otherwise, we're all dead.

Jesper sets Emma on her feet right beside me. She sways a little until he props a crutch beneath her arm. "You have what you want. Are we clear now?"

"Sure thing." In a blur of movement, Heath raises a gun

and fires. Blood sprays Emma, and she screams. My pulse hammers in my ears as I rip her behind me, then quickly grab Delta's collar just in case he decides to follow his instincts and go after the one who pulled the trigger.

All while I try to process exactly what just happened.

Jesper is on the ground, blood pooling beneath him, thanks to the bullet hole in the center of his throat. "Enjoy your payment," Heath sneers as he lowers his gun.

Emma wretches and throws up. I turn and pull her hair behind her head with one hand, steadying her with the other arm so she doesn't go fully to the ground.

"Oh, honey, you're going to need a stronger stomach. Grab her," Heath orders his men.

Two armed men come forward.

"Touch her, and I'll put you down."

"Do that, and I'll just put a bullet in you now. Save me some effort." Heath raises his gun again, this time aiming it at me. I genuinely consider taking the risk.

"Just let me go, Dylan," Emma chokes out. "Please. No more bloodshed."

I consider fighting our way out of here. They can't all fire at the same time, right? If I can get to the guy on the right—

No matter what happens, my fighting now will only result in Emma being left alone. So I swallow my anger and release her. One of the guards lifts her and steps away from me, going to stand near Heath.

"Muzzle the mutt," he tells one of his men.

"No. You are not touching my dog."

Delta growls.

Once again, Heath aims his firearm at me. "Are you thick in the skull? You don't hold the cards here, cowboy. Now, let them muzzle the mutt, or I'll decide to adopt rather than take yours."

Do I even have a choice?

God, why is this happening? Lord, be with us.

"*Sitz,* Delta." He takes a seat, and a man comes forward with a muzzle. Delta lets loose a warning growl. "Let me do it, or he'll take off your hand."

The man hesitates, then glances back at Heath, who nods. He slams the muzzle into my hands.

Turning, I kneel in front of Delta. "*Braver Hund*, Delta. Such a good boy." I slip the muzzle onto him, then, without anyone noticing, slowly press the tracker we installed on the underside of each of their collars.

A beacon, should we ever need to find each other, just in case we have to dispose of our cell phones. I'd told Tucker I thought it was overkill, but man, am I glad he didn't listen to me.

Delta whimpers, not understanding what's happening, so I pet him again before standing and facing Heath.

"Good. Now, shall we?" He gestures toward a waiting dark SUV.

Emma is staring at me, eyes wide, tears flowing down her pale face.

"I'm sorry," I tell her, then start toward the car that will likely take us all to our deaths.

"Put your hope in the Lord. Travel steadily along His path. He will honor you by giving you the land. You will see the wicked destroyed." I repeat part of Psalm 37 over and over again, and as I do, an unfamiliar peace settles over me.

You're here, Lord. I feel You. Please walk with us.

CHAPTER 26
EMMA

This can't be happening.

But no matter how many times I try to repeat that to myself, when I open my eyes, I'm still sitting in the back of an SUV between Dylan and an armed guard dressed in black. Delta is behind us, whimpering and confused.

It breaks my heart.

Sweat slicks my palms, and my heart won't seem to settle. What's going to happen to us? Where are they taking us? Will anyone ever know what happened?

God, why? Why are You not rescuing us from this? Please, God. Please. I shut my eyes tightly, trying so hard to calm my mind. But how can I do that when death is likely waiting for us when this truck stops?

As if he can sense my nerves, Dylan reaches down between us and takes my hand, threading his fingers through mine. He squeezes gently, which means the world to me, especially given how much I know simple touches can cost him. I glance over at him, but he's glaring straight ahead.

Does he think we're going to die too?

How long have we been driving?

I try to gauge our location through the window, but truth be told, I have no idea where we even are. Did we fly around and return back to Dallas?

"How did you do it?" Dylan asks.

Heath glances back at us. "Nothing a false flight log couldn't accomplish. As for Jesper, like he said—he owed me a debt. I collected."

"And even though he delivered us, you still took his life." My stomach churns as I replay the sight of him being shot and falling to the ground. Blood, so much blood. All of it still coating me.

I haven't been able to look down at my shirt since it happened. Every time I accidentally do, my stomach rolls, and I nearly vomit all over again.

"It wasn't a debt that could be repaid with anything but a life. He was just too arrogant to know that."

"What debt did he owe you?" Dylan asks.

"Let's just say your pilot had information that wasn't his to have. He then handed that information over to the wrong person, and—well—here we are. His death was a long time coming."

The SUV veers off the main road, following its twin in front of us, as it heads down a long driveway surrounded by thick trees. Dylan squeezes my hand once more before releasing it.

Is this it?

"I'd say I was excited for you to meet my mother, but you already did," Heath tells me. "How is the monstrosity that birthed me? I haven't had a chance to collect her yet but plan to soon."

"The only monster I see is you," I snap.

He glances back at me. "So you do have claws." The way his gaze rakes over me makes my skin crawl. "Good to know."

God, please don't let him touch me. Please, God, get us out of this mess.

Heath switches his attention to Dylan. "Don't worry, cowboy, I plan to let you live until after the wedding. What kind of monster would I be if I robbed Emmaline of having any friends to see her walk down the aisle?"

"There won't be a wedding," he growls, hands clenching into fists at his lap.

"And who's going to stop it?"

Dylan grins. "Oh, I was never one for spoilers. Seeing your reaction will be half the fun."

Heath's grin fades just slightly. "I can't wait to break you. It's going to make all the trouble you gave me worth every minute."

"You won't touch him!"

Dylan grabs my hand again as I lunge forward, likely to keep me from doing something stupid like hitting a man who would probably enjoy it more than anything.

Heath turns back to look at me again. "You have no idea what I'm going to do. But that's okay because you will. Pretty little small-town princess. How I am going to love ruining you." He shifts his gaze out the windshield. "And look, we're here."

The SUV comes to a stop, and my stomach lurches. Dylan releases my hand as the doors open. A man grabs him by the arm and yanks him out, while the man who was sitting beside me drags me out of the car and lifts me into his arms.

I want to kick.

Scream.

Fight.

But Dylan is maintaining his composure, so I follow suit. Does he have a plan? He always has a plan, right? Didn't he say that there wouldn't be a wedding? That someone is coming to stop it?

God, please let that be true.

Delta is unloaded from the back, the poor animal looking just as terrified as I feel. A leash is clipped to his harness and held by a man wearing all black. They're all in black.

My breathing is ragged, panic making my heart race. I

survey the boat dock in front of us. A massive yacht is parked straight ahead, bobbing slowly with the movement of the water.

"No." I shake my head. "No."

"You afraid of the water, little dove?" Heath taunts.

"She can't swim," Mattheus offers up. "Told us that at dinner."

Heath chuckles. "Fantastic. That only makes this even more fun."

"It'll be okay," Dylan tells me.

But I'm starting to think it won't be. I don't know why this is happening, but unless God grants us a miracle, I don't see a way out.

There's a yellow sports car parked at the end of the dock, and as we get closer, a leggy redhead climbs out, wearing a black dress that barely covers to her upper thigh. Her hair is the color of the blood still saturating my shirt, her long, pointed nails the same shade.

"Did you bring me a present?" she asks, eyeing Dylan.

"No, darling Tori. I brought my wife and the guy who thought he was going to keep her from me."

We come to a stop in front of her. She looks me over first, her dark eyes narrowing. "What's wrong with you? Can you not walk?"

"She's injured," Heath replies.

"Hmm." The woman saunters over toward Dylan and

comes to a stop. "You are stunning." She grips his face, and I watch as he pales.

"Let him go!" I yell as I thrash in the guard's hold. He drops me, and pain shoots up through my injured leg. But I'm on my feet, so I lunge toward her, only to be ripped back by the same guard.

All while she continues pinching his face.

His body trembles, and he's barely breathing.

Delta whimpers and pulls on the leash, trying to get closer to Dylan.

If he loses it here—a shudder runs through me. What will happen if he loses his head here? Will they shoot him without thinking? Or use his trauma to further torment him?

"I don't take orders from you," she says as she glares at me. "You need to learn your place in this house, darling, and it's not as the head. You're merely a trinket to get us everything we want." She releases Dylan's face but scrapes one of her sharp-as-a-talon nails over his cheek.

Blood droplets slide down the side of his face. He doesn't even flinch.

Delta growls, low and deep, pinning his ears back against his head.

"What's with the animal?" she asks, tone flat.

"Consider him a trophy," Heath replies. "I plan to bend him to my will just as I'll do his owner. A living reminder of my wedding day."

"Do you always let your girlfriend do all of your intimidation?" Dylan asks, regaining at least some of his composure now that she's released him.

"Oh, honey, I'm just the appetizer," she replies, leaning in closer.

"What a shame. I'm not hungry."

"You will be," she replies, then turns, flipping the long tail of red hair behind her as she turns to the rest of the guards—and Mattheus—who have joined us near the dock. "Mattheus. How lovely to see you."

"You too, beautiful," he replies, then claps his hands. "Shall we get this going?" he asks. "I can't wait to join our families."

"Have some patience," Heath tells him, then heads for the yacht.

Like moths to a flame, everyone follows. The woman falls into step beside him, while the guard who'd been carrying me lifts me again and starts walking after them. Dylan is right behind me, being escorted by two guards, while Delta is being walked beside him.

Behind all of us, a small army of armed men ensures we don't take a single step out of line.

Venom stings my veins as my stomach rolls with every step toward the floating death trap. There will be no quick getaway. Not once we hit the water. We'll be trapped.

Lord, where are You? Please don't let us die here.

We walk up a ramp and onto the top level of the yacht.

There are at least a dozen loungers surrounding a small round pool. A man wearing a captain's hat stands in the doorway that likely leads to where they steer the boat. He falls into step beside us.

"Everything ready?" Heath asks him.

"Yes, Mr. Slater. We are prepped and ready for our voyage."

"Good. I want anchors up in five minutes."

"Yes, sir." The captain veers off to the right while Heath's girlfriend stops beside a lounger and removes her dress, revealing a black bikini beneath. She takes a seat on a lounger.

"See you soon, cowboy," she calls out to Dylan.

Anger momentarily pushes past the fear. I glare back at her, and she smiles at me, completely unthreatened.

An armed guard pulls open a door and steps aside as Heath descends a set of steps. We follow, and the walls close in around us, with only dim light to keep us occupied.

I turn to watch Dylan. His eyes are wide, his body tense. He pauses at the top of the stairs, clearly terrified. Is he reliving his past? The worst moments of his life? His gaze meets mine.

It's okay, I want to tell him. But I can't bring attention to it, or it'll just be another tool in Heath's twisted toolbox. *God, please help him.*

The guards shove him down the first step, and he takes a deep breath, eyes closed. By the time he opens them again, he's calmer and takes the rest of the steps one at a time.

Once we reach the bottom, Heath pushes open a door to the left, and the guards drag us inside. The guard drops me on a cot toward the right, then quickly shackles my wrist to the wall. The metal is cold on my skin. Cold and tight.

Dylan is held standing in the center of the room, one guard on either side of him.

Above his head, there are two shackles bolted to the ceiling.

No.

"Do you understand your place yet?" Heath asks him.

Dylan doesn't respond.

Heath rams his fist into Dylan's gut. He grunts but maintains eye contact with Heath, something that only makes our captor angry.

He hits him again.

Once more, Dylan barely reacts.

I thrash against the chains bolting me to the wall. "No! Stop it! Leave him alone!"

Heath hits Dylan again, then turns to me and smiles. "Oh, little dove, if this bothers you, then I hate to see what you'll think later." He hits Dylan again, this time slamming his fist into Dylan's chin.

Dylan straightens and grins at him, blood dripping down from his lip. "There's nothing you can do to me that hasn't already been done," he replies. "I lived through that hell once. I'll do it again."

"There is *so* much more I can do. I'm far more imaginative than most."

Dylan grins again, blood dripping down onto his teeth. "They all think that."

Heath glares at him. "Kneel."

"No."

"Compared to you, I am a king. You will kneel."

"I kneel to no man," he replies. "And the only king I have is Jesus Christ."

Heath glances back at the three men who followed us in here and Mattheus, then laughs. "You think God will save you now?" He throws his head back again and barks out an exaggerated laugh. "You're already here. Now, bow."

"No."

Heath hits him again. "Submit to me, cowboy, and we'll take this slower."

"I will never. I kneel to no man," he repeats.

"We'll see about that," he growls right back. "Chain him up. Let's let him think on his choices for a bit." Before he pulls away from Dylan, though, he leans in closer. "Before this is over, you both will bow to me."

The two guards rip Dylan's arms overhead, all while he continues glaring straight at Heath. They shackle him to the ceiling, then turn to leave, following their master like beasts on a chain.

Delta is nowhere in sight. I didn't even realize that they hadn't brought him down here with us. Is he scared? Confused?

My breathing turns ragged now, the panic setting in as they seal the door. We're trapped. In the bottom of a boat.

That's about to be out on the ocean.

Where we can't escape.

"Breathe, Emma," Dylan tells me.

"I'm—trying."

"Slow, deep breaths."

"But—I—we're trapped. We're trapped, Dylan. He's going to kill you."

"It's going to be okay. Have faith."

"How are you calm?" I turn to him. "How are you so calm?"

"I prayed," he says. "And as I was standing at the top of those stairs, I felt it."

"Felt what?"

He smiles, and despite the ugliness of our situation, there's beauty in it. Joy. "We're going to be just fine. No matter what happens. But I need you to keep your head and *believe* it. This isn't the end of our story, Emma. Okay?"

I try to cling to his words, to tell myself that, if he's this calm, then it means he definitely has a plan. But how can I do that when all I can picture is a million different ways Heath could torture Dylan? Will he use a whip and add to those scars on his back?

Will he hurt me to torment the man I love?

Will he decide we're not worth the trouble and just kill us both?

"Keep your head and believe it," Dylan said. I take a deep breath and try to steady my racing heart.

"You're bleeding." Blood drips from his lip where he must have bitten it when Heath hit him. It's dripping down to the floor near his feet. Not a lot, but enough that I imagine it hurts pretty bad.

"It's just a scratch," he replies calmly. "We're going to be okay, Emma. God is with us here, right? And if He's at our side, what do we have to fear?"

God is here with us.

Seeing the vast change in Dylan on those stairs is proof of that. He went from panicked to calm nearly instantly.

God is here with us.

He has to be.

I take another deep breath. *Okay, Lord. I put my faith in You. Please help us. Please.*

CHAPTER 27

DYLAN

ONE DAY LATER

Emma's curled up on her side near the edge of the cot. I can see her face, and based on the tense expression she wears, I imagine she's not resting peacefully. But she's at least resting—which is a win. Especially since, if he's going based on some sort of twisted torture pattern, Heath will be back in here for another round with me within the hour.

Betrayal aside, Jesper was right.

Heath is sadistic.

I've been cut, burned, beaten, all in less than twenty-four hours—but I won't give him the satisfaction of knowing just how badly it all hurts.

And even though I'm reliving the worst moments of my life, I feel a calmness over me. A peace that settled on my heart the moment I surrendered to God at the top of those stairs. I can't explain any of it, but I'm grateful for the clear-headedness and for the understanding that, even though we're suffering, we're not alone.

One way or another, this suffering will end. And for the first time in years, I know where I'm going when this life is over.

I've been forgiven.

Redeemed.

And that's something Heath Slater can never take.

I shift my attention back to Emma. She's still wearing Jesper's now-dried blood. Her shirt is covered in it, the side of her face crusted from where it sprayed her. I wish she'd never seen that. The horror of watching the life fade from someone.

Oh, how I wish she'd been spared that nightmare.

And the one we've been living since yesterday.

Emma opens her eyes.

"Hey," I say, my voice hoarse. "Did you get any sleep?"

She nods. "Are you okay?"

I shake the cuffs binding me to the ceiling above. "Hanging in there."

She glares at me. "That's really not funny."

"It's the truth. How are you?"

"At any moment, he could come in here, kill you, and force me down the aisle. So I'm going to say—not good."

"It's going to be okay."

"You keep saying that, but we're still here." She sits up. "I'm losing hope, Dylan. I'm trying not to, but—" Tears fill her eyes. She cries all the time now, and the light within her is slowly beginning to dim. Is that why he's leaving her here with me? Why he's doling out the pain in front of her? Because he wants to use me to break her?

"Emma. Don't lose hope. For the first time in my life, I'm seeing things clearly. Sinful people do evil things. But that doesn't mean that God has forsaken those of us who follow Him. He's still there, standing beside us, even in the pain."

"You told me you thought He had forgotten you. How are you so sure He hasn't forgotten us now?"

"Because we're still alive," he replies. "And even if we lose our lives, that just means we'll find the peace promised to us. Can't you see it? Can't you feel the light surrounding us even in the darkness?" How can she not see? How can Emma, who has always been such a bright light, lose her hope now?

She closes her eyes and shakes her head. "I'm trying."

"'When the wicked are in authority, sin flourishes, but the godly will live to see their downfall,'" I say, repeating one of my favorite Proverbs verses. My mom had us memorize them when she homeschooled us. That one always stuck with me. "We will see his downfall. Even if he takes our lives, God is still in control."

"I'm not afraid to die," she whispers, tilting her face to look up at me. "But I am terrified that he is going to make me watch you die."

My chest tightens at the pain on her face. *Lord, I trust in You. No matter what happens. I feel You there. But please let her survive. Please let her suffer no more.*

The brokenness is all over her face, the light slowly fading from her eyes. I know what it feels like to lose all hope. I did when I was in that jail cell. I know what it feels like to surrender to the darkness because you've lost all hope that the light will ever find you.

I won't let Emma suffer that fate.

It's worse than death.

I clear my throat. "'Christ be our sure foundation. Christ be our cornerstone,'" I start singing.

Emma looks up at me, and a smile slowly lifts the corners of her lips.

I continue the hymn I memorized after a week at church camp when we were in eighth grade. "'Build up from every nation a people of your own.'"

"'Blest through your font of mercy, blest be each living stone of faith alive in witness. Fair Christ by all be known,'" she starts.

I grin. "You still remember it."

"How could I forget? We had to listen to Riley belt that out during the talent show."

I laugh. "Yeah, he may be a charmer, but singing is not his strong suit."

Emma laughs. "Do you remember how he froze partly through it, so Elliot stood up and started singing with him?"

Nodding, I recall how embarrassed Riley looked but how relieved he was that his big brother came to help him. "Elliot's voice was just as bad."

"But then you, Bradyn, and Lani all got up on stage too. Somehow, together, you all sounded just like a church choir."

"If I recall, you jumped up there with us too."

"Only after Lani ran downstage and pulled me up," she replies with a soft smile.

There it is. The light.

I laugh, remembering the fear on her face when Lani brought her up there with us. The memory is so clear that it's like watching a movie play out in front of me.

Simpler times.

Before war.

Pain.

Loss.

"I love you, Dylan. I know I told you that before, but I need to say it again, just in case."

I meet her gaze, praying with all I have that we still have a chance at a future together. "I love you too, Emma."

The door swings open, and Tori saunters in, wearing a navy-blue dress. "How sweet, but I'm afraid we'll be cutting this little love fest short. Get her ready," she orders two women in personal service uniforms as two armed guards come for me.

"My Heath did a number on you, didn't he, kitten?" She

squeezes my face, but when the panic starts, I give it to the One who can keep me calm.

"I can do all things through Christ, who strengthens me."

"Poor guy. Don't worry, soon it'll be my turn, and I'll make sure you feel no pain." Tori leans in. "Well, not a lot, anyway."

"Get your hands off of him," Emma growls.

She turns to Emma as the women unshackle her and pull her up to her feet. A hand cracks out, and Emma falls backward.

I lunge forward against my chains. "Keep your hands off of her," I warn.

"Or what?" she asks. "Tell me, cowboy, what will you do to me if I don't?"

Because I sense a fight is just what she's looking for, I don't respond. Instead, I continue glaring at her, letting her believe she has the upper hand—for now.

"That's what I thought." She turns back to Emma. "As I said, you will learn your place. Now, get her ready," she snaps at the women. "Get him upstairs, and make sure you keep a tight leash on him, m'kay? Good. Master is waiting."

"Dylan?" Emma whispers.

"Have faith, Emma," I tell her, clinging to mine with all that I have. *God, be with us.*

BY THE TIME the guards get me upstairs, I've already planned our escape.

If I can get to Delta.

Otherwise, I'll get Emma out, then follow suit as soon as I've rescued my dog. I will *not* leave him here.

There's a single life raft on the starboard side of the yacht. All I need is a gun from one of these guards, and I can get us there.

Hopefully.

We reach the bow of the ship, where an archway of flowers has been set up. The captain is standing beneath it, while Heath and Mattheus stand beside a table, talking. There's a stack of documents in front of them, a pen right beside.

Marriage license? Or something else?

"So nice of you to join us," Heath tells me as he glances over.

"Where's my dog?"

"A lot to handle, but he's fine. Didn't really find it appropriate to make him watch you die. He is just an innocent bystander in all this, isn't he?"

My gaze scans the rest of the bow. A large safe sits off to one side, its door open. A strap is wrapped along the bottom and connected to a crane that they likely used to move it. I assume they are planning to use it when they dump it in the water—with me inside.

If I'm reading the situation right, anyway.

Emma will be forced to watch me slowly sink into the ocean as I drown.

"Can't stomach watching me die?" I click my tongue. "I knew you cared," I add dryly.

"Hardly. I just want to watch her watch you die, and I imagine you're a strong swimmer." He turns to Mattheus. "Are we ready now?"

"Once my sister is married to you, I'll sign it."

The fact that I haven't seen Gio isn't lost on me. "You decide to cut your dad out of this and make a deal to save yourself?"

"My father was weak. Just as my mother was. He needed to go."

"Matricide and patricide, huh? You're just checking all the boxes."

Mattheus' cheeks redden, and he balls his hands into fists.

"Get a handle on yourself, Mattheus," Heath scolds. "He's taunting you, and you're letting him."

"He's talking really big for a guy about to die."

Overhead, lightning splits the sky seconds before thunder claps so loud it's nearly deafening. The air charges around us, winds whipping up out of nowhere. The boat begins to rock.

Bring the storm. I smile.

"Was it supposed to storm today?" Mattheus asks the captain.

"Nothing was on the radar," he replies as he looks around nervously.

A storm breeds chaos. Chaos means mistakes will be made. And that can mean our chance for escape is a lot closer than we think.

"Here comes the bride," Tori calls out in a sing-song voice moments before Emma is pulled out by the two women who were told to prepare her.

Despite the death we're likely facing, my breath is stolen by the sight of Emma in white. It's a simple dress, falling to her knees. The bodice is tight while the rest of the dress is loose and airy. Wind whips at it.

It tugs at her hair.

She's pale, her eyes wide.

"Good. We need to get these papers inside. Sign them so we can get his ceremony going," Heath tells Mattheus. Emma's birth brother grins happily, then leans down and signs his name.

I turn my attention back to Emma.

Armed guards surround us. They'll make the escape a lot harder—but not impossible if I can disarm the guy next to me.

"There. Signed. Now, when will my money be in my account?"

Heath looks down at the papers, then smiles, closes the folder, and hands it to the captain. "Right away." Heath slings an arm around Mattheus's shoulders and guides him toward the edge of the ship. "Brother," he adds.

Mattheus grins at him, victory etched in every line of his face.

Because he doesn't see what's coming.

I do.

Heath shoves Mattheus overboard into the angry sea. He screams as he falls, but I don't wait for him to do the same to me. I slam my heel down onto the foot of the guard who's on my left. He loosens enough that I rip my arm free. I slam it into his gut, then rip his weapon from its holster, aim at the guard closest to me, and fire.

He goes down.

Chaos erupts as I sprint toward Emma.

Tori withdraws a knife and presses it to Emma's throat. "Uh-uh-uh," she says. "Put it down, or I'll paint her pretty neck."

I freeze.

A foot slams into the back of my left knee, then my right, dropping me moments before the gun is wrenched from my hand.

"Just what was your plan? Fight your way off a ship full of armed guards?" Heath comes around in front of me. "What a shame."

As he's glaring down at me, a man comes forward, wearing slacks and a white polo shirt. "Mr. Slater," he says.

"What is it?" Heath snaps, though he keeps his gaze on me.

"You said to contact you if there was another ship in the vicinity?"

"Yes."

"There's one approaching now. Looks like a fishing boat, but—"

"Better to be safe than sorry. Okay. Time to speed this up. Grab him." He snaps his fingers, and two of the guards rip me off of the ground.

I fight, thrashing my body, but the grip they have on me is far too strong.

"If you ask me, you're getting off easy," the guard to my left growls.

I don't bite—because my focus is on the open safe in front of me. Just large enough for two people to slowly suffocate to death.

They shove me inside.

Emma screams.

"Don't worry, little dove, you're going in there too."

"No! Leave her alone! This is between us. I'm the one you're mad at." If she makes it off this boat, she stands a chance at escape. My brothers will come for her. I know they will.

Heath shoves her into the safe with me. "I have no use for her. Mattheus just signed over the entire Karver fortune to a corporation that I own."

"Your plan all along?" *Keep him talking.*

Heath grins. "Now I want you to die knowing that I plan to tear that ranch apart even if it means burning the entire town of Pine Creek to the ground."

Rain falls in a single sheet, soaking the boat deck in an instant. The ship rocks, creaking as it rises and falls with the waves. Emma closes her eyes tightly, her hands squeezed into fists right in front of her face.

"This isn't the end," I tell him. "Even if we die here today, what's coming to you is so much worse."

"And what's that?"

"Judgment day."

He smirks. "I don't fear fiction, cowboy."

"My God is very real, and you're going to find out way too late if you go through with this."

"I'll take my chances." He steps back, gun still aimed at Emma. "Seal it up, then throw it over."

Emma sobs, her entire body shaking.

The door to the safe slams shut, and the locks engage, plunging us into darkness.

God, be with us. Please, Lord. If it's not good, then I know You're not done.

"Baby, breathe."

I can feel rather than see Emma shake her head.

Outside, I hear the faint hum of a motor seconds before the safe is lifted. I pull her closer to me, hugging her to my chest. Step one, make sure we survive the fall.

Thunder booms.

Step two, find a way to get out of the safe.

Step three—*Lord, please let there be a step three.*

The movement stops.

And then—we fall.

I hold her tightly, pressing one foot on the floor, one hand above us to try and brace for the fall. "Dylan," she cries.

"I've got you, baby."

We hit the water with such force that it slams the side of my head against the steel of the safe. Water begins to pour in from the bottom. Considering how quickly it does, I imagine they drilled holes to make sure it sinks nice and fast.

My heart rate remains steady. I didn't lean on God back in that cave, and it cost me a piece of myself I only recently got back. I won't make the same mistake.

I only wish I could see her face.

"This isn't how I pictured your wedding day," I whisper.

"Drowning? No, I can't say I did either."

"No," I say. "Walking down the aisle toward anybody

but me." I trace her shoulders until I find her face, then I cup her cheeks and pull her forehead against mine. "I am so sorry I wasted so much time."

"I'm so scared," she cries.

"I'm not," I tell her. "Because I know He has us. Even now, Emma." The water is up to our hips now. We have a minute—maybe less. "I'll see you on the other side."

She laughs, and I brush her wet cheeks with my thumbs for a moment before guiding her toward me and pressing my lips to hers.

It's just a kiss.

But for me, it's deliverance.

Not from sin—no, Jesus Christ did that on the cross. He died so that we could be cleansed by His blood and stand spotless before God.

Her lips tremble beneath mine, fear rooting in her heart. I wish I could take it all away so she could feel the peace radiating through mine.

And if this kiss is my final act on this earth, then it was time well spent. My only regret is that I couldn't free her from this fate.

Emma pulls back slowly, then presses her cheek to my chest. Her shoulders shake as she cries, and I wrap my arms around her, holding on tightly as the water continues to climb. It's up to her shoulders now.

"Put your legs around my waist." I lift her, and she does, keeping her in the oxygen a little longer. "Listen to me, okay? I love you. We're going to be okay. No matter what happens, everything is going to be okay."

"Okay," she cries.

"'The Lord is my Shepherd,'" I start, using the King James version of Psalm 23 that I memorized when I was a kid.

"'I shall not want,'" she says.

"'He maketh me to lie down in green pastures: he leadeth me beside the still waters.'"

"'He restoreth my soul: he leadeth me in the paths of righteousness for His name's sake,'" she adds, voice trembling.

"'Though I walk through the valley of the shadow of death, I will fear no evil: for thou art with me.'"

THE COLD WATER hits my shoulders, and I know we're seconds away now.

It climbs my neck, brushing the bottom of my ears.

"Dylan," she cries.

"I'm right here, baby." I hoist her up higher, trying to keep her toward the top. "God, we ask that You be with us in this moment. Even if it's not to take us to safety, we trust in Your plan. Because when life is not good, You are, and Your promises are waiting for us. Thank You, God, for the time you did give us." The water hits my chin. "I pray this in the name of Your Son, Jesus Christ. Amen."

"Amen," Emma chokes out.

Water covers my mouth.

I close my eyes and wait, surrendering everything I have to the understanding that bad things might happen, but God is always good. Because it's not what happens in this world that matters but what happens next.

And I finally know where I'm going.

The water begins to lower.

"What's happening?" she asks, breathing ragged.

"God," I tell her, joy surging toward me. "Thank You, God! Thank You!" I kiss her loudly and lower her so she can stand on the bottom of the safe, though I keep her close so I can brace her if we fall again.

The water continues lowering until we hit something hard. My head bangs on the back of the safe once more, but it doesn't knock the smile from my face.

Because I'm not sure how I know it, but I *know* it won't be Heath on the other side when that door finally opens.

Seconds tick by in the dark silence, with just our ragged breathing to keep us company.

Muted voices carry outside. Someone yells, but I can't make out what they're saying.

A loud whirring fills my ears, so I do what I can to protect Emma's face as I imagine a steel cutter slicing through the hinges.

And then light.

Air.

Sweet oxygen fills my lungs as the door is lifted. Sunlight blinds me, but then a man comes into view, blocking it so my vision can clear.

He's grinning at me.

"Tucker, I have never been happier to see you," I say.

"You too, brother." My twin grins and reaches in to help Emma out and to her feet. She's shivering, her entire body trembling.

"Here," Riley offers Emma a towel, and she wraps it around her shoulders.

I sit up, and Bradyn tugs me to my feet. "You guys took long enough," I joke.

"We had to find a boat," Riley says. "Silas came through for us. Seems the two of you share a friend who was more than happy to help us get you out of deep waters."

My cousin comes into view, and I surprise him by pulling him in for a hug. He's wearing a wetsuit, his hair soaking. Which means he was likely the one who dove down to hook the safe up to the crane they used to pull us out. "It's good to see you, cousin," he says.

"You too." I pull away, then take a deep breath. "I'm sad I missed the action." Heath is kneeling on the ground, his hands zip-tied behind his back. The captain is right beside him, Tori on his other side, and—to my surprise—Mattheus Karver is right beside her. Wet and furious.

Seven of the guards are dead, the others kneeling.

"Did you find Delta?" I ask.

"Nova and Elliot went to look for him. We assumed he was here when he wasn't on the plane."

"You found Jesper, then?"

Tucker nods. "When you didn't show up in Maine, we tracked his financials and saw a payment of half a million dollars had hit his bank account. Then we tried to trace his plane, but it was untraceable. Had Delta's tracker not come on when it did, we wouldn't have found you."

Right as he finishes, Delta, happy and unmuzzled, bolts around the side of the ship. I drop to my knees as ninety-five pounds of furry German shepherd slams into me like a speeding bullet. He spins in a circle, rubbing against me and doing what I've always called his happy dance.

"I love you too, buddy. I know. I love you."

Nova and Elliot come around the side of the ship right behind him, both of them wearing relieved smiles.

Knowing my dog is safe too, I stand and turn toward Silas. "So which mutual friend do I have to thank for our rescue?" I ask, right as a man I never thought I'd see again steps into view.

His blonde hair is mostly covered by a worn baseball cap with an anchor on the front. He's wearing a black sweater and holds out his hand when I cross toward him. "Dylan Hunt. It's good to see you—alive."

"Captain Knox," I say, taking his offered hand. Zane Knox was lead of the SEAL team I trained with years ago, back when I was still in the service. He and Silas served together for a short period of time before my cousin was reassigned. "Thank you."

"I'm just glad we got here in time," he replies.

"Me too. Thank you," I say again as I meet his blue gaze with my own. "Seriously."

"God is the only One who gets the thanks. He cleared the skies for us," he replies.

I tip my face to the sky and close my eyes. *Thank You, God.* When I open my eyes again, it's to look at Emma. Nova is beside her, talking calmly to her as she rubs her arms on Emma's shoulders. She's shaking—but there's a smile on her face.

Needing to hold her, I close the distance between us and wrap my arms around her. She leans into me, resting her head on my chest.

"We need to redo that kiss-s-s," she stammers.

"Anytime." I cup her cheeks and tilt her face up to mine. "See, I told you He had us."

She smiles. "He did."

Leaning in, I capture her lips with mine.

It took nearly dying—again—for me to fully surrender to God. But I see now that He was always there. Waiting for me to accept Him and forgive myself for surviving when I lost all of my friends. I'd turned into the pain instead of laying it down at His feet.

A mistake I'm going to try really, really hard not to make again.

But even if I do, I know He will still be right there—waiting for me.

Because He is always good.

And if it's not good, then He's not done yet.

CHAPTER 28
EMMA

It feels surreal to be standing in my living room again. To be back here, in this place that's been my home since I was a baby.

Everything looks the same—but I feel so different.

The broken glass that was all over the kitchen has been swept up, and the floor has been mopped, courtesy of Talia, who called me this morning to let me know she's expecting me at the diner in an hour for a makeup birthday dinner.

Ash is already lying in his favorite spot on the back of the couch, and I smile over at him before shifting my attention back to the box I'd left on the coffee table. I breathe a sigh of relief when I look inside and see the photograph of Dylan and me, alongside the corsage he'd given me all those years ago, sitting on top.

I'm not sure who took them out of the trash can, but I'm so glad they didn't end up getting thrown out.

Dylan.

He'd told me I could stay in his guest room as long as I wanted, but I needed to be back in my space. Even though I'm genuinely afraid to be back in the place it was so easy for Mattheus to get to. As it always does whenever I think about him, my pulse kicks up a notch. A nice dose of fear left behind by everything I've been through the past couple of weeks.

He's in prison.

After we delivered Heath, Mattheus, Tori, and the other armed guards to Frank Loyotta's contact in the FBI, they finally had what they needed to get a warrant for both the Slater and Karver estates. And with Harlow's testimony, Heath and Mattheus will both be going away for a long, long time.

We've been assured they'll never breathe oxygen as free men again.

But the nightmares don't seem to care about that.

Every night since we've been back, I've seen Heath when I close my eyes. Standing there, taunting me—hitting Dylan.

Cutting him.

Burning him.

Hurting him. Over and over again.

My heart rate begins to increase again, sweat beading at my temples. At the onset of the panic, I rest my hand on the back of the couch as I take a deep, steadying breath.

Lord, please help me breathe. Please help me.

Someone knocks on the door, and my pulse skyrockets. Black spots invade my vision, and I rapidly blink to try to clear them.

It's not them. It can't be them.

Logically, I know that's true, but my body doesn't seem to care about that.

"Emma?"

At Dylan's voice on the other side of the door, I take another deep breath, then cross over to pull the door open with trembling fingers. The sight of him eases my panic just enough that the weight on my chest lessens.

"Hey there," I greet, forcing a smile on my face.

He's standing there, looking incredibly handsome and holding a bouquet of wildflowers placed inside a beautiful vase with golden veins threaded through the glass. "Hey. Sorry. I know you wanted to get settled, but I didn't want to wait."

"I'm actually really happy to see you," I say, my bottom lip quivering as the tears fill my eyes again.

Dylan's smile falls, his expression turning to concern in an instant. "What's wrong?"

I shake my head, the emotion burning in my throat. Because I can't trust myself to speak without completely losing it, I step aside and gesture for him to come inside. The moment he does, I shut and lock the door behind him.

I rarely used to lock my door during the day. Probably not smart, and not something I will *ever* forget to do again.

Dylan sets the vase down on the coffee table, then turns to me. "What is it?" he asks, reaching forward to brush some hair behind my ear.

The casual touches are getting easier for him—at least, that's what he tells me—but I know there are moments he still struggles. Occasionally, I still see a bit of darkness reflected in his gorgeous hazel eyes.

Still, he's doing a whole lot better than I am these days. I'm barely managing to shower, since the water on my skin is a burning reminder of the water rising in that safe as we sank to the bottom of the ocean.

"I'm just struggling. I don't know how you do it." I wipe the tears away.

"Do what?"

"Not let the fear consume you." I whisper the words, almost ashamed to speak them. After all, I didn't suffer the way he did. Not in that prison cave all those years ago, and not in the bottom of that ship.

He was the one who was burned, cut, and tortured.

Not me.

So why am I having such a hard time moving forward?

"For a long time, I let it consume me," he says, stepping closer and running his hands over my arms.

"And now?"

"Now I'm actively choosing to give it to God. It hasn't

been easy, but it's the closest I've felt to actual peace." He moves in even closer, only inches from me now.

"It's silly." I shake my head, almost ashamed to even look at him. "I'm not even the one he hurt, but I can't stop thinking about it."

"Emma." Dylan wraps an arm around my shoulders and guides me over to the couch. I take a seat, and he sits beside me, taking my hand in his own. "It may have been me he hurt, but it was you he tortured."

My eyes so full of tears I can't see, I shake my head. "No, he was hurting you, Dylan. It's all I can see. The pain on your face as you pretended you weren't hurting. I can't unsee it. It's branded in my brain. On repeat, alternating with the sight of Jesper—" My stomach rolls just thinking about it.

"Baby, we survived. I'm right here." He takes my hand and presses it to his heart. "God brought us through it. I'm sorry you had to see what happened to Jesper, and I'm so sorry Heath used me against you. But we're okay. We're here," he says again.

I nod, but I can't speak. No thanks to the lump burning in my throat. One single word, and I'll completely lose it.

"You can't let it fester, or it'll eat you alive. Trust me. I've been there. For the first time in my life, I'm fighting the demons I buried deep within me. The parts of me that I let blacken because I was so angry."

"I'm trying to let it go. And it's not anger I'm feeling—

it's fear. Fear that I'm going to wake up and Heath is going to be standing over me. Fear that our rescue has been a figment of my imagination, and at any moment now, that picture is going to shatter, and I'll be back in that safe—the water rising."

Dylan is quiet for a few moments, then he releases my hand to lift the vase he brought me. "Do you recognize this?"

I study the glass. "No."

"It's the vase that broke when you threw that box at me," he says with a crooked smile.

My stomach falls. "Oh, Dylan. I'm sorry. I did break one."

"No, no. Don't apologize. Look at it." He runs the tip of his pointer finger over one of the golden veins. "Have you ever heard of kintsugi?"

I tilt my face up to look at him. "No."

He smiles. "It's the Japanese art of fixing what's been broken. Instead of throwing something away, they use an adhesive to piece it back together, then dust those cracks with powdered gold, silver, or platinum to make it even more beautiful than it was before it was broken."

I follow his gaze back down to the vase, his words saturating my soul. "Dylan, that's lovely."

He sets the vase back down and places a finger beneath my chin so he can tilt my face up to his. "I was broken. Shattered into a million pieces, sure that I would never be whole again. But God pieced me back together. While I don't know that I'll ever be the man I was before, I'm on my way to being *me* again, because of Him." He turns to me. "You gave me a reason to want to change, Emma. You're the lifeline that pulled me back to Him."

Tears burn in my throat. "Dylan."

"And just like this vase, just like me, you feel broken, but He'll put you back together too. You just have to let Him and give it time."

Dylan leans in and kisses me gently, then pulls away and rests his arm around my shoulders again. I lean into him, and we relax against the back of my couch. As we sit here in silence, I stare at the vase overflowing with wildflowers. It was broken before—into a lot of tiny pieces, from the look of it. But it's back together now. Not the same as before, but beautiful because of the brokenness.

Just like Dylan.

He's a haunted man—and probably always will be on some level. But he's beautiful in his pain. A living testimony to the grace of God. A man returning to the light after spending a good portion of his life in the fiery furnace of his past.

Is that what I'll be someday? Beautiful despite the pieces that broke in the bottom of that boat?

On some level, I understand Dylan even more now. Not because we suffered the same but because I gave in to the hopelessness that was seeding in my heart during our time in captivity. And it's taking all I have to rip it out by the roots now so I can find the version of myself I was before all of this happened.

"Thank you, Dylan."

"For what?"

"For being here."

"I spent enough time away from you, Emma. I don't ever want to be separated again. I want to give you everything I promised you before. A family. A future. A house surrounded by wildflowers."

The smile that spreads across my face erases some of the darkness. I tilt my face up to look at him. "You remembered."

"I remember everything," he says, expression serious. "And if you'll have me, I promise that I'll fight to be a man who deserves you."

"Dylan. You already do."

"No," he says. "But I'm working on it." Leaning in, he kisses me again, then pulls away to stare down at me.

"On one condition," I say with a smile.

"Oh?"

"You teach me to swim."

He pulls away slightly. I can see the hesitation on his face, the concern that I'm jumping right into the deep end. Truthfully, that's exactly what I'm doing. But I trust him not to let me drown.

"Are you sure?" he asks. "You can give it some time."

"I'm sure. I don't want to live in fear anymore. I want to find my way back too."

Dylan cups my cheeks, then leans down to kiss me again. "I'll get the floaties ordered." He smiles against my mouth, and I laugh, some of the weight lessening on my shoulders.

"Good."

"I love you, Emma," he says softly. Though he's spoken the words before, as he says them this time, I feel a bit of the brokenness within me coming back together.

"I love you too, Dylan."

EPILOGUE: EMMA

"How do I look?" Turning toward Talia, Ruth, and Harlow, I lower both hands down at my sides. Their eyes fill with tears as they look at me.

"Oh, honey, you look so beautiful!" Talia exclaims, dabbing at her eyes with a handkerchief.

"The picture of beauty," Ruth agrees.

Harlow steps forward and smiles. "She would have loved to see you like this."

"Wearing white?"

"Happy," Harlow counters. Reaching into the pocket of her dress slacks, she withdraws a single silver cross on a chain and offers it to me. "This was hers. She gave it to me on one of the worst nights of my life, and told me that, even when things got rocky, I needed to cling to Him. I didn't listen, but I'm learning." She moves around behind me and drapes the cross around my neck, then fastens it.

My eyes fill as I reach up and touch it.

Neither my mother nor my birth mother could be here, but I believe they're both watching. Just like my father is. I hope they're standing there, staring down, proud of who I am today.

"Thank you," I whisper.

"You're welcome." She takes a deep breath. "Now, I'm going to go sit out there before I lose all of my makeup, okay?"

"Okay."

She takes my hand and squeezes a moment, then turns to leave.

"Whew, I am going to be red-faced when I walk down that aisle if I'm not careful."

"You're beautiful," Talia says.

"I'll go let Connor know we're ready," Ruth whispers, then kisses my cheek and leaves the room.

"Are you happy?"

"So happy."

It's been six months since I last wore a white dress. Then, I'd been terrified of what was coming. Today, there's not an ounce of fear in my heart. Because I know who's waiting for me at the end of that aisle.

Dylan Hunt.

A man I've loved since childhood.

Someone I thought I'd lost forever.

Who reminded me of God's love even as we faced certain death.

"Good. You deserve happy."

"Thank you, Talia. Thank you for always being there."

Talia cups my cheeks and rests her forehead against mine. "You are so welcome, my darling. I love you as my own, Emmaline. I hope you always know that."

"I do."

Someone knocks gently on the door.

"Come in," Talia calls out as she releases me and wipes the tears from her cheeks.

Connor's eyes mist the moment he sees me. Dressed in a black tux, he's beyond handsome, his silver hair styled expertly on his head. "Emma, you are a dream."

"Thank you."

"Dylan might pass out when he sees you. We should have some ice water handy."

Talia playfully smacks him. "Get the girl to the aisle; she's wanted to marry that boy since they were kids."

Connor chuckles as he crosses over to me and loops my arm through his. "You ready?"

"More than."

"Then let's go get him."

Music drifts toward us the closer we get to the door that will lead us to the sanctuary of the church. Mr. Peterson, the man who runs our post office, grins at me as he opens the door.

"Bridal Chorus" begins playing as I step out into the church.

Everyone stands.

My heart is so full when I reach the end and see Dylan standing at the altar, flanked by Tucker, Riley, Elliot, and Bradyn. On my side, Lani stands beside a very pregnant Alice, with Jules, Nova, and Kennedy lined up beside her.

My gaze shifts to Dylan.

His mouth falls slack, his eyes shimmering as he stares at me. I'm unable to tear my gaze from him, even as we reach the altar and Connor kisses my cheek before placing my hands into Dylan's.

Pastor Ford clears his throat. "We are gathered here today to witness the wonderous union of Dylan Hunt and Emma Franklin. I think we can all agree that these two have truly fought for each other through everything this life has thrown at them."

I keep my gaze locked on Dylan, like we're the only two people in this room.

"Lord, we ask that You bless this union. Be with Emma and Dylan, and guide them through the storms as they face this life together. Thank You, Lord, for bringing them to this day, where they can pledge their lives to each other. In Your Holy Name. Amen."

"Amen," I whisper as I open my eyes again.

"Do you, Dylan Hunt, want to marry Emma?"

"I do."

"Do you, Emma Franklin, wish to marry Dylan?"

"I do."

Dylan's grin steals my breath.

"They have prepared their own vows and will speak those now. Dylan, lead us."

Dylan clears his throat. "I agonized over these vows because nothing felt good enough. How do I tell you just how much you mean to me? How, in the darkest moments of my life, it was you who brought me peace? I know now that it was God reminding me why I needed to hang on. He's the reason I'm standing here today, and I will do my best to honor Him by loving you with everything that I am, Emma. I've loved you since we were kids, and I'll love you until the day I draw my last breath. God willing, even longer."

Tears stream down my cheeks, my heart so full I'm sure it's going to burst.

"Emma?" Pastor Ford gently nudges.

"Dylan Hunt, there hasn't been a day that has gone by where I didn't think about you. I knew from the moment we met that you were special to me. I just couldn't have imagined how special. You are my rock, my best friend, and life is better because you're in it." Emotion burns in my throat, but I push forward. "I'm so glad you're mine."

Dylan smiles, and a tear rolls down his cheek.

"Rings, please, Delta."

"*Hier,* Delta," Dylan calls.

Delta leaves Tommy's side and trots toward the altar.

"*Sitz,*" he says, and Delta sits. Quickly, Dylan undoes the chain holding both rings onto Delta's collar. Then, he straightens and hands them to Pastor Ford.

"With this ring, I vow to love you forever, Emma," Dylan says as he slides the band around my finger.

I smile through my tears as Pastor Ford hands me Dylan's wedding band. "With this ring, I vow to love you forever." I repeat Dylan's words as I slide his band onto his ring finger.

"Then, by the power vested in me by the state of Texas, I pronounce you husband and wife. You may kiss your bride."

Dylan wraps a hand around the back of my neck and pulls me in. Our lips meet, and love surges through my body like lightning. I fling both arms around his neck as he deepens the kiss.

I still remember wading into that ocean and Dylan promising that he wouldn't let me drown. Now, six months later, here I am. Sinking beneath the surface as my feelings for him carry me down into wonderful yet uncharted depths.

Cheers erupt around us.

But it might as well just be the two of us.

Him and me.

Me and him.

Until death do us part.

Which, God willing, will be a long, long, long time from now.

WHEW! What a journey! Thank you so much for coming along with me. I hope you loved Dylan and Emma (as well as all of the Hunt's) as much as I do!

If you're wondering whether or not Lani gets a happily ever after…she does! Lima is available exclusively on my website! You can get the eBook, audiobook, or paperback today!

And if you're wondering what's next, keep reading for a sneak peek at Zane's story, SEAL of Honor!

I want to thank you again for being a part of this journey with me. If it weren't for you taking a chance on my words, I wouldn't be able to do this! So, THANK YOU. I truly hope you have enjoyed these books, and I would love to hear from you! You can reach out to me at jessicaashley@authorjessicaashley.com, or find me in my Facebook group, Romance, Redemption, & Rescue: Jessica Ashley Books.

Thank you so much for reading, and be sure to turn the page for a sneak peek at SEAL of Honor!

IRON TIDE
BROTHERHOOD
SEAL
OF
HONOR
JESSICA ASHLEY

SEAL OF HONOR: CHAPTER 1

ZANE

TWO MONTHS AGO. DARK SITE. FRANCE.

A meaty fist slams into my face and pain radiates through my jaw, spreading up into my head and down my neck. It's a dull pain, not sharp or stinging anymore thanks to the dozens of times I was hit before I lost count.

I spit blood to the side and grin up at the man standing above me. His face is shielded by a mask but I can *feel* the anger radiating off of him. "Hey now, that one didn't hurt as bad. Are you going soft on me, Killer?" I ask, doing my best to keep my tone level.

It's not fear that has me wavering. No, I ran out of fear a long time ago. This is pure exhaustion, dehydration, and the fact that I haven't eaten anything in at least twenty-four hours.

Then again, if he keeps this up I'll likely never eat anything solid again.

The man rears his fist back again—

"Wait! I'll talk!" Sawyer Maddox, a member of my team, calls out from across the room. Like me and the other captured member of my team, Ryker Granger, his hands and feet are bound to a metal chair. He's sitting at the edge of the blacked-out basement, his face bloodied and swollen just like the rest of ours.

Though Killer, here, has definitely taken a liking to messing up my face over theirs.

"Keep your mouth closed," Ryker growls. He's the largest of all of us, built like an actual tank, and currently being held to his chair with chains since he managed to snap the ropes they'd bound him with the first time.

If he weren't on my side? *Then* I might be slightly intimidated. But scared? Nah. Because I know I have God with me and with Him at my side, what should I fear?

Death can do nothing to me since I put my faith in Jesus Christ.

"No," Sawyer snaps. "You might be okay with them using Cap's face as a punching bag, but I'm not, okay?" He feigns tortured emotion and closes his eyes.

I grin because I know what's coming. I've seen Sawyer stare down the barrel of a rifle with a smile on his face. There's no way he'll bow down now.

But they don't know that. And the nature of the game? Delay until the calvary shows up.

"Talk," the man wearing my blood like gloves orders, his finger pointed directly at Sawyer.

"Okay." Sawyer takes a deep breath. "It was me," he says. "I'm the one who took your sister out last night. Listen, I know we stayed out late, but it was all honorable. You have my word. I didn't even—" Sawyer's words are cut off when Killer charges across the small room and slams his fist into his face.

"I told you to keep your mouth closed," Ryker says, chuckling.

Sawyer laughs and spits his blood to the concrete floor. "Yeah but then I would have missed out on that sweet little love tap." I'm pretty sure he winks, but with one eye completely swollen closed, it's also possible he was just blinking.

"Look, how about a little quid pro quo?" I ask. "You answer my questions, and I'll answer yours."

"Do you think that's how this works?" Killer snarls and turns back toward me. Reaching down into his boot he straightens and withdraws a blade nearly as long as my forearm.

Okay, maybe things are getting a *bit* more heated now.

Lord, please be with us here in this room. If it is Your will, please let us walk out of this. Amen. As I pray, peace washes over me. Death doesn't scare me. It never has. Maybe that's why I'm as good at this as I am? Because I know that no matter what happens to me here, I'm going somewhere better.

Both Sawyer and Ryker have gone completely silent, their serious gazes trained intently on the man in front of me. So far, he's the only one in this room, though I know there are plenty more above ground. We saw them firsthand when we infiltrated this place looking for the missing teenage daughter of a French diplomat yesterday.

Unfortunately, the intel we were given was flawed and there were far more guns within the walls than we anticipated. Hence the whole being tied to a chair thing. It's also what's kept the calvary so long. Dealing with that many opposing forces takes planning and precision.

The man closes the distance between us and presses the cold blade against my cheek. "How about I start removing things and we see just how brave you are then?" he questions, dragging the blade up toward my ear.

Come on, Demo. Bring the rain.

Even as I think the thought, a roaring explosion rocks the very ground we're sitting on. Overhead, the ceiling opens and rubble rains down on top of us. Chunks of the ceiling slam into me and pain radiates through my head.

But it can't steal the joy in my heart because this is about to be nice and wrapped up in a tight little bow.

My attacker leaps backward, and I use his momentary distraction to lean down and slice the ropes at my ankles, utilizing the handy blade I'd managed to keep hidden in the hem of my sleeve. I'd managed to cut my arms free at least an hour ago, which made taking those hits even more difficult. But making a move before I knew it was clear upstairs could have led to my taking something a lot more permanent than a punch.

I kick the knife away from him and flip him over, pressing my knee to his back as dust fills my lungs.

I cover my mouth and nose with one arm and cough, hoping to get as much of it out as I can while the air continues to clear.

"You guys miss me?" Garrison Holt calls down with a sly smile on his face, a detonator in his hand.

"Took you long enough," Sawyer calls back as he stands and stretches.

"Sorry, Cowboy and I had our hands full up here. You guys couldn't have handled at least a few of them for us?" he jokes as he tosses a ladder down into the pit. "How long did it take you to break through those ropes?" he asks.

"Not long," Sawyer calls out. "Less time than Tank here—" he turns toward Ryker who is still sitting in his chair, chains around him. "Oh, sorry big guy. Forgot you were in chains."

"You let Sawyer beat you, Tank?" Garrison asks.

"Hardly. They just caught me first."

"That's because you used your brute strength to break out while Cap and I used sleuthing skills." Sawyer continues to work on Ryker's bindings so I shift my attention back to the man pinned beneath me.

"Where is the girl, Killer?" I demand, grabbing a handful of his hair with one hand and pressing my own blade against his throat. I won't actually kill him—not when the active threat is over—but he doesn't know that.

Besides, there are plenty of ways to make someone talk without threatening their life.

"You'll never make it out of here alive," he growls.

"You seriously underestimate our resourcefulness," Sawyer calls out.

Ryker eats up the ground between where he'd been chained and where I'm kneeling, so I straighten and flip the guy over onto his back. I remove Killer's mask, revealing a glorified sorority boy in *way* over his head. Apparently the government is recruiting straight out of college these days.

"If you don't tell me, I'm going to let Tank here treat you like a chew toy," I warn him.

In pure Ryker fashion, he growls and sorority boy's eyes widen almost comically.

"She's upstairs. Top floor," he sings like a canary. *Beautiful.*

"Great. Demo, care to do the honors?"

"Absolutely."

"Smile," I say as I hold his face up in front of mine so Garrison can snap a photo. Then, I throw him to the side. "Stay and be a good boy. We have someone coming to collect you. If you run, we'll find you. We love playing hide and seek. Don't we, Tank?"

"My favorite," he replies, then rears back and slams his fist into sorority boy's face. He falls back, unconscious and Ryker turns toward the ladder. "Just making sure he doesn't run," he adds when I shake my head at him.

Ryker is the first up the ladder, then Sawyer, then me. As I reach the top, Garrison pulls up the ladder. Rubble blocked the only door in or out, so without the ladder, he'll have an interesting time trying to escape.

There are at least half a dozen men on the ground, scattered throughout what used to be a foyer. Given the bullet holes in the glass and the blood spatter on the floor, I know this was Cowboy's doing. With how fast he is, he likely took the last one down before any of them even realized what was going on.

The death makes my stomach churn, but sometimes there is no other way. And in this war? It's us or them. With a teenage girl added to the death toll should we fail.

Reaching down on the floor, I lift a discarded weapon, then check it for ammunition. Since they relieved us of our weapons when they grabbed us, both Sawyer and Ryker do the same as me, arming themselves with whatever they can find.

"You know there was a door," Sawyer tells Garrison. "You didn't have to blow a hole in the place."

Garrison shrugs. "It would have taken too long to find

it. Besides, then I wouldn't have had the amazing entrance I got."

"Yeah, well let's hope they didn't hear the explosion and kill the girl." I start toward the stairs. "Cowboy, do you read?" I ask, through the earpiece our lovely hosts didn't check for when they searched us. Lungs still burning from the rubble, I cough. As is protocol, we'd gone radio silent the moment the three of us were abducted.

"Loud and clear, Cap," Weston Hayes, my oldest friend, replies. After the last few hours, his smooth southern drawl is a welcome sound. I'm far from being the rank of Captain —especially since I technically no longer serve in the Navy —but it's a nickname that's been with me for nearly a decade. "Things are quiet out here. I took out the two guards at the top of the stairs. You should be clear going up, but I can't get a visual on the girl. All the windows are closed up."

His tone is strained, and I know it's because this mission is hitting close to home. It's that way for all of us, but for a guy who lost his younger sister at the same age this girl is, he's struggling. I only hope this has a happier ending than the tragic story that ripped apart what remained of his family after his dad abandoned them.

"We'll get to her. Everything else clear?"

"Crystal," he replies.

"Great." I turn to survey my team. Even dirtied and bloodied there's no other group of men I would count on having my back. They're the best of the best. And I'm lucky to serve beside them. "Let's go find this girl and get her home."

"On you, Cap," Sawyer says as he raises his weapon at the ready.

With a final nod, I turn and raise my weapon then head for the stairs. Cowboy was right and both men at the top of the stairs are down, their eyes frozen open, pulses nonexistent.

God, please let her be alive.

Please don't let us have been too late.

I pause by the door and hold up a fist for my team to pause, too. Pressing my ear to the door to listen for any sounds, I gently close one hand around the handle and try to turn it. The door's locked, and I hear nothing on the other side.

If she were dead, they wouldn't have kept the door locked.

Either she's in there alone—or she's not. But my hope that we'll find her alive grows.

Adrenaline pumping through my veins, I shove the anger down to keep a clear head. Details matter in moments like this. Emotions will blur already distorted lines.

Glancing back at my team, I motion for Ryker to come around. He offers me a slight nod and I raise my weapon all the way, training the barrel on the door. Ryker raises a heavy boot and slams it into the door.

It splinters and we move in as one.

It takes less than a heartbeat to get inside, but that heartbeat feels like it takes hours when I see a silver blade pressed to the throat of a trembling teenage girl. Her blue eyes are wide and terrified, her cheeks dirty, trails of tears cutting through the grime.

The man behind her glares at me, dark eyes darting back and forth between me and the rest of my team. He's sizing us up. Trying to decide if he has a chance. Given that he used to be one of us, he likely knows he doesn't.

"Come on, Martin, you know the only way you're walking out of this is if you let her go," I warn, my weapon trained on him and the girl since I can't get a clear shot through her given the coward is using her as a shield.

"You're on the wrong side," he snaps.

"You've got that backward, Bud," Sawyer comments. "Good guys don't kidnap terrified teenage girls. No matter the circumstances. I always knew you were a loose cannon."

"Please," she whimpers, the word barely audible given her thick accent and the terror in her tone. "Let me go."

"Shut up!" Martin yells, pulling her tighter against him. She cries out and a bead of crimson drips down the side of her throat where the bite of the blade got her.

I glance at Sawyer. Then Ryker. Then one final look Garrison's way.

Their gazes say the same thing I'm thinking: Martin is

going to kill her as soon as he comes to the understanding that he's not leaving here a free man. He knows he's going down and he'll take her with him just to cause as much damage as he can.

Something I can't allow.

"It's going to be okay," I tell the girl. "Okay?"

Her eyes widen, but she takes a deep breath.

I squeeze the trigger.

The gunshot is deafening in this small room, and the girl screams in pain as the bullet rips through the meat of her shoulder and slams into her abductor. Martin releases her and stumbles backward. Both Ryker and Sawyer move in on him while I rush for the girl.

Garrison is already getting his med kit ready to go while I lay my weapon aside and apply pressure.

"I'm sorry," I tell her. "I had no choice."

"I—I know," she whimpers. Tears stream down her face. "My dad. I want my dad. Can I go home now?" she whimpers.

"Absolutely," I reply.

"Got the quick clot," Garrison says.

"She okay?" Cowboy asks through my coms.

"Yeah. Bullet wound to the shoulder. Make the call."

"They're already on their way," he replies. "I'm coming in."

I tear a larger hole in her shirt so I can access her shoulder, then flush it with saline. She cries out and squirms, but Garrison takes her hand in his.

"Squeeze, okay?" he tells her. "You're doing so good. So brave."

Moving as fast as I can to ensure she doesn't bleed out, I fill the wound with gauze, packing it as tightly as I can. I hate that I caused her pain. But a bullet to the shoulder, with a clean exit, is a lot better than what Martin would have done.

Cowboy comes rushing in right as I'm finished with the front of her injury.

His hazel eyes narrow on her, nostrils flaring in anger when he gets a look at the guy Ryker is currently detaining.

"You guys have no idea what you just did! You kicked a hornet's nest! They'll make you disappear, and you'll never see the light of day again!" Martin yells. He's always been a loose cannon, but I never would have picture him taking the terrorist route.

I ignore his threats, focusing only on the girl. "I'm going to gently roll you to your side, okay? So I can get the exit wound."

She nods.

Blood pools beneath her, slower now that I've got one part of the injury packed. Gently, I roll her over, feeling terrible when she hisses in pain.

"She's losing consciousness," Garrison warns.

"Shock. Stay with us, Charlotte," I say urgently as I

pack her exit wound. "Wrap," I reach out a hand and Cowboy slams a wrap into it. Placing the end on her entry wound, I wrap her shoulder as best I can given the awkward location.

Injury packed and wrapped, I gently lay her back then stand and turn my attention to the guy who'd been holding her. His familiar face is one I'd honestly hoped to never see again.

"Martin Shaw." I shake my head. "You've got that backward on the hornet's nest. You should have left the girl alone."

"This isn't over," Martin warns again, a sadistic smile on his face. "You have no idea what you just stepped in."

"That's what they all say," I reply as the door opens and four men wearing black tactical uniforms rush in, weapons drawn. When they see that we've got it covered, they lower them and two rip Martin from the ground.

He's rushed out of the room and two medics load the unconscious teen onto a stretcher, then carry her out. As they're leaving the room, our handler, Brenda Leroy strolls in wearing black slacks, tall heels, and a black suit jacket. Her dark hair is slicked down, so shiny you can practically see your reflection.

Her red lips are flattened in a tight, disapproving line. "A lot of bodies out there, Knox," she says. "You get a little trigger happy?"

"Actually, that was me," Cowboy replies, tone sharp as

a razor. "And there was no way to get to the girl without dropping them. You vastly underestimated the fire power here. That or you just decided not to clue us in."

Her disapproving look isn't unfamiliar. "You know that I am only as good as the intel I get. I was unaware of the amount of people Shaw managed to get on his side. Apparently, the corruption ran deeper than we thought."

"He claims we kicked a hornet's nest," I tell her. "My guess is this is only the tip of that iceberg." Crossing both arms, I glare back at her.

We've known Brenda for years. Ever since our last official op as Navy SEALs six years ago went sideways and she offered us off-books contracts or prison cells.

Obviously, there wasn't much of a choice there.

"Who shot the girl?"

"I did," I say, earning an arched brow. "It was that or Shaw was going to kill her."

"We'll get his bullet hole patched up and find out who he's working for. Until then, lay low. This isn't going to be a fun one to explain."

"Feel free to cut us loose," Cowboy replies coldly.

"You're cut loose when I say you are," she snaps. "And I'm not done with you just yet."

"Prison's looking pretty good these days," Sawyer comments dryly.

"Given that you just put a bullet hole in the daughter of a French diplomat, I wouldn't rule it out just yet," Brenda replies. "Now, go before I have to include your names in my paperwork. I'll be in touch with your next assignment," she adds as I pass by.

I don't miss the irritated glance she throws my way right before she starts barking orders at the men who'd come in to start cleaning up the mess.

Tomorrow there will be no evidence of anything that happened here.

They'll destroy this place, creating a new black site somewhere else unlisted to replace it. The *only* reason we haven't fought our way out from beneath her thumb is because we do good work. My team and I hunt rogue government agents and military operators.

We bring them to justice before too much damage can be done.

And today, we saved the life of an innocent seventeen-year-old.

So, despite the way Brenda makes my skin crawl, I'll keep pushing forward until the day she becomes a rogue agent in need of justice that I will *happily* deliver.

Click HERE or scan the code below with your phone's camera to find all the places SEAL of Honor is available!

SEAL OF HONOR: CHAPTER 2

TESSA

PRESENT DAY. SOUTH CAROLINA.

Pain radiates through my right leg, spreading fire through my veins, but I keep moving. Each step is agony, but if I stop, I'm not sure I'll be able to start moving again. With dawn coming soon, I have to make sure I'm out of sight.

My foot catches on something and I cry out as I fall forward, my hands scraping against the pavement. Tears burn in my eyes and I crawl into the nearest alley and out of view. With a building at my back, and one a couple yards to my front, I'm completely shielded in the darkness.

I whimper, hands trembling as I check the bandage on my thigh. It's saturated with blood. Given what I know about injuries, which is all self-taught, I don't have long before the blood loss becomes a major issue. Truthfully, I'm not even sure how I'm still alive as it is.

Keep moving.

The two words are deafening in my mind, so I use the building at my back to push myself up to standing. Doing what I can to keep weight off of my injured leg, I take one deep breath before pushing forward.

Sweat beads on my skin despite the chill in the air.

The small-town street is silent tonight, aside from the chirping of bugs in the air, but every single noise has my already-racing heart rate spiking.

Did he follow me?

Can he hear my hammering heart?

Can he sense my fear?

No. This is a man. Not a monster from a horror film. The sobering reminder does little to ease my terror given the worst monsters I've ever known have been little more than men.

As I draw in ragged breaths, I study every shadow, waiting for a hooded figure to emerge and finish me off. Wouldn't that be ironic? I fled this place to save my life, only to lose it here eighteen years later.

Different man. Same outcome.

With that sobering thought, I continue forward, crossing the street in the shadow between the streetlamps.

To my left, ocean waves crash against the shoreline.

The scent of saltwater clings to the air around me. It should be welcoming. Familiar. But all it does is send shards of pain through my still broken heart.

Focus. I need supplies. Not that I'll know what to do with them. Breaks, bruises, and cuts? Those, I can handle.

But a stab wound? This is a first—even for me.

I guess it's a good thing I know how to sew. Because that may be my only hope here. So long as I can remain conscious through the pain.

I continue limping forward, looking left and right for any sign that someone is out and about. In this small town, someone is bound to recognize me. It's only a matter of time. My only chance is getting out of sight before the sun comes up. Then I can hide until dark.

If I make it that long.

Tomorrow night, I'll make my way to that broken down trailer on the other side of town. That place is practically condemned and sitting vacant since my dad died two years ago. Unless the state's taken control of it in my absence.

Breathe, Tessa. One problem at a time.

With any luck, my old first-aid supplies will still be hidden beneath the loose baseboard in my room. The very idea of stepping foot back in that place makes my skin crawl and my stomach churn, but there really isn't much of a choice.

Going to a doctor is out of the question. They'll have to

report the injury and the last thing I need is anyone in this town knowing I'm back. Especially since I have no idea who attacked me or if they're still looking to finish the job.

What if they're monitoring police scanners?

Time to heal.

Time to think.

That's what I need.

Since it's nearly two in the morning, I have about three hours before the bakery opens and people start moving around.

Three hours to make my escape or find a place to hide.

Sweat continues to slick my skin, matting my hair, as the pain becomes nearly unbearable. My vision wavers and I reach out to steady myself against a light pole.

I'm not going to make it far. I may not know much about stab wounds, but I know the amount of blood saturating my leg is hitting dangerous levels. And if I pass out here—I shudder. I can't think about what will happen if I pass out on the street.

Get it together, Tessa. I can do this. I was in worse shape when I left this place nearly two decades ago.

Most places in this tiny town never had a need for security cameras, but there's no telling what's changed in the last eighteen years. Because that's exactly how long it's been since I walked the streets of Stormwatch Landing, South Carolina.

When I'd come for my dad's funeral two years ago, I

steered clear of town and hid in the trees of the cemetery so no one would notice me. I'd been successful then, so here's hoping that luck will carry forward.

The paved sidewalk running between the buildings on Main Street and the coastline hasn't changed much, aside from some fresh plants placed strategically on either side of the walkway.

A few new benches here and there, but aside from that, everything is pretty close to the same. As soon as I can, I step off onto the grass so I hopefully don't leave a blood trail on the pavement. In this small town that would be front page fodder.

My leg begins to throb even worse as the adrenaline wanes.

I stumble forward and catch myself on the back of a bench.

Supplies.

I need supplies.

Something to stop the bleeding and possibly some thread and a needle, or even some glue to close it up. *But where?*

Everywhere is closed and the *last* thing I need is to get arrested for breaking and entering. I can see the headlines now: LOCAL DRUNK'S RUNAWAY BRIDE DAUGHTER RETURNS AS A THIEF.

I groan.

Why did it seem like such a good idea to come back?

Because I had nowhere else to go.

As I'm stepping off Main Street and coming up on the marina, a familiar boat catches my eye. Its sails are down, and the green striping along the side is slightly faded—but unmistakable.

As is the faded *The Tessa* painted on the bow of the ship.

My heart leaps at the sight of my name. I would have thought he'd have painted over it. Renamed it something else.

Something better.

Don't think on it too much, he probably just got busy. Shoving the past back where it belongs, I change course and head straight for the marina.

Supplies.

A cautious planner, he always had a first aid kit on board. Here's hoping that, like the town, that didn't change. I can find the supplies, tend to my leg, then slip out before anyone ever notices that I crawled back to this place.

With renewed strength thanks to my plan, I continue forward until I hit the dock. My shoes thud against the boards as I limp my way toward the boat, all the while glancing behind me to make sure I'm not being followed.

As soon as I climb aboard, I head straight for the door that will lead me into the cabin. I know this place like the back of my hand because nearly *every* good memory I have of this town happened here. On this boat. With *him*.

I pull open the door and his scent hits me. Salt and teak. *Home.* Because it smells like him. Tears blur my vision for reasons other than the pain now, and emotion sears the inside of my throat.

There hasn't been a day that's gone by where I haven't thought of him.

My vision wavers again, a sobering reminder that if I don't stop focusing on the past, I won't have a present, so I fumble around for a light switch I know I can't use for long without drawing attention. But trying to find supplies in the dark, on a boat I haven't been on in nearly two decades, seems improbable.

Supplies. Maybe a little rest. Then I'll be gone before he knows I was here. Maybe the holding tank even has water in it so I can take a quick hot shower.

Man, wouldn't that be lucky.

I continue toward the right, running my hands over the walls.

But when the cool steel of a gun barrel presses against the back of my head, I freeze in place, dread coiling in my stomach like a deadly snake ready to strike.

No way. There is no way they found me here. Not this fast.

Light floods the room when a lamp is flipped on. I blink rapidly as my vision adjusts to the assault.

"Tessa?"

My heart flutters at the recognition even as my stomach

plummets to the floor. *No. Of all the people to run into, why did it have to be him?*

Right as I turn toward him, the floor gives way and the room tilts. Or, maybe it just feels that way, because everything goes dark.

"Stay with me, please!" that familiar voice orders.

If only I could tell him that I never wanted to leave in the first place.

***

A THIN LINE of sunlight draws me out of sleep, but the peaceful feeling ends there. As soon as I've crawled out of the dark nightmares, pain assaults me. There's not a single inch of my body that doesn't ache, and my left leg might as well be on fire.

The steady beeping of machines claims my focus next, and the all-too familiar sound brings a wave of nausea over me. *No. No. Did he find me? Will he find me?* My heart begins to pound, but I keep my eyes closed tightly.

Like someone trying to avoid a bear attack, I play dead —or rather, unconscious.

"Tessa, you're safe." The deep voice is comforting and familiar, but it brings an onslaught of emotions even more powerful than the fear.

Zane.

My eyes flutter open and I look up at him. He's

standing over me in faded jeans, a worn sweatshirt with the word NAVY across the front, and a tattered South Carolina baseball cap pulled low over his sun-kissed hair.

Oh, Zane. His face is glorious torment and sweet rescue all at once.

He's here.

Where is here?

"Hey, there, sweetheart! You're awake!" A woman in blue scrubs with kittens all over them comes breezing over toward the bedside. "How are you feeling?" Her expression grows more worried the longer it takes me to respond.

"Throat dry," I choke out.

"I'll get water." Zane turns to leave and I want to beg him to stay. The moment he's out of sight, my heart begins to pound again.

What if he doesn't come back?

What if he does?

"Easy, sweetie. Zane's not going anywhere." She smiles softly. "Do you remember me?" She runs her hand over my forehead in a way that brings suppressed memories to the surface with the force of a tidal wave.

Her black hair is threaded with silver, but her soft brown eyes still hold the same kindness as the woman who spent far too many years helping me with broken bones or injuries that required more than a Band-Aid.

"I do. Hi, Nurse Rose."

She smiles kindly, then finishes checking my vitals.

"Hi, sweetie. Listen, we have you checked in under a different name, okay? Zane wasn't too sure what was going on, so he convinced Leopold to—"

"Leopold? As in Officer Alan Leopold?" *No. This is bad.* I try to sit up, but whatever pain medicine they gave me has my vision swimming.

"Honey, relax. You're safe here."

"No. I can't—the cops. If they're looking for me, they'll find out—"

"Who will find out?" Rose asks, her brow furrowing.

Zane breezes in and I freeze in my bed. He sets a plastic cup on the bedside tray, then shoves both hands into his pockets.

"I'm going to go update your chart," Rose says. She squeezes my arm gently. "You're *safe* here, Tessa. You always have been." With one final smile, she turns and leaves the room, cracking the door behind her.

"Are you feeling okay?" Zane asks.

"I need to leave."

His jaw tightens. "You can't go yet. You haven't been released yet."

Our gazes hold, his green eyes having been burned into my memory since the moment I first saw him. I know them better than I know my own. And as usual, his expression nearly strips away every wall I've built over the last eighteen years.

I never thought I'd see him again.

I never dared to even *hope* to see him again.

But here I am, sitting here in a hospital gown, mere feet away from the only man I've ever loved.

CLICK HERE or scan the code below with your phone's camera to find all the places SEAL of Honor is available!

**She vanished on their wedding day. Now she's back—
with a target on her back and danger in her wake.**

Former Navy SEAL Zane Knox gave up everything
when Tessa Lane left him at the altar. Now he lives off the
grid, taking off-books missions and keeping the past where
it belongs—buried.

Until she shows up on his boat… trying to steal it.

Private Investigator Tessa Lane is in trouble. The kind
that leaves bodies behind. With nowhere else to turn, she
runs to the only man she knows can protect her. Even if
she's the last person he wants to see.

Zane's instincts say walk away. But when he realizes
how deep the threat runs, he calls in his old team. Because

the woman who once broke his heart… may be the one worth risking everything to save.

Explosive action. Unfinished business. And a second chance that might just come at the highest cost.

Grab your copy of SEAL of Honor, and get ready for another epic adventure!

ABOUT THE AUTHOR

Jessica Ashley started her career in 2016 writing romance novels for the secular world, before feeling the Lord pulling her in a different direction.

She is now a three-time award winning author of Christian romance, and has published nearly twenty novels and novellas since 2024.

She is an Army veteran, who resides in New Hampshire with her husband and their three children.

You can find out more about her and her books by joining her newsletter via her website: https://jessicaashley books.com/ or by joining her Facebook group, Romance, Redemption, & Rescue: Jessica Ashley Books.

Member of the ACFW.

Awards won:

- *First-place in the Romantic Suspense category of the Firebird Q1 2025 Book Awards. (Pages of Promise)*
- *Readers' Favorite Gold Medal Winner for excellence in writing. (Bravo)*
- *Literary Titan Gold Book Award Winner. (Echo)*

ALSO BY JESSICA ASHLEY

<u>Coastal Hope Series</u>

Pages of Promise: Lance Knight

Searching for Peace: Elijah Pierce

Second Chance Serenity: Michael Anderson

Tactical Revival: Jaxson Payne

Perilous Healing: Silas Williamson

<u>Coastal Hope Short Novels</u> (*Website Exclusives*)

Badge of Hope: Alaric Simmons

<u>Coastal Hope Novellas</u> (*Website Exclusives*)

Pictures of Hope (*Coastal Hope Prequel Novella*): Alex & Lilly

A Coastal Holiday Short: Caleb & Carmen

A Coastal Valentines: Lance & Eliza

A Coastal St. Patrick's Day: Elijah & Andie

A Coastal Easter: Michael & Reyna

A Coastal Thanksgiving: Jaxson & Margot

A Coastal Christmas: Silas & Bianca

The Hunt Brothers Search & Rescue

Bravo: Bradyn Hunt

Echo: Elliot Hunt

Romeo: Riley Hunt

Tango: Tucker Hunt

Delta: Dylan Hunt

Hunt Brothers Short Novels *(Website Exclusives)*

Lima: Lani Hunt

Hunt Brothers Holiday Novellas *(Website Exclusives)*

A Hunt Brothers Valentines: Bradyn & Kennedy

A Hunt Brothers St. Patrick's Day: Elliot & Nova

A Hunt Brothers Easter: Riley & Jules

A Hunt Brothers Thanksgiving: Tucker & Alice

A Hunt Brothers Christmas: Dylan & Emma

Iron Tide Brotherhood

SEAL of Honor: Zane Knox

SEAL of Bravery: Garrison Holt
